ALL I HAVE TO KEEP

THE SUCCOURI SAGA
BOOK FOUR

MERIDITH GIBBENS

STAY INFORMED

Be the first to hear about new releases and receive special offers by signing up for my newsletter at:
http://succourisaga.com

.

CONTENTS

CHAPTER I

THE NIGHT

No night had ever felt so long or so dark. Callie stood in the sterile silence of Doctor Navarro's medical lab, fighting with clenched fists against every cell in her body as, with one voice, they commanded her to go to Ben. Though the compulsion was relentless, she held her ground, anchoring her resolve in the whispered call for sacrifice required by selfless love. She wouldn't take the chance of hurting him, even if it meant she could never touch him again.

The invisible boundary line Doctor Navarro had designated to keep Ben safe only afforded her a blurred image of his face, so she depended on others to watch for signs of a return to consciousness. Helplessly, she listened to his steady breathing, in and out, as each torturous minute ticked by ever so slowly.

Everyone in the house took turns standing or sitting by her side, doing what they could to comfort her. Each attempted to persuade her to eat or rest, but she had no appetite, and she knew she wouldn't sleep while Ben's condition remained tenuous.

Presently, Grace slept in the back corner of the large lab, awkwardly slumped in a chair near Donovan's bed. Privately, she'd been suffering her own sorrows. Though no one wanted to speak the words aloud, they all knew if Ben couldn't meet with the grieving Succouri, there was likely no one else who could reach him in his troubled state. Without the transfer of Ethan Devereaux's gift, there was no chance of saving Donovan's life. Even if Ben did wake up, he'd need to focus on his battle to survive. Wordlessly, each woman pained at the misery of the other.

Maggie and Doctor Navarro stayed close by, one or the other continually monitoring both patients. Each had offered Callie encouraging words, but as the hours advanced and nothing changed, words failed as exhaustion and fear heightened. As the hour approached three a.m. and Ben still didn't stir, it took every ounce of Callie's willpower to keep from hyperventilating as she began to fear that he might never open his eyes again.

A few hours ago, Taylor's words had comforted her as they were almost the same as those Ben's Succouri spoke on the beach during their brief honeymoon. Upon hearing them, hope had lifted her spirits as it seemed to be an unmistakable positive sign, but as each passing hour brought no change in Ben's condition, that precious hope was sliding through her fingers, like fine grains of sand.

Though she continually probed at the hollow place in her heart left by their missing bond, she couldn't detect the slightest trace of a connection to Ben. Each time the shadow of her roaming thoughts fell near that space, her stomach contracted, but she'd long since emptied everything in her. Methodically, she breathed through the nausea until it subsided, only to have it return moments later. After the first few episodes, she got better at hiding it, though Grace was aware and had already repeated her plea to inform Doctor Navarro about her symptoms as well as the reason for her suffering. But Callie wanted the doctor's focus to remain on Ben and Donovan as he could do nothing for her anyway. Curing Ben was her only hope for recovery.

Another hour passed. Second by second, the roots of despair plunged deeper into her soul, suffocating her and blocking out the light of hope.

With a sigh, Lee rose from his chair and stepped in front of her, halting her uncharacteristic pacing. "Sis, please, leave the pacing to me. I'm much better at it on account of all the practice I've had. You need to rest. You can't keep this up. You'll wear yourself out, and you won't be able to help Ben when he wakes up. Please, try to eat something and get some sleep. I swear, I'll stay with him and come get you as soon as—"

Shaking her head and patting his arm, she cut off his plea. "I can't, Lee. I'm not being stubborn; I just can't leave him." Tears filled her eyes, and Lee raised his hands, relenting as he didn't want to cause her additional distress.

"Why isn't he waking up this time, Lee? What if he never wakes up?"

"Cal, don't do that. Keep the faith. We don't know how long he was out the last two times since you were asleep when it happened, and you didn't know he'd fallen unconscious until you woke up. This might not be as bad as it seems."

"But we roused him before. Nothing's worked this time."

Lee sighed in frustration, having no good answers to

offer her. "Is there anything I can get you? Please, let me feel useful, do something."

Though she didn't want it, she sent him for a bottle of water.

Doctor Navarro and Silvia had graciously opened their home to the group, offering their spare bedrooms and a stocked kitchen for their free use. Silvia had prepared a meal for them the prior evening that everyone, except Callie and Taylor, partook in gratefully.

Ben's father, Wes Taylor, was nearly as distraught as Callie, though he didn't suffer the physical discomforts. Having just begun to enjoy a relationship with his son after twenty-seven years of separation, the possibility of losing him so soon after their reunion was unbearable. His way of coping, however, was to keep busy, chasing leads and researching potential sources for answers.

Taylor, Callie, and Lee had planned to fly to Philadelphia that afternoon while Ben met with Ethan Devereaux. A man named Antonio Carozza lived there, and Maggie had mentioned his name as a source of knowledge about the Succouri sought out by her late husband, Owen Briggs. Taylor and Callie had intended to ask him together about Ben's odd illness, but now it seemed Taylor would likely travel alone.

"Callie!" Maggie's excited voice halted her pacing and sped up her heart. "He just blinked."

Callie held her breath and almost rushed to his side, but she remembered the assigned distance just in time. Hopeful but anxious, she hugged her arms around herself.

"Ben?" Maggie whispered, leaning over him.

Though there was no answer, Maggie lifted her head to speak to Callie, a smile in her voice. "He's blinking, and his eyes look good, Callie. There's life in them."

Callie continued to hold her breath.

"Ben. Can you hear me?" Maggie asked.

He swallowed, then spoke Callie's name so softly and desperately that it healed and crushed her simultaneously as she ached to throw her arms around him.

"She's here, Ben," Maggie comforted.

Though something lightly fluttered in the vacant space in her heart, the hole didn't fill.

For an excruciating moment, Ben didn't speak or move, but at last, he lifted himself onto his elbows.

"Easy," Maggie cautioned, putting her hand on his back to help him sit up. Pulling the sensors off his chest, he turned toward her.

"Callie." He reached out his hand, but she stepped back, the action breaking her heart into pieces.

"Ben, I can't." Fresh tears blurred her eyes and spilled onto her cheeks.

"What? Why? What in the world's going on?" With a soft moan, Ben grasped at his chest at the same spot where the discomfort of their vacant bond throbbed in hers.

"I'm going to get the doctor," Maggie announced, rushing from the room.

"Callie, please come to me," Ben begged, again reaching for her. The intense strain in his voice made it barely recognizable.

"I can't. I'm sorry," she sobbed. "I love you, but I'm the one who hurt you. It's my fault, Ben, all my fault."

Abruptly, he rose to his feet, and she had to stumble backward to keep him from catching her around the waist.

"Please don't! Please, stay back, Ben. I won't hurt you again."

"Sweetheart, what are you talking about? There's no way you could hurt me except by keeping your distance from me like this. Please. I can't feel you." His voice cracked. "I need to feel you." Profound sorrow at the absence of their bond and the perceived rejection by her overtook him, and he struggled to breathe.

"I can't feel it either. It's breaking my heart, too." She lifted her hand to her heart as she sobbed, and Ben held out both hands, inviting her, once again, into his arms, but though it was all she wanted, she couldn't go to him.

Callie doubled over in torment of the heart and body, and Doctor Navarro came up behind her, placing a comforting hand on her back.

"Oh dear! I know this is painful, but it will be okay," he soothed, showing genuine concern for Callie before turning to Ben. "She's trying to protect you, Ben. She's doing this because she loves you. Please, sit, and let me explain."

Hesitantly, Ben sat back down on the hospital bed, but though she couldn't see his eyes, his face never turned away from her. Doctor Navarro stepped closer to him but stayed to the side, ensuring he didn't block their view of one another.

Soberly, he explained to Ben what had happened, his theories about Ben's condition, and the reasons for his collapse and unconscious episodes. Silent and unmoving, Ben didn't acknowledge the doctor or ask questions, and Callie wondered if he was hearing the doctor or if, like her, the trauma evoked by that vacant space in his chest was making it near impossible to concentrate.

When the doctor finished his explanation, he looked at Ben's tortured face and set a hand on his shoulder. "Are you also unable to feel your bond?"

Ben dropped his head in a single nod. "But it doesn't matter," he said, tightening his jaw. "She's my wife, and I won't keep my distance from her. The last two times this happened, things returned to normal when I came out of it."

"But this time, it's different. Neither of you can detect your bond, and as far as I know, that's never happened to a Succouri couple before." The doctor stroked his chin and looked between them. "Callie, try coming just a bit closer, but Ben, you must be straight with us if you feel anything unusual."

"I can't," Callie protested. "I won't take the chance of him collapsing again."

Doctor Navarro walked up beside her. "Ben and I won't let that happen, I promise. We'll take it nice and slow." He put her hand around his arm, and she reluctantly stepped forward.

Though she couldn't see it, Ben must have nodded his head because the doctor urged her forward again. After one more step, she heard Ben suck in a breath, and the doctor stepped back with her. When he released her, she retreated to the spot she'd originally occupied.

"What did you feel?" the doctor asked, his voice low and hoarse.

Ben didn't respond.

"I recognize this is frightening and painful for both of you, but to make headway at understanding what's happening here, I need as much information as you can give me."

Grieved by the need to speak what he'd prefer to ignore, Ben's words came out halted and tinged with frustration. "As I described to Callie a few days before our wedding, it feels like I'm being sprayed with a hose, like strength is rushing at me too quickly and powerfully, but none is sticking. It's just passing right through."

"And is the sensation weaker, stronger, or the same as last time?"

Again, there was an extended silence before Ben finally whispered his answer. "Stronger."

"That's consistent with my present theories. Because of the diminished Succouri presence in your body, you're unable to process the strength coming from Callie. It's too much for your system to handle."

Sharply inhaling through his nose, Ben clenched his teeth as he spoke his next words. "It doesn't matter. I'll find a way to deal with it. I can't... I won't keep six feet of distance between us. That's not an option."

"We don't have a choice, Ben," Callie cried, frantic for him to understand her need to keep him conscious and well. Though she hated the distance as much as he did, his voice and presence with her were a thousand times better than watching him lie still and silent. She wouldn't, couldn't let him fall back into that state. She needed him, even if this was all she could have of him.

Doctor Navarro let out a slow, empathetic breath, revealing genuine distress at their anguish. "I understand, and I sincerely hope this situation won't last long, but we can't allow you to check out on us again, Ben. Nothing I attempted was effective at waking you. Next time, you might not wake up at all. Then, imagine the pain she'll face. This is harder on her than it is on you. Though this is some-thing most Succouri partners develop after many years, it's evident that she's experiencing an increased drive to help you in your weakness. Trust me when I say, it's taking everything this courageous woman has to hold back rather than rush into your arms. Please, don't make it harder for her."

Defeated, Ben's shoulders sank. "Can I... Can I at least

have a moment alone with her, Doc?" He held up his hands. "I promise not to get too close."

"Of course." Doctor Navarro moved to the door, catching Lee on his way in and directing him back into the hallway.

For a moment, Ben didn't speak, wiping his finger under his eyes and attempting to control his breathing.

"Sweetheart," he finally said softly. "I promise not to move. Please, come a little closer."

She took two small steps toward him and lowered her head.

"I know you can't read my face from that distance, so let me express how desperately sorry I am for putting you through this." His tears were audible as his voice conveyed a deep sorrow she'd never heard him express. "You did nothing wrong here. This is all my fault."

"That's not true. Not at all true."

He put a fist to his forehead. "Once again, I'm hurting you because of who I am. The Succouri in me is tearing us apart."

"Please don't say that. Our Succouri helped bring us together and made our bond possible. It's saved my life and yours repeatedly. It's not punishing us or trying to hurt us. Something's wrong, there's no denying that, but it isn't anyone's fault, least of all yours or our Succouri's."

"Regardless, I can't bear this, Callie. This is a hundred times worse than those cursed gloves. I need to touch you, to hold you in my arms, especially since I can't—"

"I know," she interjected, protecting him from having to speak the truth about their absent bond. "This is a nightmare, but you're awake and talking to me, and that's a lot more than I had ten minutes ago. For better or worse, remember? I know it feels like it can't get any worse than it is right now, but the last seven hours were infinitely worse." Another sob shook her before she could finish. "I wasn't sure you'd wake up again. I thought I might not get the chance to tell you how much I love you, Ben Sawyer: bond or no bond, far or near, Succouri or human."

Momentarily covering his face with his hands, he shed tears of utter torment. "And my love for you will never have limits or conditions. But I'd freely trade everything I own for the chance to touch you right now." The words were so sweetly spoken that a bright light temporarily lit up her dark world.

"Callie, I can't sense your feelings, but you're very pale, sweetheart. I know you're exhausted and afraid, but beyond that, what's wrong? Please, tell me the truth, even though I can't confirm your words."

Her mind raced. She knew what the truth would do to him, and right now, her heart couldn't bear causing him additional suffering. But she couldn't lie to him either. Though their Succouri bond had vanished, she still had a human bond with him, a covenant. She'd promised to honor him and share everything, good or bad, with him. Lying broke that sacred vow. But he already blamed himself for their misery, and the truth would compound his sense of guilt.

"Um, I..."

Before she could finish her sentence, the alarm on Donovan's monitor sounded, startling them as it sharply pierced the silence in the room. Doctor Navarro and Maggie rushed in, followed by Lee and Taylor. With a gasp, Grace jumped from her chair, her eyes wide with fear.

Instantly, Ben hurried toward Donovan, causing Callie to shuffle backward to keep him from getting too close, but before Ben reached him, Taylor moved to intercept.

"Son, no!" he commanded, grabbing his arm in an unyielding grip.

"I have to!" Ben tried to shake off his father's hand, but Taylor held firm, and Lee joined the effort, standing as an immovable stone wall in front of Ben.

"Not this time, son. You probably couldn't help anyway, but we won't let you take the chance."

"But this is a life-or-death situation," he argued. "It doesn't violate my promise."

Taylor shook his head and held his ground.

Dumbfounded, Ben's gaze moved between Lee and his father, unable to believe they were restraining him against his will.

Cautiously, Callie took one step toward him. "Ben, the doctor said you can't help anymore, no matter the circumstance. It could kill you. Please. Let the doctor handle it this time." She gripped her stomach as a strong wave of nausea rose in her throat. "Please, we're trying to save your life. We... I can't lose you."

As the doctor and Maggie worked frantically over Donovan, Ben stared speechlessly. Even without their bond, Callie knew him well enough to know this was breaking his heart. He'd risked much to get Donovan there, Donovan's health as well as his own. They'd come so far and escaped so many close calls only to have it all come crashing down around them. Ben felt responsible for the outcome as the perilous journey resulted from his hopeful attempt to save his friend's life. If Donovan died, Ben would never forgive himself.

"I must try. I'm sorry, but please understand." His words were directed at her, but after he spoke, he turned to the two men blocking his path. "Please, let me pass. This is what I'm meant to do."

Callie held her breath, fearing Ben might try to force his way past Lee and Taylor.

"If you do," Taylor warned, shifting his weight to allow for a firmer grip. "You may very well be responsible for killing not only yourself but also your wife."

Aghast, Callie put a hand over her mouth, and Ben jumped back, dragging Taylor with him.

"What?" Anger mixed with fear resounded in his exclamation.

"She's deathly ill. Can't you see that? Your friend's not the only one whose life hangs in the balance. You can't protect Callie without protecting yourself. The moment you collapsed, she fell ill. That's quite a coincidence. My gut tells me it's much more than nerves."

"Callie?" Ben's voice was frantic as he turned to her for confirmation.

Her heart pounded. Though she felt it wasn't Taylor's place to share this secret, she couldn't deny that if Donovan's condition hadn't suddenly faltered, she would likely have been forced to tell Ben the truth herself. The words were spoken in desperation, arising from a father's love and desire to protect his son. What Taylor saw in Ben's eyes must have convinced him that Ben wouldn't relent without a fight. Though Ben was willing to sacrifice his life for Donovan, Taylor knew he wouldn't risk hers. Therefore, revealing this truth was perhaps the only way to stop him.

As Grace cried and the frenzied efforts to save Donovan continued to play out in full view, the four of them remained suspended in silence, Ben awaiting Callie's answer, and Lee and Taylor watching to see what Ben would do. Besides the night when Ruiz had attacked, and she'd almost been forced to watch Ben die right in front of her, Callie couldn't recall a bleaker night than this one.

Somewhat comforted by the fact that she couldn't see the pain in his eyes, she slowly nodded.

With a sudden burst of inhuman strength, Ben shook off his father's grip, turned his back to them, and rushed out of the room. Lee came to Callie, and she leaned against him, covering her eyes as new tears wet her cheeks.

As Lee appeared unshaken by Taylor's dramatic pronouncement, Callie recognized that her feeble attempts to hide her condition had utterly failed. Lee knew her too well, and Taylor was an investigator who was trained to maintain heightened situational awareness at all times.

Momentarily still, astonished by his son's outburst of strength, Taylor slowly exhaled and turned to Lee and Callie.

"Dear one, I'm sorry," he whispered. "I didn't know how else to stop him."

She extended her hand, and Taylor tenderly placed it between his, grateful for the gesture of forgiveness. "I was about to tell him before Donovan's monitors went off. It's alright. I understand. You may have saved his life once again."

"You know him best," Taylor said. "Should I go after him?"

"Let's give him some time; let him stay away from this," she said, gesturing toward Donovan's bed. "It's too hard for him to watch without being able to help. He's torn between his love for me and his duty to save lives. It isn't fair to him."

Though her heart broke for Ben and she wanted to go after him herself, she was unsure how to help him given their awkward situation. The distance she had to maintain was a chasm between them, cutting her off from his eyes, expressions, and touch. How would she comfort him when they hadn't yet figured out how to relate to one another within the confines of their current reality? Her exhausted mind and weak body robbed her of strength and clouded her typically clear thinking.

For the moment, she couldn't help Ben, so she went to Grace and put her arms around her, praying fervently for the dreadful night to end.

CHAPTER 2

THE ACCEPTANCE

Ben sat on a fallen log, watching the first rays of dawn streak across the horizon. After he'd left the Navarro home, he'd wandered aimlessly in the dark, not caring where he was going.

The country roads wound through forests thick with tall trees whose branches whistled and swayed in a cold, steady morning wind. Eventually, he'd encountered a small stream and, feeling too weak and defeated to continue, he stopped to rest.

Every part of his body ached, but that was nothing compared to the anguish that was ripping giant bleeding wounds in his heart.

What had he done? He'd brought his friend here, promising him a cure and giving his word that he'd offer all he had to help him. Now, Donovan lay dying and Grace despaired because they'd trusted him.

Worse yet was what he'd done to his own wife, the one he'd pledged to protect and cherish. From the very beginning, he'd feared this; that he'd hurt her, bring nothing but pain and hardship into her life. Though he'd dared to hope that the depth of his love might somehow shield her from the inevitable consequences of his inhuman identity, it had not. Though they'd experienced short periods of joy, the river of tears she'd cried since falling in love with him cut him to the core.

And if all that weren't devastating enough, now he'd trapped her in a doomed fate, her life tethered to a rapidly sinking ship. Every protective instinct he'd had from the beginning was proving to be correct, though unfortunately, his realization came too late. He'd worried he would add to her burdens, and he had. When he discovered that his physiology wasn't human, he panicked, concerned about the potentially negative consequences of close contact with him. Though the possible threats he'd imagined were terrible, they couldn't compare to the horror of the revealed truth. Loving him hadn't simply hurt her, it would kill her.

And now, he had no way to change it, to go back and protect her from himself. What was done couldn't be undone. Even if he walked away, never touched her again, she'd still perish. His love had brought her pain, and his death would deal the final blow. Jessica Hughes had been right. Ben's curse would crush Callie, and he could do nothing at all to stop it.

Unable to contain the rage inside him, directed at himself alone, he stood and, with a cry of desperate anguish, violently punched the tree in front of him. The pain of the reckless blow shocked him as it lingered in his hand and arm. When he looked down, he stared in a daze at his bloody knuckles, which showed no sign of rapid healing.

"Well, that wasn't too smart, but I've been there."

Startled, Ben whirled around and found Lee leaning on a tree, an amused grin on his face.

"You're mostly just plain human now, so you might want to go easy on the punching. It doesn't solve anything anyway; just gives you bloodied knuckles. Trust me. I'm speaking from personal experience here."

"Lee. How'd you find me? I don't even know where I am?"

"There's not a lot of options out here. I just followed the dirt road."

Putting his hand to his forehead, Ben sighed and turned back toward the stream, sitting again on the log. Lee stepped over it and sat beside him, but neither spoke for a long time.

"Is Donovan—"

"They stabilized him," Lee answered before Ben finished the question. "He's alright."

Another sigh passed through Ben's lips.

Ben lowered his head into his hands, waiting for Lee to express his righteous anger, but he said nothing. Casually, Lee picked up a small rock and tossed it into the stream. Why wasn't he livid? Ben deserved the worst Lee could throw at him, disappointment, rage, even hatred. He'd just lost his father, and now, because of Ben, he may very well lose his sister, too.

But as Ben glanced over at him, there was nothing but genuine affection and concern in Lee's eyes.

"I'm sorry, Lee. Please believe me. I never wanted to hurt her in any way. I love her, more than I can ever express. Do you remember when I told you I was no good for her, that I shouldn't be with her?"

Lee nodded.

"Turns out, that was exactly right. I wanted to give her a happy life. I hoped that somehow, despite who and what I was, that would be possible. I should have run away, left her be. If I had, she'd be safe and healthy right now. I couldn't live without her, but it was selfish of me to risk her future."

For a silent moment, Lee watched the stream as it gurgled happily over the smooth rocks. Then, he turned toward Ben, shaking his head repeatedly. "Without a doubt, you're the best thing that ever happened to my sister, and she's the best thing that ever happened to you. You were meant to be together, and it isn't selfish to love someone, Ben. You weren't right at all. You're the only one who could have ever made her happy, and she is very happy with you, happier than I've seen her in her entire life."

Ben dropped his hands, holding them out in total bewilderment at Lee's lack of condemnation. "How can you say that? I'm killing her, Lee! Right in front of your eyes."

Still unshaken, he leaned back and placed both hands on his knees. "Well, that's an entirely different topic. You had better be damn sure that doesn't happen, brother."

Ben grabbed Lee by the arm, desperate for him to understand. "I have no control over it. Don't you see? This isn't something I can save her from, protect her from."

"I'm not so sure about that. Maybe, Ben, the man, can't protect her, but there's a whole other part of you that I believe can."

"But that part's dying or broken or something." Ben threw up his hands. "I have no clue. It's not like I can communicate or reason with it."

"But it did communicate, with Callie. And I'm willing to bet some real money that it isn't as dormant as the doctor thinks it is."

Ben straightened, surprised that Lee knew about Callie's experience on the beach.

Lee smiled. "Last night, when you were unconscious,

your dad said something to try to lift Callie's spirits, and it sure worked. She suddenly turned and hugged him, and then she told us the story of her vision on the beach. Kind of weird and creepy if you ask me, like some kind of *Twilight Zone* thing, but I know my sister, and if she says it was real, then it was. You two are in the middle of this swirling tornado right now, and it's clouding your hope, but I got plenty as I believe in you, Ben, every part of you, even that crazy alien thing inside you. You told Callie it has to happen this way, so I guess it does. Maybe your Succouri wants to let you be plain human for a while." He pointed to Ben's knuckles. "Let you see what it's like for the rest of us mere mortals, walk in our shoes. I don't know." He shrugged. "But you said that, in the end, it would work out, so it will. If there's one thing I know about you, you don't lie."

Astounded by Lee's unwavering faith in him, Ben stared, unsure how to respond. "But I don't remember any of that. I can't vouch for that part of me. I don't know its motives or its character."

"Really?" Lee wrinkled his brow in confusion. "Didn't your Succouri pick Callie for you, even before you did? Doesn't the healing you give come from it? Doesn't it give Callie sight every day, and didn't it offer Dad one last moment with us? Wasn't it your Succouri who warned you with a feeling of dread when Callie was in danger, and didn't it save your life when you were twelve and dying of leukemia? Geeze, Ben, I know you have some serious trust issues, but I think it's done more than enough to prove itself worthy."

Callie had recently said a similar thing to him. They both regarded his indweller as generous and well-intentioned, possessing integrity that paralleled his. But Ben would never alter someone's entire being without their consent, nor would he leave them to suffer in utter confusion and fear at the tender age of twelve.

"If it's so noble, so harmless, why did it let me struggle for fifteen years? Why didn't it find a way to communicate with me, like it presumably is now?" Ben was surprised by the intense anger that accompanied his accusation.

"Aww." Lee put a finger in the air. "I see. That's where all this pessimism comes from. You resent it because you think it abandoned you, betrayed you, and you just can't let that go, even though you know it saved your life and is giving you the chance at a life that is far more exciting and meaningful than you would have had without it. Look at you and Callie, for example. I mean, seriously! Who gets to be that close and connected to another human being? As Allie said, you two practically share a soul. That's real living, Ben, and some of us are a little jealous that we'll never experience that kind of life or love. Just sayin'."

Lee's words hit him like a bucket of frigid water being dumped on his head; shocking, but precisely what he needed to wake him up.

Surrendering to the undeserved kindness of his big-hearted brother-in-law, Ben sighed. "I think you would have been a much better choice for the Succouri life. In my humanity, I'm not sure I'm the adventurous type."

Grinning broadly, Lee patted Ben's knee. "It picked you, so you're just the man for the job. But do me a favor. Try to forgive it, or yourself, for those rough years now far behind you. After all, you were willing to forgive your dad. I'm confident you have many happy years ahead that will more than make up for whatever you feel you lost."

"I will try," Ben promised. "I don't know what you, or your sister, saw in me, see in me that prompts you to continuously extend such unending forgiveness, but I know for certain I don't deserve it."

Lee softly chuckled and punched Ben's knee playfully. "You don't lie, but you also don't see yourself very clearly either. As I said at your wedding, you're humble to a fault, which is a condition I personally don't suffer from."

Despite Ben's heavy heart, he smiled. "Well, regardless, I don't know how to thank you for that healthy dose of tough love, not to mention the positive perspective and encouragement."

"Don't sweat it. Just hurry back to the house and help my sister, would ya? I know she's usually the stronger one between you two, but right now, she needs you. She's weak and exhausted. She hasn't eaten anything since the plane ride, and she threw everything up last night after you collapsed. We've gotta get her to eat and rest, or she's gonna be the one to collapse on us next." Lee slapped Ben on the back. "You're probably the only one who can influence her to act in her own best interest."

Ben's heart sank, and he felt ashamed and selfish for running away and leaving her alone. "I didn't realize she'd suffered all of that," he whispered.

Rising to his feet, Ben headed back to the house, moving as quickly as he could manage, Lee close behind him. Though his adrenaline had propelled him forward on the way out, that advantage was lost on the return trip, though his worry for Callie provided ample motivation. He felt discomfort in his stomach that he thought might be nausea, but since he hadn't experienced anything like that since childhood, he wasn't sure how to define the sensation.

When they entered the house, Taylor met them, looking worried and apologetic.

"Ben, I—"

Ben gripped his shoulder. "Dad, it's alright. You did the right thing. I needed to know, and if you hadn't told me, I probably would have fought you to get to Donovan. I'm not sure what to do next, but right now, Callie is my main focus. We need to get her eating and it looks as if everyone in this house could use some rest. In a couple of hours, I have to meet with Mr. Devereaux, but maybe Lee can stay here with her and—"

"You're still going?" Taylor asked in surprise.

"I have to. Since I can't help Donovan with my touch anymore, this is my last hope to save his life. I need to finish what I started." Ben held up both hands. "No Succouri powers required, and I promise, I won't do anything to put Callie in danger."

Grateful for his son's forgiveness and his renewed promise, Taylor gave up arguing with him. "I'll head to Philly then, see what I can learn from Carozza."

"And I'm going with you."

Ben, Lee, and Taylor turned around to find Callie standing just outside the door to the lab.

"Callie." Ben took a step toward her, but she backed away, so he halted his advance.

"We'll let the two of you talk," Lee said, patting Ben's back and joining Taylor as they headed for the kitchen.

Ben gazed into his beautiful wife's emerald eyes, tormented by the exhaustion and fear he saw there. No words could express what was in his heart, but as she couldn't see his face from that distance and he couldn't touch her, words were all he had.

"I'm sorry for running off."

"It's alright. I understand you couldn't stay and watch

your friend suffer without being able to help him." She smiled. "But I'm glad you came back."

"Your brother can be very persuasive, not to mention incredibly kind."

"Yes, he can," she agreed as she held her weary smile.

Ben took a deep breath, dropping his hands to his sides. "Callie, I'm wrecked by what I've done, what I'm doing to you. You have to know that this isn't at all what I wanted. In fact, it's exactly what I feared most from the very beginning. My love has harmed you in the worst possible way and that kills me, as all I've ever wanted is to protect you and make you happy." Ben balled his hands into fists. "The worst part of it is that, now, it's too late. I can't go back and change it, though I swear to you if I could, I would. If I had known that your fate would become entangled with mine, I never would have asked that of you, never would have wanted that." Ben dropped his head as sorrow overtook him. "I'm helpless, powerless to save you this time, as the danger lurking in the dark shadows, threatening your life, is me."

Folding her hands together over her heart, she shook her head vigorously as tears shone in her eyes. "Beloved, do you imagine that I have a single regret about my fate being tied to yours? Do you think I want to live if you die? Do you think I want to laugh if you cry, win if you lose, or grow strong while you grow weak? Do you think I want to let you walk down a road I can't travel or shoulder a burden I can't share?"

She paused, but Ben didn't know what to say, so she continued.

"The answer to all these questions is a resounding 'no'. I don't. I married you to share everything with you, and that's just exactly what I want to do."

"But, Callie, those vows didn't include this. This wasn't part of the deal. You agreed to do life with me, not death."

She waved her hand in the air. "So, we won't part at death. That suits me just fine. I'm happy to make an amendment to my vows and promise to love you eternally. I'll gladly throw out the escape clause as I have no desire to escape from you, Ben Sawyer."

"But I don't want this for you. I don't want you to die with me. I want you to live, thrive, be happy."

"We will. I don't want to die either and we're not going to. We will find a way out of this mess. But I could never thrive, live, or be happy without you. Our Succouri knows that, and that's why it fused our fates together. I know it's hard for your heart to accept, but please, hear me. This is what I want, Ben. It's exactly what I would have chosen if offered the choice."

Unable to accept what she was saying, Ben put his hand to his forehead. "But it isn't what I want, not what I would have chosen for you."

She smiled and crossed her arms, as Ben continued to watch her reactions with bewilderment. "Then it's a good thing you didn't get to decide. You have no cause for guilt as you had no knowledge, nor did you have a choice. It is our Succouri who linked our fates and I'm grateful it did. I'll happily die by your side if it comes to that, but I'd rather live with you, so let's focus on that goal, alright?" She took a small step forward and put out her hands as if freely offering him her life. "But know this. I regret nothing: meeting you, loving you, bonding with you, marrying you, none of it. I'd do it all again without a moment's hesitation."

"Callie, I..." But Ben couldn't finish, overwhelmed and undone by her extravagant love. He stood in humbled silence, knowing he could never find the words to express how he felt. She should be enraged, disgusted by where her trust in him had left her. At the very least, she should be afraid, scared of the suffering she might have to endure as she shared his fate.

But instead, she was willing, even honored to stay by his side through the darkest of valleys. The noblest of deeds couldn't hope to earn that kind of favor. It was a gift, a sacrifice of the truest kind, revealing, once more, the infinite value of her unparalleled love.

Suddenly, the distance between them was insufferable and Ben's hands began to shake. He needed to hold her, to touch her, as there was no other way to communicate the depths of his emotions.

"Callie Sawyer, I'm going to live because I need the rest of eternity to pay you back for all you've given me. I promise you, one day very soon, I will change this. I'll fill your life with joy and laughter instead of sorrow and tears. Somehow, I will find a way to be worthy of the gift of your heart."

She reached her hand into the space between them. "You already are, beloved. More than worthy."

Unable to resist his urge to touch her, he took a small step, feeling nothing at all, no bond, but also no inflow of strength.

"Ben, stop." Her back was against the door, but she put her hand around the knob.

"Hold on, sweetheart. I think... I think it's okay." He took another step, but still nothing.

"Please don't come closer. I don't want to hurt you. It would kill me if you collapsed again."

"It's alright. I don't feel anything. Nothing at all." He stepped again, now almost close enough to reach for her hand."

"Ben!" Her eyes were wide with fear but also a flicker of hope.

Inhaling deeply, he stepped again and reached out to wrap her in his arms, laughing with ecstatic joy and relief.

She melted into him, kissing his face, and clinging to him as if she hadn't touched him in years. Even without their Succouri bond, Callie in his arms was home, life, hope, wholeness, and bliss. Though the mountain before them was steep and their path unsure, with her beside him, he now had the strength to face it.

He pressed his cheek to hers, alarm halting his laughter.

"Callie, you're hot, really hot, like you have a fever."

"I know," she said with a casual shrug, pulling him close again.

Though he continued touching her, her skin didn't cool. "I need to get the doctor."

"There's nothing he can do for me. We need to get some answers, so I have to go with your dad to Philly."

As Ben stared into her eyes, considering whether she was well enough for such a trip, she blinked but her eyes didn't focus on his face. He felt no draw from her, but that wasn't unusual as that had been the case since their wedding ceremony. He raised his hand to her silky cheek, gently stroking it with his fingertips, noticing the scabs beginning to form on his knuckles. She smiled, but the light he was used to observing in her eyes at his touch was noticeably absent.

"Sweetheart, can you see me?"

Leaning forward, she softly kissed his lips. He could feel the heat still emanating from her feverish face. Keeping her eyes open, she gazed into his. Then, she turned her head to the side and collapsed into his shoulder, her whole body falling into him as exhaustion weighed her down. Though he had very little strength, he held her against him, vowing never to take a single touch for granted.

She hadn't answered his question, but she didn't need to. He already knew. The Succouri in him had fallen silent. He had no healing to give. The strength coming from her hadn't overwhelmed him because there wasn't enough Succouri left in him to detect it anymore. He was just a man now, something he'd wanted all his life, but a reality that would kill them both if they couldn't reverse course, and fast.

CALLIE AND BEN spent the next half an hour sitting side by side on a hospital bed as Doctor Navarro cleaned and wrapped Ben's hand, took new blood samples, and ran more tests. Ben wasn't surprised to find out he was also running a fever, and at the mention of food, his stomach twisted uncomfortably. These physical pains were all but new to him as his memories prior to becoming Succouri were distant and faded.

It wasn't long before Lee and Taylor rejoined them, their presence comforting as they confronted the stark truths about their current condition.

"Be straight with us, Doc," Ben urged. "What does it mean that my touch no longer has any Succouri healing power?"

Doctor Navarro rubbed his hands together and diverted his gaze. "It likely means that the Succouri activity is continuing to decline and has perhaps reached a critical low. You're still conscious, so it hasn't diminished to a debilitating level yet, but if we can't quickly counteract the regression, my guess is it won't be long until the normal functioning of your organs and systems begin to shut down. We must get you two eating and drinking. Otherwise, I'll have to put you on IVs to keep you from getting dehydrated and weak."

There was silence in the room for a long moment as everyone absorbed the unfavorable prognosis.

"Have you ever seen anything like this before?" Ben asked, looking over at Callie. "Partners' fates linked like this?"

"Never," he answered solemnly. "After the ripening, when a Succouri dies and the partner is left behind, there's a normal adjustment period during which she may experience fatigue, headaches, and, of course, intense sadness. But I've never seen a partner suffer an acute illness." He paused to shake his head and fold his arms. "But then, I've never seen a Succouri experience illness either, Ben. Everything about this situation is unprecedented."

Before continuing, Ben momentarily glanced over at Lee. "Do you still believe in the benevolence of the Succouri nature?" Ben's tone wasn't sarcastic; he asked the question with sincerity.

After pondering for a moment, the doctor sighed and nodded. "If the Succouri you possess has ill-intent toward either you or Callie, it would be the first time that's ever been the case. In my own work, as well as my research, I've never heard of or come across any evidence that would support the notion that your Succouri is harming you or Callie on purpose. Therefore, I believe it is far more likely that something about the manner of your acquisition and the transformation it initiated in your physiology is the cause of the problem. We've always believed children could not become Succouri. Though your acquisition seems to defy that forgone conclusion, perhaps our present situation exposes the underlying justifications for that incompatibility."

"Or maybe there's another explanation," Lee interjected. "Something we just don't know about yet."

"That's an entirely plausible theory as well," the doctor freely acknowledged.

"This is the same Succouri that was in Owen Briggs," Taylor said, stepping forward. "It certainly never harmed him, Maggie, or me during the short time I possessed it."

The doctor picked up his clipboard, tapping it repeatedly as he spoke. "Over the next couple of hours, I'm going to comb through all the data from these tests and do my very best to find some answers. The two of you should try to eat, drink, and rest."

"Doc, I'm going to meet with Mr. Devereaux. It's Donovan's only shot." Ben glanced toward the corner of the lab where Donovan rested peacefully. Maggie had convinced Grace to rest for a couple of hours, promising her that she wouldn't leave Donovan's side until Grace returned.

"It's not a good idea for you to drive or go alone," the doctor cautioned. "You could pass out again or worse."

Lee came up beside Ben. "No worries, Doc. I'm going with him."

Surprised, Callie looked at her brother. "If you're determined to go to Philly, you've got Taylor to help you," Lee explained. "Ben feels he has to do this, and he needs help. That's what family's for. I'll drive him and make sure that he gets back here in one piece. I know you'll be a lot less worried knowing he's got someone looking out for him."

Nodding, Callie smiled appreciatively at her brother.

Though profoundly touched by Lee's offer, Ben shook his head. "I need to meet with Ethan alone. I doubt he'll be comfortable if he feels ganged up on or—"

"I'll stay in the car or go for a walk or something while you meet with him, but I'm driving you, and I'm going to be there just in case." Lee's tone was uncompromising, and after a few seconds of hesitation, Ben relented with a sigh, and smiled. "Alright. Thank you."

"Then it's all settled. Lee will go with Ben, and I'll be going with you," Callie declared, turning to Taylor.

Doctor Navarro put up his hands. "I strongly advise against that as well, but I'm guessing it won't matter."

Taylor circled around the bed to stand beside Callie. "The clock is ticking and we need answers. The longer we wait, the weaker these two will get. I need someone with me who knows the whole story, everything about Ben's past and experiences. If that can't be Ben, then Callie is the next best choice. We'll get in and out quickly, learn what we can, and I'll get her right back here to you, Doctor."

Concerned, Ben focused his gaze on his father. Taylor put his hands on Callie's shoulders. "I know you'd be trusting me with the most precious person in the world to you, Ben, and I recognize that there's been insufficient time and opportunity for that level of trust to develop between us but..."

Callie smiled reassuringly at Ben and squeezed his hand.

"I trust you, Dad," he said softly. "But please, please be careful."

"Alright then," Doctor Navarro reluctantly conceded. "At least grant me this: everyone rest. You have a couple of hours before you have to leave, so take advantage of them. I'll give the two of you some medication to help with the fevers and nausea."

Lee and Taylor moved toward the door, and Ben

jumped down from the bed, putting his arm around Callie to help her as she stood.

Before they left the lab, Ben turned a compassionate eye to the distressed and exhausted doctor who was doing everything he could to save their lives despite having very little information to work with. "You rest too, Doc," Ben advised. "Don't wear yourself out. While we appreciate what you're doing for us, this isn't all on your shoulders. Science can't solve every problem. I'm beginning to believe that the cure for this particular infirmity also includes a generous dose of patience, faith, and hope."

Patting Ben's arm, the doctor tried for a smile. "I sincerely hope you're right."

AFTER SHOWERING and changing into comfortable sweats, Ben and Callie lay side by side on the bed in one of the guest bedrooms of the Navarro home. Though he'd been unconscious all night, Ben was nevertheless exhausted, as was Callie. It felt as if twenty-pound weights had been strapped to his arms and legs, making every motion tiring and slow. They had both nibbled on a few crackers and drunk a glass of ginger ale, but that was as much as either could stomach.

"Ben, are you awake?" Callie whispered.

Despite their current trials, Ben smiled, the situation reminding him of their late-night chats at his former home in Boston. "Yes, my love."

"How does it feel?"

Without their bond to connect their thoughts, he wasn't sure what she was asking.

"Which new and bizarre sensation are you referring to?"

She turned onto her side so she could get the clearest

view possible of his face. "How does it feel to just be you, without the Succouri voice in your head?" Her tone was gentle, conveying concern for the potential loss he was experiencing.

Turning onto his side as well, he stroked her hair as he answered, still craving closeness after the agonizing distance they'd been forced to endure, yet also understanding that she needed this in order to read his expressions. "It's not as empty as the hollow void left by our missing bond. That, and my inability to help you see or take away your sickness, are the worst parts of this by far. I'd always imagined that breaking away, no more powers or promptings from my alter ego, would be liberating, like being released from prison." He grimaced. "But that's not the case. It's more like walking out of jail only to find myself in a scorching hot desert. Suddenly the cool, damp shelter of the prison seems hospitable. And if I get to be in there with you, with that sweet connection to your heart, then it's a palace."

"I'm with you," she vowed. "Prison, desert, or palace."

Ben smiled and softly kissed her forehead. "Without that anchor, I'd be adrift." His smile faded. "I won't have any trouble relating to Mr. Devereaux. I feel the emptiness, similar to what I felt before I met you, but noticeably stronger. My whole being aches from missing you, even though my eyes inform me that you're still here." He ran his hand down her arm. "The only thing that eases the pain is touching you; temporarily filling up the hole where our bond should be. If we'd had to continue to maintain our distance from one another..." A tortured grimace contorted his expression. "I think I may have gone crazy. At least this provides temporary relief, but I'm greedy. I want it all. I want you back inside my heart and head. I'm incomplete, broken without you, more so than without my Succouri partner."

Callie put her hand to her heart, rubbing it like it was a sore muscle. "I know exactly what you mean. It feels like a limb was removed."

Ben put his hand on hers, intertwined their fingers, and then moved their linked hands to rest over his heart. "At least this is some way for us to connect, feel the nearness of the other, even if it's not everything we're used to or want."

"After last night, this feels like a lot," she replied, shifting closer to him. "Tell me everything you're thinking right now."

Ben chuckled. "Everything?"

"Yes, all of it."

"Well, I was thinking how much I'm going to hate watching you leave with my dad today and how I won't be able to take a full breath until you're back safely. I was thinking that I now understand why your brother has always been such a comfort to you as his positive, direct approach to life is refreshing and contagious. I was wondering what in the world I'm going to find this after-noon when I meet with Mr. Devereaux and how I'm going to convince him to help Donovan, and I was thinking..."

"Go on."

"I was thinking how irresistibly beautiful you are. If in the end I must die, I want to die like this, with you in my arms; that way I'll be going from heaven to heaven."

She flashed him a radiant smile.

"Your turn," he prodded.

"I was recognizing how much better I feel about you traveling today now that Lee's going with you. I was replaying Louis' reassuring words about our destiny, drawing hope and strength from them. I was wondering about our home in Cape Cod and when we might actually get to stay there, and I was thinking…"

"Go on."

"Do you remember that night in the park when I told you that even without the bond I'd still want you just the same, still need you just as much?"

He smiled as he nodded.

"Though I desperately miss our Succouri connection and my clear view of your spellbinding blue eyes, my feelings for you are exactly the same. No matter what changes, one thing will always remain: I love you with my whole heart, soul, and body."

Ben leaned down just as she lifted toward him. They shared a kiss so full of passion that all weakness, exhaustion, and pain vanished. A new kind of flame ignited between them, quickly strengthening into a raging fire. Callie wrapped her arms around him, sliding her hands under his T-shirt. Pulling him with her, she rolled onto her back.

"Callie!" Ben panted, using his elbows to keep some of his weight off her, even as she countered the effort by tightening her embrace. "There's nothing I want more than to be close to you right now, as close as possible, but I need to let you rest. I don't think we should—"

"Please, Ben. I almost lost you last night. I thought I might never get to hold you like this again. Then, I couldn't get near you for hours, even though everything in me, human and Succouri, desperately needed to touch you. I don't know what will happen tomorrow, but I don't want to waste a single minute. We have right now, right here together. I need you, much more than I need rest."

As gently as he could, Ben took Callie in his arms and loved her with his whole being. Without their Succouri bond, the experience was different, but no less exciting or fulfilling. As they got lost in the sweet pleasures of sharing their hearts and bodies, the ache of their missing bond temporarily eased. Exploring new paths of intimacy, they relied on their human bond, whispering tender words to express what they could no longer innately discern.

Afterward, as Ben lay holding Callie as she peacefully slept on his shoulder, he smiled, pondering how the experience had in some ways, been less intimate, but in other ways, more so. Her pleasures and desires weren't automatically transferred to his consciousness, so he had to pay attention, tune into her reactions and whispered affections, and she the same with him. The encounter was uniquely human, but it had absolutely proven the words he'd spoken to her on their honeymoon. He'd told her that even without their Succouri bond, making love to her would be heavenly, and indeed it was. Though he still longed for the day when their special connection would return, he knew this experience would bring them closer, make them even better lovers as it provided them with the opportunity to deepen the other bonds they shared.

As the passion ebbed, the exhaustion returned, and Ben kissed Callie's forehead before settling back into his pillow to grab what was now only about an hour of sleep. Though he regretted keeping her from the longer period of rest he knew she needed, Callie had been right. Tomorrow wasn't guaranteed. Their experience with Ruiz had taught him that. Treasuring each moment with her, loving her while he still could; these were the choices that would leave no regrets behind, no matter what came next.

CHAPTER 3

THE MEETINGS

At noon, Callie and Taylor boarded a private plane bound for Philadelphia. Though she continued to feel weak and she still had no appetite, the medication Doctor Navarro had administered had lowered her fever and eased the nausea, making travel more tolerable. Taylor kept a protective eye on her, watching for any change in her condition and looking for ways to make her more comfortable. She smiled, knowing the special attention was his way of keeping his promise to Ben, but also arose from genuine affection for her as his daughter-in-law. It reminded her of her own father's loving care for her, and those warm memories strengthened her as she battled the fatigue and discomfort of the strange illness.

In addition, Callie was pleasantly surprised by how adept Taylor was at assisting her with her visual limitations. Since she'd met Taylor, there hadn't been many times when Callie had been separated from Ben's healing touch, so she knew this knowledge didn't come from observation or personal experience. It was evident that either Ben or Lee had intentionally instructed him on the basics of what she would need. Since Ben had demonstrated this kindness before, she wasn't surprised by the thoughtful provision, but she was still grateful for it as it made their interactions easier and allowed them to remain focused on the goals of this trip.

"Have you learned anything new about Carozza since we last talked?" Callie asked as they made the thirty-minute drive to the man's home.

"He lives with his son, Roberto Carozza, who has never been married nor does he have a family of his own, and is—from what I was able to dig up on him—of questionable character. When I made the arrangements, Roberto, who goes by Bobby, was hostile and defensive. In no uncertain terms, he let me know his father's physical and mental health were extremely poor, and he tried very hard to dissuade me from coming. I got the definite feeling that his objection came primarily from his disdain for Carozza's philosophies and ideas about the Succouri. He's certainly not a believer, and that's likely an understatement.

"Does he know you're FBI?"

"Heavens no!" Taylor exclaimed. "I have no doubt he would have hung up on me if he'd known that. The guy's skittish, which is understandable given the subject matter and his father's outspoken and apparently unorthodox views. But I suspect it's more than that. As it was, I had to improvise quite the tall tale—something about scholarly historical research—before he'd even admit that his father was the man I was looking for. I didn't reveal anything about our situation, and I advise caution, especially around the son. I don't trust him."

"If he's a skeptic and doesn't believe his father's in his right mind, how did you manage to convince him to let us come at all?"

No immediate answer was given, but when Taylor did speak, there was a sly smile in his tone. "I can be very persuasive when I need to be."

Callie held up both hands. "Enough said. I'm glad you're on our side. I would never want to go up against you."

Reaching over, he patted her hand. "And I'd never bet against you, dear one. My son's a lucky man to have found someone so strong and courageous. I've wanted to tell you this for quite some time but haven't had the chance. I know for certain that Ben's willingness to offer me undeserved forgiveness was, in large part, because of you. His mother and I wounded him deeply, and he had no reason or obligation to give me a second chance. If he'd found out about me before meeting you, I'm quite sure he would have walked away from me but through your love for him, he's learned to trust again. Though Ben is kindhearted, the neglect and rejection he endured was unforgivable. I know you loved your father and had a close and healthy relationship with him. Through you and Lee, Ben saw what a family should be, which, I'm sure, deepened the hurt in some ways but also planted within him seeds of hope and longing. Knowing you as I do now, I have no doubt you watered those seeds, so when he learned about me, he didn't slam the door in my face. Thank you for all you said and did to encourage him to take a chance on me. I owe you a very great debt."

Callie lowered her head for a moment before turning to smile at him. "It didn't take that much encouragement. When he read your letter—the part where you said you loved him—he wept for a long time. Something inside him knew those words were genuine. His heart wanted them to be true. On our road trip to Boston, he told me he always believed you knew about him, even though he had no evidence to support that belief. Perhaps it was that conviction that kept the door from shutting permanently. You owe me nothing. The reward of watching your hearts come alive as you grow in love and trust for one another is all I want or need. Ben's heart is more whole with you in his life, and as my heart beats in rhythm with his, so mine is as well."

Taylor smiled. "I'll say it again: my son's a very, very lucky man."

Silently, Taylor pondered for a moment before speaking again, his voice unsteady with raw emotion. "Right before I donated marrow, I went to see Ben in his hospital room."

As she continued to look at him, her smile shifted to an expression of surprise and when Taylor saw it, he rushed to explain. "They had him sedated, probably because of the pain he was suffering. I hadn't intended on going in, but when I saw that he was asleep, I couldn't help myself. I sat by his bed and quietly wept, wishing with all my heart that I could change everything and be this incredible boy's father. His innocent face was so... beautiful, but even in sleep, his expression was far from peaceful. Perhaps it was the torment of that terrible disease, I don't know, but as I sat there, staring at the pain etched on my young son's face, I knew my life, my work, my efforts to change, my very existence would never mean a thing until I could take that pain away." He paused to chuckle softly. "Little did I know that it would actually be a remarkable, beautiful young woman who would beat me to it."

"Did he ever open his eyes or seem to notice you there?" Callie asked, wondering if at some level Ben's subconscious had been aware of his father's surreptitious visit and that's why he believed his father knew about him.

"No. He never stirred, and I left before anyone knew I'd been there, but the experience changed me, gave me one goal in life to work toward. I decided that day to get out of undercover work as quickly as I could so I could be with my son and try to undo the damage his mother and I had inflicted. Unfortunately, it took far longer than I hoped, and then, when Ben didn't return my correspondence, I worried that my hopes were only an unattainable dream, but I was determined never to give up trying."

"That's why you kept paying for the box all those years?"

"I knew the odds of him changing his mind and forgiving me were slim, but I couldn't let go of the hope."

Placing her hand on his arm, Callie smiled. "It's a very good thing you never did."

"I'm not giving up this time either. I have two precious children to protect now, and I'm every bit as determined if not more so, to get the answers we need." Unyielding resolve as well as genuine fear of losing what he'd finally found resounded in his promises.

"I appreciate that and your determination comforts me, but don't underestimate the value of your love and presence. Those are powerful medicines themselves."

As they pulled into the driveway of an old, run-down house, Taylor shut off the engine and turned to smile at her. "They certainly are, dear girl. Medicines of the most potent kind."

AFTER BEN LEFT Callie in the care of his father, he and Lee set out on the drive to Ethan Devereaux's remote cabin. Though he trusted Taylor, and knew that, right now in particular, he was probably more capable of guarding and physically caring for her than Ben was, he still felt uncomfortable with the distance between them. Though presently he might be mostly human, his Succouri instincts to protect his wife and partner were ingrained in his being. A shift in the chemistry of his blood couldn't change that.

Though Ben missed their intimate Succouri connection, he was comforted by the realization that what he and Callie felt for one another hadn't changed whatsoever. The love they shared could stand and thrive on its own.

Since their first date, when he'd pressed against her to keep her from sliding in the snow, the fire had drawn them together, overwhelming them continuously as they'd tried to control it. Even after they married, the enticing pleasure in the connection it provided couldn't be resisted. As every moment they'd shared had been affected by that powerful force, it had been impossible to know how different their feelings might be without it. But their passionate moments together that morning had proven that the physical love and attraction between them was also firmly rooted, unshaken by the drastic changes they were experiencing.

Despite these comforting discoveries, Ben couldn't deny that the connection provided by his Succouri identity was precious and nothing could satisfactorily fill that hole. If it were possible for them to survive as they were right now, they could live out their days, sharing a deep and beautiful love, but Ben knew that neither of them would ever stop yearning for the extraordinary intimacy offered exclusively by their Succouri bond.

Ben hadn't been exaggerating when he'd told Callie that he could now fully empathize with Ethan Devereaux. Whatever remnant of Succouri remained inside him, it was ample enough to torment him with the abiding emptiness typically suffered by Succouri who have lost their partner.

No matter how many times he reminded himself that Callie wasn't lost, he couldn't shake the sorrow. And, without her nearby, it was becoming increasingly difficult to manage the heaviness that pressed down on his heart.

In addition, the now noticeably silent space in Ben's consciousness where his inconspicuous, yet omnipresent Succouri partner had previously resided troubled him. Until it was gone, Ben hadn't recognized that his Succouri had been such a significant source of comfort and strength as well as a subtle voice of wise counsel. Separating its influence from his own inner thoughts had been challenging until its absence shone a spotlight on the vacated space.

"Do you have a plan?" Lee's voice interrupted Ben's reverie.

It took Ben a moment to respond as his mind refocused. "Um... not really. I don't know exactly what to expect, so it's hard to strategize. I suppose I'll share my experiences, do a lot of listening, and try to make a connection somehow."

"Why does the doc seem so sure you're the one who can convince this guy to help Donovan?"

"I'm the only Succouri he's ever known who stayed sane despite fifteen years without a bond. Since Mr. Devereaux lost his wife fifteen years ago, I think the doctor's hoping our similar experiences will generate a connection."

"So, the guy's crazy?"

"Probably 'broken' is a better word."

"You sure you don't want me to come in with you?" He pointed at Ben's bandaged hand. "You might need backup if he goes nuts on you or something."

Ben shook his head. "I doubt he's violent, but I'll keep you on speed dial just in case." Ben smiled at Lee's willingness to rush to his aid.

"How will you explain that?" he asked, nodding toward Ben's hand.

Ben sighed as he stared at it. "I have no idea. I don't even know how to explain who and what I currently am to myself. I'm not really human. My biology can never return to its original chemistry and my blood is still full of Succouri... substances, even if they're malfunctioning . But I can't claim to be Succouri either since I can't help anyone with my touch, heal myself, or bond with my wife." Ben threw up his hands. "I thought defining who I was before was difficult. Now, it's impossible."

"How about just being Ben, then. I mean, most of us never give a single thought to what is, or is not, swimming in our veins." He shrugged. "Take me, for example. I'm just Lee. What you see is what you get. I don't think you really need to give Mr. Devereaux a chemistry lesson. It's not really his business anyway. Just be Ben. That's good enough for me, and it's definitely good enough for my sister."

Once again, Lee's simple, straightforward perspective brought a smile to Ben's face and a lasting sense of peace to his heart. "There aren't too many other people's opinions I care about, so that suits me just fine. Have you heard from Allie?" Ben asked, knowing that her surgery had taken place nearly twenty-four hours earlier.

"I got a text that said 'I'm alive! More later'." Lee grinned as he stared out the front windshield. "I'm sure the recovery is long and hard, but I'm taking that as a good sign."

"I think it's a very good sign."

Inwardly, Ben rejoiced at the fact that his Succouri touch hadn't failed during that flight. If he hadn't been able to help Allie or get Donovan at least this far, the guilt of their deaths would have haunted him all his life. Though

Donovan's situation was far from resolved, the transport had been the time of greatest risk for both him and Allie, and as it seemed that his subsequent decline was inevitable, he was at least grateful that it hadn't rendered his touch powerless any earlier.

Abruptly, Ben began to wonder if his Succouri had been aware and perhaps even planned or adjusted the timing of these happenings. His negativity toward his silent partner—a habitual state of mind that Lee had kindly pointed out—inclined him to dismiss that notion, but as he'd committed to try to be more generous in his assumptions, he permitted the idea to linger and develop.

Assuming Callie's vision on the beach was everything she believed it to be, his Succouri knew this illness or decline was coming; perhaps it even intentionally caused it. Though some warning signs had manifested in the previous weeks, the loss of healing power hadn't happened until just after Donovan and Allie were safely delivered to their destinations. The timing was undeniably fortuitous. Until the last few hours when its absence had marked a discernable 'X' on the psychological spot it had previously occupied, hearing its voice had been difficult, yet there was no doubt that they shared experiences and destinies. Assuming it knew the desires and intentions in Ben's heart and had the power to delay the approaching crisis, choosing to do so would indeed demonstrate a deference and affection for him that would warrant a shift in his attitude.

Nevertheless, the fact remained that it was the Succouri's withdrawal that was killing him and Callie, and try as he might, he couldn't conceive of a defensible reason for putting them through this misery. Therefore, though the concept of an altruistic and cooperative cohort was appealing, even comforting, their present circumstance made it hard to justify a change of heart.

Still, he couldn't deny that he'd felt the same way about his father before he'd heard his story. He'd been sure that there was no defense for the abandonment Ben had suffered as a child. But after learning the truth and getting to know him, Ben had indeed changed his mind and forgiven him. That experience had taught him to be more cautious in forming judgments, especially when all the cards weren't yet on the table. When he'd met her, he'd underestimated Callie's ability to accept his secret and love him for who he was. Were the remnants of distrust and skepticism he still carried causing him to underestimate the good will of his Succouri usurper as well? Ben wasn't sure, but he had the feeling he would soon find out.

After Taylor knocked on the door of the Carozza home, he and Callie waited for a long moment before it finally opened just a crack. The home's occupant peered out at them through the small space, giving Callie the clear impression that their visit was far from welcome.

"Bobby? I'm Wes, and this is Callie." Taylor introduced them, his voice strong and confident despite the rude welcome.

The door swung open, and Taylor guided Callie past a thin, slumped figure. Though she couldn't see well enough to observe much about the man's features, his posture and the distance he maintained from them as they moved into a small, dark living room spoke volumes.

The house smelled of mold and cigarette smoke, and the combination churned Callie's already queasy stomach.

"You're wasting your time," the man growled in a gravelly, low voice, which revealed years of chain smoking. "My dad's just a crazy old man. He drove my mother away years ago with his rantings, and if I weren't a raging alcoholic and chronic gambler with no money and no friends left to use, I wouldn't be here either."

Bobby lit a cigarette and stared at them, without bidding them to sit. Defensively, Taylor kept himself positioned between the gruff man and her, and she was grateful as Bobby made her uneasy.

"It's our time to waste, now isn't it?" Taylor countered calmly but with an air of authority. "Kindly show us to your father's room and we'll finish our business here and leave you be."

"What is your business with the Succouri anyway?" the man asked accusingly. "You don't look like one to me, and I know she certainly isn't." Without a doubt, this man was trying to bully them, but Callie had a feeling he'd met his match.

Taylor crossed his arms and subtly patted Callie's hand before stepping forward. She understood the signal and stayed where she was, remaining safely behind him as she breathed a prayer of thanks that her father-in-law had more than enough experience with thugs worse than this one to have the situation firmly in hand.

"My business is with your father, not you, but if you insist on making yourself my business, I'm all too happy to oblige. As we discussed on the phone, I'm well acquainted with several of those old friends you mentioned. Some of them are anxious to reunite with you. Shall I let them know where to find you, or would you rather I focus my attention on the matter I came here to discuss with your father? Your choice."

As a silent standoff ensued, Callie's heart pounded.

Taylor's presumed bluff was flawlessly executed and his tone so confident yet chilling that it sent shivers up her spine. If she didn't know the man he truly was, she'd be frightened by him. As it was, she had to keep reminding herself that he had spent twenty years undercover with drug dealers and murderers and he'd survived because he knew how to handle situations just like this one. Still, it was hard to reconcile the street-smart man before her with the kindhearted one she knew as Ben's father.

"This way," Bobby at last conceded, backing away and turning to head down an adjacent hallway. Taylor stepped back to offer Callie his arm again, and they followed the man to a closed door.

"Don't say I didn't warn you," he huffed as he spun around and moved away.

"You alright?" Taylor whispered near her ear before entering the room.

She let out an anxious breath she'd been holding since they'd entered the house and tried for a smile as she nodded her head. "As I said, I wouldn't want to go up against you."

Taylor chuckled and softly patted her hand. "Are you ready?"

Raising her chin, she nodded once more.

The small bedroom they entered was even darker than the rest of the house and the smell hit her like an unanticipated punch. A combination of urine and dirty laundry, the pungent odor triggered the nausea that was barely under control, and she placed her hand over her mouth as she inhaled deeply, struggling to prevent it from rising into her throat.

Throwing aside a pile of clothes that covered it, Taylor pulled over a folding chair, and Callie sat down. She rested her elbows on her knees and leaned her head into her hands, breathing steadily until she finally regained her equilibrium. Taylor squatted next to her, gently rubbing her back as he watched her face intently.

"I'm okay," she finally assured him with a relieved sigh.

Taylor felt her forehead. "I think your fever's back. We'll make this as quick as possible."

"Who are you?" a voice called from the small bed in the far corner of the room. The voice was weak and shaky, but not aggressive like the son's had been. The remnants of an Italian accent were audible in his pronunciation.

Taylor stood and stepped forward. "My name is Wes Taylor, and this is Callie Sawyer. We're pleased to make your acquaintance, Mr. Carozza. We've come to talk with you about the Succouri."

Callie heard fabric shifting, and she guessed the man had sat up. "The Succouri?" he asked, as if surprised to hear the word spoken out loud.

"Yes. My friend and mentor, Owen Briggs, came here many years ago to inquire about them. We're hoping you can share with us what you remember about that conversation and ask you some questions ourselves."

"How did you come to know about the Succouri?" Each time he said 'Succouri,' he held out the last syllable until there was no air left in his lungs, making the word sound mystical.

"Someone I love deeply is one, and he needs help."

A low, rhythmic chuckle billowed from the man. "You had best go to his partner. You and I certainly can't help him."

"Please, Mr. Carozza," Callie pleaded, hating that she had no power in this case to help Ben.

The man shifted again, and Taylor looked her way,

making her believe Carozza had also focused his attention on her.

"Are you his Datouri?" The man's voice was filled with awe, as if in the presence of royalty.

"I'm his wife," she answered, not knowing what he meant, but hoping her answer provided the requested information.

"Then there is no need for my help, Bella Signora. You already have everything he needs."

Callie lowered her head.

"Her husband, my son, has Owen Briggs' Succouri," Taylor announced.

Carozza let out a long, heavy breath, informing Callie that, though neither of them had any idea of the significance of this fact, Taylor's shot in the dark was about to pay off.

To say that Ethan Devereaux's residence was remote was an understatement. Ben and Lee got lost twice trying to find it, and as cell service was spotty, they'd had to stop at a gas station and ask a local man for directions before they finally located the unmarked dirt road that eventually dead-ended at the camouflaged cabin.

Though it was small and simple, it wasn't run down as Ben had somehow expected. There was no yard to speak of, as it was surrounded on three sides by the tall trees of an ancient forest.

"This guy's a hermit," Lee observed as he parked the car far enough away that no one could see Lee inside it from the home's windows.

"I'm guessing there's a good reason for that," Ben said as he took a deep breath and unbuckled his seatbelt.

"You're sure you'll be okay out here?" Ben asked, feeling bad about leaving him with nothing to do.

"I'll probably do a little exploring," Lee said excitedly. "But don't worry, I won't go too far, especially since the speed dial thing is a bust."

Ben pulled his phone from his pocket, nodding at Lee when he saw that he had no signal. He wondered how Doctor Navarro had reached Mr. Devereaux in the first place.

Before exiting the car, Ben unwrapped his hand, hoping to avoid an immediate suspicious reaction from Mr. Devereaux that would inevitably arise if he noticed Ben's injury. The sight of his scabbed knuckles was so foreign that he couldn't help staring at them as Lee watched with an amused grin.

"Good luck, brother," Lee offered, patting Ben on the shoulder.

Wearily, Ben exited the car, but before he moved away, he bent down to speak to Lee through the open window, offering him a grateful smile. "You were right, you know."

"Usually am, but feel free to elaborate."

"When you said we needed you, and you could help us. In less than two days, you've already become invaluable to me. I couldn't have made it this far without your encouragement and assistance."

Lee shrugged his shoulders. "This is what family does, brother Ben. You'd better get used to it 'cause you're stuck with lots of it now."

With a slight nod of his head, and one last grateful smile, Ben turned toward the cabin, his heart full as he reveled in the comfort of finally being part of the kind of family he'd only ever dreamed of. Staring at the solitary dwelling before him, he whispered a prayer of thanks that isolation and loneliness were unlikely to be burdens he'd have to carry again, and he sincerely hoped he could free Ethan Devereaux from that unbearable existence.

When he approached the thick, wooden front door, he took a deep breath, feeling the fatigue of his illness worsening by the hour. Placing the back of his hand to his forehead, the heat alerted him to the return of his fever. If he was experiencing these symptoms, so was Callie. Though comforted by his father's presence with her, Ben was eager for them to reunite and to have her firmly back under his watchful eye.

Before he could knock, the door swung open, catching Ben off guard. The man that stood before him looked to be about fifty, though Ben knew he had to be closer to seventy. His medium brown hair and thin beard were peppered with gray, and his tired, light blue eyes were framed by deep creases. As he had with the cabin, Ben expected the man to be unkempt, perhaps even wild-looking in his appearance and hygiene, but besides the obvious pain etched into the lines on his face, Ethan Devereaux was well-groomed and appeared perfectly sane.

"Mr. Devereaux?"

The man crossed his arms and smirked. "Ben Sawyer?"

"I'm sorry, yes." Ben extended his hand, forgetting all about the scabbed knuckles, but Mr. Devereaux kept his arms crossed and his eyes remained locked on Ben's, so Ben dropped it back to his side.

He waited for an invitation to enter but Ethan only stared at him.

"May I come in?" Ben finally asked.

Stepping aside, Ethan gestured for Ben to proceed, so he moved past him, entering a small room with one straight-backed chair and a fireplace. Though his current condition made sitting appealing, it didn't feel right to take the only chair in the room, so he stood next to the fireplace instead. Ethan closed the door and took up a position on the opposite side. As there was no fire presently burning, which was regrettable to Ben, they both looked somewhat silly standing there. Whether from the fever or the cold reception or both, occasional waves of chill began to plague him.

"I appreciate your willingness to talk with me," Ben started. "It's my sincere hope that we can find a way to help each other."

"You're not what I expected," Ethan complained as he stared into the cold fireplace. "You're much too young to even be a Succouri, much less to have suffered as one."

Ben shook his head. "You'd be surprised."

At that, Ethan turned his head to look at Ben.

"I've been Succouri for fifteen years, Mr. Devereaux and for all but the last couple of months of that time, I had never heard the word nor did I have any notion whatsoever of what I was. I lived in confusion and isolation, running and hiding."

Ethan laughed mockingly. "You're a fraud, Mr. Sawyer. I know Succouri look young, but you can't be more than thirty."

"Twenty-seven, actually." Ben let the statement hang in the air for a moment before continuing. "I became Succouri when I was twelve years old."

Ethan spat into the fireplace as he angrily glared at Ben. "Children can't be Succouri."

Keeping his eyes firmly locked on Ethan's, Ben folded his arms, desiring to be compassionate, but determined not to let this man bully him. "It turns out, they certainly can, though it seems not without some rather dire consequences."

Pushing a puff of exasperated air through his lips, Ethan finally broke eye contact and stared back into the cold fireplace. No one spoke for a long moment, and Ben waited patiently, letting Ethan choose the direction of the conversation.

"So, you didn't bond because you were a kid." He shrugged. "That's not the same as—"

"I didn't bond because I didn't know anything about the bond. I was an adult for many of those fifteen years, but I only knew I felt empty and incomplete. I never knew why." As he spoke of the past, the fresh ache of his and Callie's lost connection throbbed in his chest.

Ethan's jaw tightened and his hands balled into fists as he spoke his next words. "Much better not to know what you're missing than to know all too well and have to live with the consequences of that knowledge every day and every night."

Lowering his head, Ben answered softly. "I completely agree." He couldn't argue with Mr. Devereaux as, even though Callie wasn't gone, the torment he presently suffered was more acute than anything he'd endured before he'd met her. If he had to contend with that hollow sensation alongside the actual grief of losing her, he had no idea how he'd survive it.

Surprised by his response, Ethan returned his gaze to Ben, and Ben saw the flicker of a connection ignite in his dull eyes.

CHAPTER 4
THE CONNECTIONS

As Callie sat, suspended in hopeful anticipation, Taylor took a step toward Carozza's bed. "There was something unusual about Brigg's Succouri, wasn't there?"

Another rumbling chuckle vibrated in the air. "Tell me, Mr. Taylor, which do you find more unusual, or perhaps the word should be unnatural: the wild wolf or the tame lapdog? The fierce lion or the coddled pussycat?"

"I don't understand," Taylor answered.

"Then I will ask you a different question. How did Owen Briggs come by his gift?"

Taylor was silent for a moment, and Callie wondered if perhaps this was a test to see if they really were acquainted with Owen Briggs. "While on a dangerous mission in Central America, he was anonymously saved by the blood of a Succouri after being beaten nearly to death. He had no memory of the rescue and Owen didn't know what he was for a long while, until he spoke with you."

"Where did you hear this fictional tale?" he asked, amused curiosity in his tone.

"From his widow."

Carozza sighed in sad resignation. "So, he never believed. That's regrettable, quite a shame, indeed. But perhaps your son will be the one."

Though she knew the fever was clouding her mind, Callie was lost, unable to follow the winding path of this man's words. Maybe Bobby Carozza was right. Perhaps age had already robbed his father of sound reasoning.

"Mr. Carozza," Taylor persisted, calmly but with a sense of urgency. "My son and his wife are very ill. We don't have time for riddles. Please, if you know something about Owen's gift that might help us solve this mystery and return them to health, I implore you to share it."

"Ill?" Carozza questioned with surprise. "Mr. Taylor, neither Succouri nor Datouri suffers illness. Has it left him?"

"No," Callie spoke up. "He's only twenty-seven, too young for the ripening."

"His age is of no consequence," the man said dismissively. "Has the gift departed?" He repeated the question with more interest.

"No, well, yes, but..." Callie stammered, not sure which answer was correct.

Taylor stepped back and placed his hand on Callie's shoulder. "Mr. Carozza, my son became Succouri when he was a child. It transformed his body, irrevocably merging the human and Succouri physiology. He can't lose it. If he does, he will die."

The man gasped, then took several shaky breaths before responding at a volume barely above a whisper. "Mrs. Sawyer, may I ask, does your husband's touch release healing to all, even others who possess the gift?"

The question contained such hopeful anticipation that

Callie's heart began to pound, wondering what this unique ability foretold. She looked up at Taylor as he looked down questioningly at her. How did Carozza know about this? Perhaps he wasn't as mad as they presumed, after all. "Until this morning, yes it did."

Carozza's sharp, audible inhale gave Callie goose-bumps, and when he spoke, his voice was so breathy that she had to strain to hear the words. "Then, it is true. He indeed is the one."

DESPITE HIS TIREDNESS and the new throbbing in his head, Ben straightened his posture and faced Ethan Devereaux. "I know all too well the emptiness of living without a partner. It consumes you and makes you feel hopeless, weak, and desperate. It relentlessly whispers lies, day and night, defining your future as desolate. Without someone to share the burdens of this sacrificial life, the gift is a curse, setting you apart from the rest of humanity. Until just weeks ago, I'd had no aid during the draw, so I hated it and resented the strength taken from me, even as I couldn't resist the compulsion to give it to anyone in trouble. Like a helpless puppet, I was forced to live a life outside my will and choos-ing. And I was certainly convinced that no one could or should ever love or accept me. I regarded myself and my unusual abilities as destructive, even dangerous, so I never let anyone get too close."

"We are puppets, Mr. Sawyer," Ethan seethed. "Pathetic, pitiful pawns haplessly maneuvered around a game board we can't see."

Rubbing his temples, Ben's mind struggled to stay focused as his thoughts scattered, like fallen leaves in the wind. "That is one way to look at it. It's the view I also chose to adopt for a long time, and admittedly still slip back into frequently. But there is another perspective, Mr. Devereaux, one that offers a great deal more hope and fulfillment."

"Let me guess," he said with a mocking chuckle. "Your wife helped you see the light."

Like grasping a lifeline, he fixed the image of Callie's face in his mind, and it temporarily settled his thoughts. "She did," Ben admitted, smiling at the truth despite Ethan's skepticism. "But not in the way you probably think. My wife was born almost completely blind. Though her world was, and in some ways still is, limited by her circumstances, her inner peace, strength, and contentment continue to inspire and challenge me. In a way, she's a puppet too, living with challenges she didn't ask for and can't control. Her limitations could isolate her and rule her destiny if she let them. But she turns her weaknesses into strengths, and through her struggles, she builds bridges to those in pain. Without question, she believes that what we go through has a purpose, but we must accept who we are, the good and the bad of the hand we've been dealt, in order to discover it." Ben sighed. "Her courage astonishes me, forcing me to stretch and grow to keep pace."

For a moment, the expression in Ethan's eyes softened, but then he turned his face away from Ben and balled his hands into tight fists. "And what would happen to you if every time you closed your eyes, you had no choice but to see her crushed body, her caved-in skull, her blood pouring out on the ground like water? Would you maintain your hope and optimism then?"

A shiver ran through Ben, and he lowered his head. "I've

faced the terror of losing her too many times already, and I'm not done suffering it yet. I can't fathom your pain. I have no words, no magic, no fix for your broken heart, Mr. Devereaux. I didn't come here to cure your grief, for if I were in your shoes, no one could ever cure mine."

"Then, you simply want my Succouri," he accused, pointing at Ben. "You want to save your friend, and I'm your only hope," he shouted, taking on a contemptuous tone as his volume rose.

Intentionally, Ben countered by lowering his voice to just above a whisper. "I want to save my friend, that's true. Donovan is dying and this is now the only way I can help him. But I came here hoping to offer you more than a chance to escape your Succouri chains. Once they're gone, I sincerely hope the pain of losing your wife eases, but there is no guarantee. No one can give you back what you've lost, but you can forge new connections or reconnect with those who care about you. I want to help you do that. This"—Ben gestured into the space around them—"is no way to live."

Through the mask of pain, the brokenness of the isolated years, Ben caught a glimpse, the tiniest spark of something warm and kind in Ethan's eyes. It retreated quickly, but the impression lingered in Ben's heart even as the man gritted his teeth and spoke with conviction. "I don't want to live. I haven't wanted to live for fifteen years, but it's hard to die when you heal nearly before you bleed."

Saddened by the desperate admission, Ben's heart twisted in empathy, but he didn't look away. "What about your family, those who love you? Until I met Callie, I had no one else in my life who cared about me, but you do. You matter to them. You might be able to find a different, but no less meaningful bond with them. They—"

"Jessica hates me and rightfully so," Ethan interrupted.

"I ran, left her alone with the aftermath. I couldn't help her; I couldn't be anything to her or the baby. Without Lexi I was, I am, hollow, empty. I have nothing to give anyone. Jes wasn't alone. She has a husband and a child. And I knew, eventually, she would heal, get over the grief of losing her mother. My incurable sorrow would derail that healing. I can't... I'm not like you. My heart was already opened and then crushed. I have nothing left to give anyone. I'm shattered glass, the broken pieces of a former man. Time hasn't changed anything, hasn't granted me a single moment of relief from the agony. But they're not Succouri. They've had fifteen years to move on. If I return, I'll pull them under with me." He shook his head and spoke through gritted teeth. "The best thing I can do is leave them be, keep them as far from me as possible."

The words flowed out in a torrent and Ben did his best to absorb them despite the advancing fog that clouded his thoughts. Still, his mind fixed on one particular word: Jessica."

IN DESPERATION, Callie stood to her feet. "What does that mean? Please. If you know something that can help him, save his life, please tell us."

Taylor put his hand under her elbow, trying to lend her support as she swayed unsteadily on her feet.

"*Non aver paura.* Don't fear, Signora," he said soothingly. "If what you tell me is true, neither of you are ill."

Taylor put up a hand. "Let's back up. What was different about Briggs' gift? If the story we've been told isn't accurate, what did happen?"

"Owen Briggs did not pass out from the beating he suffered, nor did he forget what happened to him. Because his mind was closed, he convinced himself that he fell unconscious, and that's why he couldn't recall certain events he decided must have occurred. Before he came to me, he spoke to many others, but their information didn't align with his experience, so he kept searching. I tried to help him accept the truth and embrace the priceless treasure he possessed, but as I was a lone voice, one of the few who still speak for the Succouri Antico, it appears my voice was drowned out by the unanimous chorus of the ignorant."

Putting her hand to her head, Callie was beginning to feel that this trip, this meeting was pointless as every answer they received only led to more questions.

"What did Briggs remember?" Taylor followed up, trying to focus the man's attention on a singular topic.

"He remembered the touch and the deep blue eyes of the man who saved his life." Carozza paused and switched his tone to one of curiosity. "Eyes like Owen Briggs' and like yours, Mr. Taylor. He remembered renewing strength pouring into his veins and watching his wounds close and disappear. He remembered the stranger walking him back to his hotel room, speaking all the while in a tongue Briggs didn't know, yet somehow understood. The man spoke of a gift, one he'd received twenty years prior. He described its healing powers, and its magical spell that enabled two human hearts to unite as one. He told Briggs that his giver had possessed it for a brief ten years and that the Antico still sought a terminal union with its destined partner. Briggs' giver knew his time with it was ending, and when it passed to Briggs, he was overjoyed, believing Briggs was the one."

"But... but," Callie stammered, disoriented by Carozza's story, which countered nearly everything they'd been taught. "I don't understand. How could it have transferred after only ten or even twenty years? And, if Briggs remembered everything, why did he say he didn't recall the blood transfusion?"

"That was the myth he adopted but it was only a fantasy. You see, Signora, there was no blood transfusion." Carozza forced out an exasperated sigh. "I see you too have fallen victim to ignorance. Let me attempt to correct your erroneous education, just as I did with Briggs. Perhaps your heart, as the Datouri of the chosen one, will be more open to it. The Succouri is a wild thing, Mrs. Sawyer, never meant to be domesticated and controlled by its human partner. It possesses an intelligence, a kind of ancient instinctual wisdom. The untamed Succouri seeks a perfect bond, much like you share with your husband. It craves a matching soul, a heart that is innocent, true, honest, brave, and strong, in addition to other unique qualities that pair perfectly with its nature. From the dawn of its existence, it knows exactly whom it seeks, and it sets its course, moving strategically from host to host, until, at last, it reaches its intended. Generously, the Antico offers each host along the way the chance, through a lesser but nonetheless beautiful bond, to taste the kind of connection that it desires. It often takes centuries for the two to at last rendezvous, but the Antico is patient, moving step by step, waiting, inching closer and closer to its chosen one. Along the way, it benevolently shares some of its gifts and blessings with those it in-dwells but it saves the full measure of its bounty for the man and his Datouri who reflect the heart and soul of the Antico itself."

Callie and Taylor stared as they stood motionless, their eyes wide with confusion. His explanation starkly contrasted with what they'd been told, but then, that was why they'd come: to seek out the answers no one else had.

"But I'm still not clear," Taylor finally said. "How exactly did Briggs receive the gift?"

"Aw, yes. Now, you should know the answer to that one," he challenged.

Before he finished the sentence, the answer resounded, clear as day, in Callie's mind. "Through touch," she said confidently.

Carozza clapped his hands. "Witness the wisdom of a very special Datouri!" Carozza praised. "I see your heart indeed seeks the truth. At the precise chosen time and decisive will of the Antico alone, the gift passes. Touch is the only method by which a Succouri's gift is ever rightfully transferred. There is no other way."

"But... that's not how it works," Taylor protested, shaking his head. "The only way I've ever heard of it being passed is through donation."

"And that," Carozza exclaimed furiously, pointing at them, "is why the Succouri is all but extinct. Modern medicine has transmuted the Succouri into a domesticated pet, a diminished creature, as good as dead. Imagine a lion stripped of its mane, or a de-feathered eagle who no longer soars. It's grotesque! Utterly shameful. Man's control and manipulation of the gift to serve his own purposes have stripped away its majesty, leaving us all in a diminished world; a world with one less inspirational legend and one more deserted bastion of hope."

Carozza sucked a slow breath through his clenched teeth, attempting to calm his rage. "But perhaps all is not lost. If Briggs' gift has found its intended, there remains a spark, a single ember that may yet become a flame."

"But the Succouri aren't dead," Callie countered. "Even

if the gift was transferred through donation, they still help people and—"

Carozza spat on the ground next to his bed. "Those who come to possess it through blood aren't Succouri. They're frauds, all of them, frauds." His voice was a shout by the end of his sentence and Taylor backed Callie away from him.

No one spoke for a time, the man's enraged outburst renewing their fears that all of this was nothing more than the rantings of an unstable mind.

Finally, with determination sourced in the desperation of their situation, Taylor spoke again. "How does passing the gift through blood destroy the Succouri?"

"When the host, rather than the Antico, chooses the inheritor, it disrupts the projected path, displacing the Succouri from its plotted course to its final host. Though it may try for a time, if it ultimately can't redeem its route, can't find a way to ever reach its intended, it essentially dies. Oh, it still might give its hosts the power to heal and in a diminished capacity, bond with a partner, but it has no more potency than that. It becomes nothing more than a lapdog, only good for a bit of comfort and companionship. Its will, its unique nature are lost, as are the consequential benefits that it and its final host were meant to bestow on mankind. And once the light has gone out, it can't be relit." His voice shook with distress at his own words. Crazy or not, there was no doubt he believed what he was saying.

Taylor blew out a sigh as he held out his hands, surrendering to Carozza's bleak perspective. "Okay, but you said Briggs was different, that my son is different, that he possesses the original kind of Succouri, the... Antico. But Briggs entered the ripening stage. He passed the gift to me via a blood transfusion, and I passed it to my son through bone marrow. Admittedly, I wasn't in the ripening stage and Ben was a child, so the circumstances were unusual, but..."

"Are you certain, Mr. Taylor?"

"Certain of what?

"Are you certain the gift transferred through blood?"

Silence fell for a breath. "I... I think so. I mean blood was transferred in both cases."

"Did Briggs ever touch you and did you touch your son?" Carozza was amused now, so sure of his conclusions that the conversation had become a game to him as he arrogantly mocked their ignorance.

Callie turned to Taylor. "When you went to see him at the hospital before the donation, did you touch Ben?"

Taylor reflected quietly before answering. "Yes. But just briefly. I put my hand on his. But I didn't feel anything."

"And Briggs?"

"I... I don't remember. Briggs was an affectionate man. I'm sure he set his hand on mine at some point as he sat next to me in the hospital room, but if the gift transferred that way, why didn't I recover until after the blood transfusion and the same with Ben?"

"Because this is *not* a lapdog, Mr. Taylor. This Antico has survived for centuries, evading domestication. It is clever. It is one of the last, perhaps the very last of its kind. It hasn't made it this far for this long without acquiring substantial cunning. Two possibilities exist. It may have transferred by touch but then remained hidden until it determined it was safe to integrate into the host's body. The other possibility, and perhaps the more logical one given what we now know, is that, in this rare case, the will of the hosts and the will of the Antico aligned. If the transfer coincides with the Antico's determined path, it won't resist it and the transfer won't result in its demise."

"But what about the ripening?" Taylor objected. "Why did Briggs enter that stage?"

"The ripening is a warning sign for the host, a way to alert him that his time as Succouri is ending and to be watchful for the next host who will continue the Antico's journey. Biologically, it initiates the process of returning the host's body to its original state. When a man possessed a spirited Antico, but he was not the chosen one, the period of his service was indeterminate, though ten to twenty years was average. Due to the short term, the harmful effects of the draw on his human body were minimal. Therefore, after the Succouri departed, he could live out his years as he would have otherwise. The Succouri impostor of today reaps his own due punishment as his body deteriorates quickly after the unnaturally prolonged term. Since the enslaved creature inside him no longer has the will to transfer itself, the ripening is simply a sign that his human body has become too frail to carry on. He rids himself of it, then spends his remaining days paying for his insolence." He laughed mockingly. "How do you say it here in America? The chickens come home to roost."

Sitting back down, Callie hugged her arms around herself, feeling chilled, perhaps by the fever, but also by the vitriol directed at good men like Raul and Louis, who had given their lives and strength to help everyone they could. Even if Carozza was right about the unnatural passing of the gift, neither these men nor those like Doctor Navarro who helped them, deserved such scorn. They were acting on what they knew, the limited information available about this extraordinary phenomenon. Their goals were noble and their hearts pure. If Carozza knew better, he should have shared his wisdom with the network and participated in solving the problem rather than vilifying everyone involved. These were their friends, people who had rescued them, cared for them, provided them with the best answers they had. There was no allowance for grace and compassion in the old man's heart, and because of that, his words, though perhaps true, cast an empty darkness into the room.

Callie began to understand why Owen Briggs had been reluctant to accept the man's theories. His pride, as well as his obvious personal biases, were odious, hindering the effectiveness of his message. Nevertheless, their desperate situation didn't allow them the privilege of walking away because of the man's bad attitude. Despite his assurance, she and Ben were in trouble, and this bitter man was, perhaps, their only hope.

"Mr. Devereaux," Ben interjected, leaning forward, and looking him squarely in the eyes. "Is Jessica Hughes your daughter?"

Ethan straightened as shock played out in his narrowed eyes. "How did you know that?"

Ben shook his head, unable to accept the coincidence himself. "We all traveled on a medical transport plane with her and your very lovely granddaughter yesterday."

"My... my granddaughter? Why were they on that kind of flight?" Once more, for a little longer this time, Ben glimpsed the gentle heart of the man behind the wall of pain.

Closing his eyes, Ben searched for his Succouri's voice, wishing to draw upon the enhanced skills of compassion and empathy it provided, but he came up empty.

All at once, a crushing wave of panic crashed over him. What if it was gone forever? The eerie hush deep in his soul where a soft voice had unceasingly spoken for most of his life was painfully deafening. He'd grown so accustomed to it that he hadn't recognized it for what it was, but now he couldn't tolerate the silence. With each passing minute, the sting of its absence, alongside that of his missing bond with Callie, was spreading like an invading mist, into his mind, jumbling his thoughts. If he couldn't find the voice, couldn't entice it to speak again, Ben knew that, biology and science aside, it would ultimately be the silence that would kill him.

Unable to stand any longer, Ben sat, rubbing his head. He attempted to stay present in the conversation, but he couldn't remember Ethan's question. "Um… what…"

"Mr. Sawyer, are you alright?"

"I… I'm sorry, I don't think I can…" Ben couldn't focus his thoughts, and he covered his face with both hands. It didn't feel like he was losing consciousness, he simply couldn't think straight.

Ethan suddenly gasped. "Mr. Sawyer, your hand!"

Without looking, he knew that Ethan had spotted his scabbed knuckles. He'd want an explanation, but Ben couldn't give him one. Something was dreadfully wrong.

He needed to get out of there. He couldn't help Mr. Devereaux anymore. He needed… needed something, but he wasn't sure what it was.

Confused silence hovered as Ben focused all his effort on organizing a single, coherent sentence. "My brother-in-law… outside… Please."

Ethan rose and disappeared, and a few seconds later, Lee's face appeared before him.

Squatting, Lee set his hand on Ben's shoulder. "Brother. What's happening?"

"His eyes suddenly went blank," Ethan explained. "And his hand!"

"Can you hear me, Ben? Are you with me?" Lee coaxed.

Though he shut his eyes against the turmoil cycling in his mind, Ben managed a nod. He comprehended the words, but he couldn't answer, couldn't make his mind send the words to his mouth.

Abruptly, something shifted inside him, and he knew exactly what he needed. Setting his jaw, he took several deep breaths and focused on Lee's familiar green eyes, hoping he'd understand. "Callie!" he managed.

Lee nodded at once, put his strong arms around Ben, and helped him to his feet. "Alright, brother. I've got you. Let's go."

"Wait," Ethan protested. "What's wrong with him? He shouldn't have scabs on his hands, and he shouldn't be... ill. Was this all some kind of sick trick? Is this man not Succouri?"

Ignoring Ethan's questions, Lee turned, moving with Ben toward the front door, but Ethan grabbed Lee by the arm. "He knows something about my daughter and granddaughter, something he was about to tell me, I need to know, I need him to—"

Lee spun around. "Look, Mr. Devereaux. I don't know what you're talking about, and I don't frankly care right now. I need to get Ben back to our doctor. My brother most definitely is Succouri, but something is happening to him that none of us understand. Nobody's tricking you here. He risked his life, and perhaps the life of my sister, by coming all the way out here to no-man's land to chat with you today. Unlike Ben, I'm not the diplomatic type and I don't have the luxury of being sensitive to your feelings right now. If you want more information and if you want to help Donovan, you're welcome to come with us. If not, then stay here and live with the truth that you're going to cost one man his life and another man deep and permanent regret because, despite giving you his last ounce of strength, you were too stubborn to see past your own pain and help someone else."

Without looking back, Lee and Ben rushed out the door toward the waiting car.

"Let's get back to Ben," Taylor insisted. "Why did the Succouri change him, alter his physiology?"

"In its wisdom, his Antico found him while he was still young enough to be changed, to be strengthened so he could endure the draw and remain a part of the union for an entire lifetime."

A surge of life-giving hope flooded Callie's heart, and she jumped to her feet. "Do you... Do you mean Ben won't go through the ripening, won't transfer the gift, and won't... won't die young?"

"Mrs. Sawyer," Carozza began, his tone now filled with delight. "Once an Antico unites with his final host, he has reached the end of his quest and will never again transfer to another. As long as the union remains intact, the three of you will thrive and live a long, meaningful life. As this merging is extraordinarily rare, occurring once in hundreds, if not thousands of years, its timing is not accidental. There is a reason for it, a crucial impact the three of you are meant to have on this world."

As her heart rejoiced, Louis' similar predictions floated like sweet music through her mind.

"So, why is he sick?" Taylor asked, his emotions finally overtaking his calm façade.

"I assure you, Mr. Taylor, neither he, nor his Datouri are sick," Carozza declared, returning to his bemused tone. "Their Antico is up to something, I can't tell you what, but it will become clear in time."

"It warned me," Callie said softly. "In a vision, it told me it would be alright. But then we both became ill at the same exact time and—"

"Just as your hearts are united, so too are your fates. That is yet another generous gift offered exclusively within the union of the terminal triad. The bond that ties the three together is simply too strong. If severed, survival is impossible."

"Are you saying that if Callie died, Ben would as well?" Taylor asked.

"Of course. And if either of them perishes, so will the Antico. What was once three is now one, inseparable, unbreakable, and"—he smiled—"unstoppable."

At the old man's words, Callie placed both hands over her heart just as something began to stir inside her.

"Will... Will they ever die?" Taylor asked hesitantly as the question seemed ridiculous, but in light of what they'd learned, not as ridiculous as it would have sounded half an hour ago.

Carozza chuckled. "As I know all too well, humans aren't immortal or invincible, even with the Antico's help, though they do come close to the latter. After a long, wonderful life, the host's body, or that of his Datouri, will perish and all in the union will cease to exist."

"Then, if the Antico also perishes after this final matchup, wouldn't that mean that, eventually, there will no longer be any Succouri? I mean, Succouri couples can't have children, so how do they, procreate or... continue to exist?"

As Taylor's question hung in the air, the stirring intensified, centered around the hollow space where her bond with Ben had resided. It began to throb, then pull at her, urging her to do something, but she wasn't sure what that was.

"That is a mystery I haven't yet solved. Even if I shared my beliefs on the subject, it would only be a guess. As there hasn't been a Succouri like your son in centuries, I'm afraid the knowledge regarding this question has been lost. When I was younger, I sought the answer with great fervor, but my quest was in vain. It's painfully regrettable that I at last have a way of answering this lifelong quandary, but I won't live long enough to learn the truth."

Callie tried to listen to the conversation in the room but though the nausea had vanished, the urging in her chest had intensified and was now a deep ache. Unable to bear it any longer, Callie grabbed Taylor's arm. "Dad, we need to go. Something's wrong. I need to get to Ben!"

Taylor turned to face her. "What is it?"

"I'm not sure exactly, but I feel... I can feel him, but in an unusual way. I can't explain it, but I think... I know he needs me."

"You must go," Carozza urged. "Always trust his Datouri. She's had the answers all along. But please, I would beg one thing of you before you leave."

Taylor and Callie turned to him, nodding in acknowledgment. "Please, bring him here when you can. I've spent a lifetime waiting for this, enduring scorn, mockery, and loss because of my outspokenness. I want to meet him, know the one the Antico has chosen, and shake his hand."

Callie approached his bedside, still harboring mixed

feelings about the man and his philosophies, but sincerely grateful for the hope he'd given her. She placed her hand on his. At her touch, the man's eyes grew wide, as did hers. "I promise we'll come back. I know Ben will want to meet you and he'll have many more questions. Thank you for your help."

Carozza reached with his free hand, laying it on top of hers. "Bless you, Donna Bellissima. Bless you."

CHAPTER 5

THE RUSH

Lee helped Ben maneuver into the back seat, where he lay down on his back, putting his hands over his face as he tried to understand what was happening to him. The closest comparison he could make was the feelings he'd experienced just after the fire rescue when he'd felt pulled, like a rope encircled him and Callie was drawing him to her. But in that case, he'd been nearly unconscious. Right now, he was aware of his surroundings, but he couldn't interact. It was almost as if the confounding silence of his Succouri was manifesting in his mute tongue; like he couldn't speak because it couldn't speak. Two abiding aches pulsated deep within him: the first wrought by the missing voice of an almost lifelong counterpart and the other by his sorely missed connection to Callie's heart.

As Lee started the engine, the passenger side door opened, and Ethan Devereaux climbed inside.

"Good choice," Lee said with a touch of sarcasm.

"I have to know about my daughter."

"Right," Lee huffed.

Turning the car around, Lee drove significantly faster

than the speed limit, down the dirt road and then onto the paved highway toward Cape Cod.

The car was quiet for a time, though Lee continually glanced in the rearview mirror watching Ben carefully. Ben stared back, blinking his eyes as he tried to communicate that he was still conscious, but still unable to speak. Lee nodded in response, each time increasing his speed as his worry intensified. As he drove, he tapped the steering wheel nervously.

"Where is his wife?" Ethan finally asked.

"My sister had to make a trip with Ben's father. They're trying to get answers about this illness or... whatever it is. Ben stayed behind so he could meet with you. They should be on their way back from Philly by now."

"And she's sick too?"

Lee nodded.

Ethan stared out of the front windshield. "That makes no sense. I haven't been sick since the change and Lexi never was either."

"Their situation is... complicated."

"Yes. He told me about being a child when he received the gift and he said something about dire consequences but... Why in the world did he come all the way out here if he wasn't well? He should have stayed with your sister."

Lee shook his head. "You don't know the half of it. He's been having symptoms for weeks. We knew using his gift was a risk, but he and my sister were determined to save Donovan's life and the life of a young girl, who he'd promised to deliver safely to Baltimore." Again, Lee glanced at Ben. "My kindhearted brother can't say no to anyone, even when his life's at risk."

"What girl?" Ethan inquired, looking intently at Lee.

Lee smiled. "A charming girl with a contagious smile.

She had a life-threatening heart condition and there was a doctor in Baltimore with the skills to fix it. But getting her there was risky. It turned out to be a damn good thing Ben was there as she likely wouldn't have made it without his…" Lee held a hand up in the air to demonstrate the rest of his sentence. "And neither would Donovan."

"What was her name?" Ethan probed insistently.

"Um, I don't think that's really my place to—"

"Was her mother Jessica Hughes?"

"How did you—"

"Please, what was her name? Ethan's jaw was tight as he pleaded with Lee.

"Allie," Lee relented. "Well, Alexandra, but she goes by Allie."

Helplessly, Ben watched Ethan's anguished expression as tears formed in his eyes.

As Taylor and Callie moved swiftly to exit the house, Carozza's son stepped in front of them, blocking their path.

"Did you get what you came for?" he snarled as he folded his arms.

Without hesitation, Taylor stepped forward, once again keeping Callie safely behind him. "For now. When we return, we expect to see that your father's care has significantly improved."

"Mind your own business. If you're doing research and profiting from the access I gave you to his"—he chuckled sarcastically—"rare knowledge, I think some compensation is appropriate."

Callie's heart began to pound. There was a clear demand and a not-so-subtle threat in his words and posture.

Mirroring the man's stance, Taylor confronted Bobby's challenge head-on. "I think the most profitable and certainly the safest thing for you to do right now is to let us pass. I won't ask twice."

"I have debts to pay, mister, and I let you in here, gave you something you wanted so—"

The man never had a chance to finish his sentence. With one swift motion, Taylor grabbed his neck with one hand and his arm with the other. The next thing Callie knew, he was on his knees facing away from them screaming in agony as Taylor bent his arm back unnaturally. Callie gasped and put her hands over her mouth.

"I warned you, I don't ask twice," Taylor said, his voice as calm as if engaged in casual conversation. "Do we have an understanding, or would you like to continue to block our departure?"

"No!" the man panted, gritting his teeth in torment. "You can go!"

"That's a wise choice. I will be back, and I'll be gratified to see that your father's situation has improved significantly."

Taylor released his arm, and Bobby collapsed into a fetal position on the floor. Taylor stepped back to retrieve Callie and they hastily left the house.

When they were safely in the car on their way to the airport, Callie finally let out the breath she'd been holding.

"That was... really scary, but you were... that was amazing, what you did! I'll be sure to let Ben know he had no cause for worry by leaving me in your care."

Taylor chuckled, but his smile soon faded. "It's sad really. That man must be in deep to have behave that way. Undoubtedly, he owes a lot of money to a lot of debtors who are far scarier than I am. I hate the thought of Carozza living in that filth and in such a dangerous circumstance. Bobby's 'friends' may show up any day and they won't be discriminating about who they hurt to get what they're owed."

A shiver ran through Callie at the thought. "How can we help him?"

"Leave that to me. It shouldn't take much more than an anonymous report of elder neglect to get him removed from that house."

"Do you... do you believe what Carozza said about Ben and the Succouri?"

Taylor looked over at her, his brow creasing as he considered his answer. "I'm not sure. His explanations did address most of our unanswered questions, but it's all so different from what we've been taught, and I can't reconcile the fact that, evidently, Owen never believed it. If he had, I'm confident he would have told me or Maggie about it."

"But," Callie countered, "Owen didn't have the same unexplainable anomalies as Ben. Without that evidence to back up, or at least give more substantiation to Carozza's theories, his unfair and confrontational demeanor would probably have led me to outright reject his ideas as well." Callie paused to sigh. "I haven't known many Succouri, but I don't accept his characterization of those who give and receive the gift through blood, or of those, like Doctor Navarro, who help them. Carozza was much too harsh in that regard."

"No question," Taylor agreed emphatically. "Still, if it is true that passing the gift that way has destroyed the... the Antico, as he called them, I can understand the passion behind his words, even if the anger is misplaced."

Nodding, Callie contemplated her next question, even as she contended with the urgent pull in her chest, which was growing stronger by the minute. "Do you believe what he said about Ben and me? That we're... chosen, the last recipients of this Succouri?"

Taylor took his time answering, but at last, he put his hand on hers and smiled. "Yes, dear one, I do believe it, and I do believe his predictions about Ben's lifespan and this... whatever it is you're suffering through right now. I'm now convinced it will work itself out and, at some point, we'll understand why it happened." He exhaled in relief. "That reassurance alone made this trip well worth it."

"Do you think Ben's Succouri really waited, searched specifically for him for centuries?"

Taylor scratched his head. "That one's a bit harder to swallow. It takes a large measure of faith to believe it knew about Ben long before he was even born. I'm not sure I can wrap my mind around that one, but that doesn't mean it isn't true. Anyway, you would know far better than me. If the three of you are interconnected, then you likely have the answer already, even if you've never directly considered the idea before."

Staring straight ahead, she tried to think or perhaps feel her way to an answer, but every thought was shouted down by the urgent outcry to reach him, and fast.

"I can't think right now," she said, shaking her head in frustration and pressing her hand to her heart.

"What are you feeling?"

"It's like... like a burning where our bond should be. It feels like I'm supposed to touch him or tell him something or... I'm not sure exactly." She lowered her head, covering her face with her hands, and Taylor pressed down on the gas.

"Callie. Call him."

"But what if he's with Mr. Devereaux? I don't want to interrupt if—"

"Then call Lee."

Callie nodded and moved to retrieve her phone from her purse.

BEN WATCHED Lee's confused expression as he cycled his gaze between the road, the rearview mirror, and Ethan Devereaux.

Though he was still unable to speak, Ben had put it all together in his mind and he couldn't believe the incredible coincidence. No wonder Jessica Hughes harbored such bitterness toward the Succouri. After Lexi Devereaux's tragic death, she'd lost her father as well. Unable to manage his own grief, Ethan had run away, leaving Jessica alone. As Ethan didn't seem to know even the name of his granddaughter, it was unlikely he knew that Jessica's husband had died a year earlier, once more leaving her on her own to manage Allie's serious heart condition. She'd suffered hardship after hardship, and her father had been absent through it all. No wonder she felt crushed by the consequences of what she perceived as her father's Succouri curse.

"Mr. Devereaux," Lee started, but before he could finish his thought, his phone buzzed.

"Finally, a signal," he mumbled as he pulled his phone from a compartment in the console and glanced at the caller ID.

"Ben, it's Callie," Lee announced as he again made eye contact with him in the mirror.

Ben sat up.

"Cal," Lee said, hitting the speaker button and setting it on the middle console.

"Lee! Is everything alright?" She was frantic, and Ben's heart twisted in worry but also relief at hearing her voice.

"Um, well, I'm not really sure. Ben is…"

"What's wrong with him?"

"He's awake, but he can't communicate for some reason, except by nodding his head. The last thing he said was your name."

"Can he hear me?"

Ben nodded at Lee.

"Yeah, he's listening."

"Ben." Her voice shook. "I can feel it, too. We're on our way, almost to the airport. I don't know what's going on, but I know I need to get to you as soon as possible. We learned a whole lot from Mr. Carozza, information that changes everything. I'll tell you all about it when we get there, but please meet us at the airport. I love you. Please hold on."

At the sound of her voice, something in the empty space in his heart fluttered, sending a mixture of pleasure and pain through his body. Though their shared drive to reunite with one another caused her to speak with sober urgency, there was excitement in her tone as well and Ben wished he could ask her more about what she'd learned from Carozza. But his present condition made that impossible. Ben nodded several times at Lee.

"He heard ya, sis," Lee relayed. "We'll meet you at the airport. Ben's okay for now, so don't worry."

"And Mr. Devereaux?"

"He's actually in the car with us."

"That's… That's great news!"

"Text me your ETA when you've got one. And I'm very interested in what you learned in Philly, as it sounds legit."

"It is. Lee, thank you for everything, and please, hurry!"

THOUGH IT WAS a short flight back to Cape Cod, it felt like an eternity. Callie fidgeted with her seatbelt, rubbed her hands on her knees, and bit her lip as the urgency inside continued to pull at her, fraying her nerves.

"Is the nausea completely gone?" Taylor asked, watching her closely.

"Yes, but I think I'd rather be nauseous. This... tugging is making me crazy!" More from nerves than from need, Callie grabbed her water bottle and took a long sip.

"Doctor Navarro will be pleased that you're eating and drinking again."

Callie sent Taylor a weak smile.

"This started right after Carozza told you about Ben— about him being changed so that he could live a full life as Succouri, and about all three of your fates being inter- locked. Do you think that's just coincidental timing or was there something in that information that prompted this?"

"I'm not sure. I think I have something he needs imme- diately, something I have to give him, or... give back to him." She spoke the last phrase as if her own words surprised her, and indeed they did, but as they registered in her mind, she was struck by a sudden conviction that they were absolutely true.

Silently, she contemplated whether to share the next part with Taylor, as she had intended to wait to talk with Ben first but given the urgency of their situation and Ben's present inability to speak, she decided to proceed. "When I touched Carozza's hand, I felt something very weird and unexpected. When Ben revived my father, through the bond, I was able to share a piece of his experience, so I somewhat know what the draw feels like. What I felt when I touched Carozza was like... like a very weak draw, and from his reaction, I'm pretty sure he felt it too." She shook her head, confounded by the incident.

"But you can't—"

"I know!" Callie exclaimed, unnerved by the thought. "I can only give to Ben, and I never feel a draw when I do."

Taylor rubbed his chin, pondering quietly before responding. "What if the Succouri in Ben hasn't been lost or gone dormant? What if it passed to you, at least some of it?" Obviously, you couldn't have much or you'd be capable of curing your sight loss, but maybe you possess just enough to cure the nausea and give off a small amount of healing."

"But that's impossible! I'm the Datouri, not the Succouri. I've never heard of a partner acquiring the gift."

"But Carozza said the three of you were essentially one, and the gifts offered to the last host and his partner were greater, which I take to mean above and beyond what normal Succouri are empowered to do. Maybe, for reasons we don't yet understand, the Antico needed to withdraw from Ben, or at least decrease its influence on him for a time. If it sought somewhere safe to go, you would have been the only logical choice since it knew you'd stay close to him, and it trusted you as you're part of the triad. You're also the one it chose to warn about all of this."

Though his words struck a chord in her heart, her mind struggled to accept them. "I've never heard of a Succouri being able to move between people like that, except during the transfer, but that's complete and permanent."

Taylor chuckled. "Well, if we're embracing Carozza's theories, we must begin by accepting that the Succouri in

Ben, and now perhaps in you, is no ordinary Succouri. I don't think the same rules apply."

As the reality of Ben's acquisition and transformation had already shattered the established norms, Callie couldn't argue with Taylor's statement.

As he leaned forward, the passion in Taylor's voice grew. "Perhaps the Antico is spread so thin between the two of you that it can't function normally in either one. Ben maintains just enough to stay alive, and you have just enough to manifest small signs of its power."

"But... How could I have acquired some of his Succouri?"

Taylor lifted his shoulders in a gradual shrug. "If there's one big takeaway from our time there, it would have to be what we learned regarding the Succouri's preferred method of transfer." He paused to smile. "I don't mean to get too personal here, but I'm fairly certain you and Ben have engaged in plenty of touching over the last couple of weeks."

Feeling awkward but unable to deny the truth, Callie momentarily looked down and leaned back against her seat. "Maybe that's what's been happening this whole time!" she exclaimed. "Maybe Ben didn't pass out just because of the strength flowing from me to him. Maybe he also lost consciousness because of what was flowing from him to me. If the Antico was attempting to do something that bent the rules, so to speak, it would follow that there might be unexpected or at least unusual side effects for both of us, like passing out or nausea, or nightmares. Maybe I've been unknowingly receiving small portions of his Succouri for weeks, since the first time I woke up and couldn't rouse him. This would also explain why each time Ben uses his gift, the consequences are more dire. If he's been gradually passing some of it to me, then each time he offers someone his healing strength, he's drawing from less and less Succouri power, so the effects on his human body are harsher, longer lasting, and more debilitating. And as the Succouri in him decreases, so does his ability to receive strength from me. No wonder the inflow was too powerful to handle. If what I'm offering him has been enhanced, augmented by the presence of actual Succouri additive in my blood, then it's probably a lot more potent. Since he can't even tolerate the normal flow, how could he possibly handle the increase?"

Slowly, Taylor shook his head and whistled in amazement. "Wow! This opens up a whole new can of worms, Callie."

She nodded, but her mind continued to follow the new trail blazed by their proposed theory. "You're right in concluding that the amount of Succouri I possess must be extremely small or I'd be manifesting many more of the typical gifts. As Ben's Succouri has integrated into every part of his body: muscles, organs, and tissues, his health relies on a precise balance. Losing even one or two percent may be all it takes to throw his whole system off kilter." She closed her eyes to concentrate, and after a few seconds, she heard Taylor chuckling softly.

"What's so funny?" She raised her eyebrows at him.

"You really did have the answers all along. I barely gave you a nudge and you ran away with the baton."

Callie shrugged. "You possessed this Antico for a few days yourself, remember? You may still have remnants of its knowledge and nature tucked into the corners of your mind and that may be influencing your thoughts more than you realize. And anyway, I don't know how we prove any of this, but it just feels..."

"Right?" he asked with a smile.

"Possible," she corrected. "As the Datouri, I'm not meant to carry this. It belongs to Ben, and he needs it. This isn't a sustainable situation. Perhaps the Succouri has now accomplished whatever its objective was that initiated the transfer in the first place, and it's ready to put things back the way they should be. That would explain why I'm feeling desperate to get to him, to touch him."

"It's strange that your nausea suddenly vanished. If the gradual transfers were causing it, why the sudden improvement? You're feeling better and, it seems, Ben's feeling worse."

"If we're right about the rest of it, that actually does make sense. It may be that the amount of Succouri I've now received from Ben has reached a threshold where it's adequate to offer me a weak dose of self-healing, just as it offered Carozza some healing when I touched him. But for Ben, the lack is reaching a critical low, and it's wreaking havoc on his body, and perhaps"—she put her hand to her heart, rubbing it anxiously—"now even on his mind. Of course, in the end, we will all share the same fate anyhow." Callie took a shaky breath. "Still, I really need to get to him, Dad. This isn't good for him; the human part of him. I think... No, I'm sure the Succouri in me knows that too. It doesn't want him permanently damaged by this."

Taylor also began to look worried. "Just another twenty minutes and we'll be on the ground. Hang in there. If we're right about all of this, that still leaves us with one unanswered question."

Callie laughed. "Only one?"

Taylor smiled, acknowledging her point. "Let me rephrase. That leaves us with one essential question."

With a single nod, she bid him continue.

"Why? Why did any part of Ben's Succouri need to leave his body, hide away inside you, and put the two of you through all this turmoil? If the Antico's fate is linked to yours, why would it risk hurting you or Ben? It doesn't make sense."

Shaking her head repeatedly, Callie sighed. "I wish I had an answer for that one. I really do."

BEN LEANED against the car next to Lee and Ethan Devereaux as they watched Callie and Taylor's plane land and taxi toward them.

Though he was still unable to communicate his thoughts and his body continued to ache, his heart was relieved to have her firmly on the ground and moments from his arms.

Glancing briefly over at Ethan's stoic expression, Ben felt regret at the timing of the day's unanticipated events, knowing that watching their affectionate reunion would be painful for him. After the phone call, Ethan remained quiet, not inquiring further about his daughter or granddaughter, which surprised Ben. Nevertheless, his distress was written on his face, and Ben had no doubt that as soon as he got past the shock, Ethan would want to know more.

As the plane rolled to a stop, Lee leaned close to Ben so he could hear him over the roaring engine. "This will be interesting if you can't talk and she can't see. You two sure know how to keep things fresh and unpredictable. Never a dull moment with you two." Lee chuckled, but Ben only offered a polite smile, sincerely craving nothing more than some quiet, uneventful time with his new bride as their marriage was barely more than a week old.

When the airplane's doors opened, Ben's father

appeared, waving to them as a set of boarding stairs were pushed to the doorway and secured. When Ben's eyes fixed on Callie, the burning in his chest swelled, and it took all his willpower to restrain himself from running up the stairs to take her in his arms. Though he knew she couldn't see him yet, she looked his way and grimaced as she placed her free hand to her heart. This wasn't exactly the bond they were used to, but it was a connection, nonetheless. But why now? Why were they suddenly being pulled together so forcefully?

Ben advanced toward the plane, but when Callie and Taylor were halfway down the stairs, she halted and turned to speak to Taylor, looking alarmed. Unexpectedly, Callie let go of Taylor's arm and remained where she was as he descended the remaining steps, heading straight for Ben.

Holding his breath as he continued to fight the consuming urge to run to her, Ben blinked questioningly at his father as he approached.

He put his hand on Ben's shoulder, his eyes communicating his distress as he took in Ben's weak appearance. "She's worried she might cause you to pass out again, son," Taylor shouted over the noise. "Trust me, she wants to get to you as badly as you want to get to her and now that you're so close, she's convinced it's extremely urgent that she does so as she's got something you desperately need, but she wants to speak with you first. But not out in the open like this."

Glancing around, Ben looked for a place where they could retreat. He pointed to a nearby hanger and Taylor nodded, then retraced his steps to retrieve Callie. Ethan remained with the car, but Lee and Ben circled around to the back of the building, approaching from the south, while Taylor and Callie did the same from the north. The building blocked the view of any prying eyes and reduced the noise of the plane.

As they moved toward one another, Ben focused on the welcome sight of her exotic eyes, noticing that she looked worried, but much less ill than she had when she and Taylor had left for Philly. As his condition had worsened considerably, including this new inability to speak, he was puzzled by the improvement.

"Ben." Though the noise of the plane was distant, she still had to speak louder than usual for her voice to carry across the ten feet of distance between them.

"Are you alright?" She wrung her hands as she spoke, both uncomfortable as the force of the pull overwhelmed them.

He nodded and Taylor spoke into her ear.

"This is going to sound crazy, but I think we've figured out what's going on."

Frustrated at his mute tongue, Ben blinked, trying to encourage her to continue.

"I think some of your Succouri has been transferring, little by little, to me over the last couple of weeks. Not like what we talked about on our honeymoon, not just to heal my wounds, but the... the gift itself, the part you need, the part that speaks to you and gives you the ability to heal yourself and others."

"Whoa!" Lee exclaimed, looking between Ben and Callie. "Can a woman even be Succouri?"

Emphatically, Ben shook his head, knowing that what she was saying wasn't possible.

She put her palms together in a pleading gesture. "I understand your skepticism, but we've learned a lot today, a lot of new information that challenges what we presumed about everything, especially when it comes to us, you and me, and our Ant... Succouri specifically. Please, I don't want to get into it here in the open like this, and time is of the essence as I believe it's urgent that we act quickly or the damage to your body may be permanent. Please, you'll just have to trust me. I... I felt a draw today, Ben. Just a slight one, but I recognized the feeling."

"What?" He mouthed the word, but no sound accompanied it. He put his hand to his forehead, astonished by her statement.

"That couldn't have happened unless I possessed some Succouri additive. But I have to give it back to you. It doesn't belong to me. Temporarily, it's curing my nausea, but since you don't have what you need, your condition is getting worse."

Raising a hand, he vigorously shook his head. If whatever she had was making her better, he wanted her to keep it.

Without Taylor speaking into her ear, Callie stepped forward, her jaw set and her eyes focused on him. "No! I'm not keeping it, Ben. If we don't immediately put things back the way they should be, one of us will die, and the other will soon follow."

Ben clenched his teeth, desperate to speak, but still unable to make his body cooperate.

"Wait, I'm confused." Lee spoke up. "If you... you know, then Ben will too? I thought it was the other way around."

Keeping her eyes on Ben, she answered Lee. "It works both ways, actually, all three ways. We're all tied together now: you, me, and our Succouri. That's how a part of it was able to temporarily transfer to me, but I'm absolutely sure now that it's time to return it to you. That's why we're feeling the strong pull toward one another. I don't know why it moved into me, but whatever our Succouri needed to do, it's done, and it doesn't want you harmed. We must fix this before it's too late."

The conviction in her eyes was unwavering. She had no doubts, no hesitation. He didn't understand any of this. How could Callie have received some of his Succouri? He wasn't in the ripening stage, and he'd transferred no blood to her. He'd never heard of a woman becoming Succouri, nor a partner experiencing the draw.

Taking another step toward him, she put her hands out like she wanted to give him something. "Please, my love, we must hurry. I know this is confusing, and I'm not giving you all the information you need to understand why I'm so confident about this, but I'm asking you to trust me. I promise I'll explain it all when you're whole again, when we can sit and talk and hold each other. What I don't know for certain is what might happen when I touch you. It's possible you will pass out again, but even so, we must do this. If you do lose consciousness, I'll keep contact with you until I've returned the Succouri portion I'm carrying, and you're able to heal yourself again. It might be rough, but we don't have a choice. Please, please believe me."

As he got lost in her tear-filled eyes, he sighed, recognizing that no explanation was necessary. If she asked him to swim to the bottom of the ocean to bring her up a prized pearl, he would dive right in. If she asked him to walk through roaring flames to get her jacket so she wouldn't be cold, he'd enter the inferno without a question. He loved her and trusted her with his whole heart, soul, and body.

Closing his eyes, he breathed in and out, doing his best to focus on his instincts. Though he still couldn't detect the whisper of his Succouri companion, he listened for a soft footstep, a faint echo of its voice that might yet reverberate through the caverns of his mind. But all he could see was her face, radiant and full of dreams as she stared into his eyes at the altar, pledging her life and heart to him forever. He heard her voice when she had called his name just before he lost consciousness as he knelt on the floor surrounded by smoke and flames. The smell of her filled his senses as he traveled back to their wedding night when he'd at last loved her freely and completely. Though he wondered if these visions were a way of communicating it, he didn't need his Succouri's confirmation. He believed her and trusted her with his life.

Opening his eyes, he locked his gaze on hers and moved forward without doubts and with no intention to stop.

CHAPTER 6

THE BEGINNING

Callie's heart pounded as Ben closed the gap between them. She knew this was right, what had to be done, but she was afraid for them both as she suspected that Ben's weakened condition, the increased level of Succouri power in her, and the abrupt return of the missing portion of his Succouri might be a shock to his system.

When he was right in front of her, he reached out his hands, and Callie grasped them tightly. For a few seconds, he stood firm, smiling at her reassuringly. Her heartbeat began to slow, but before it could resume a normal rhythm, Ben's smile faded, and he fell forward, knocking her off her feet.

Instantly, Taylor rushed to her aid, catching her as Ben's weight propelled her backward. Lee, who hadn't let Ben get more than a few feet away, also jumped into action, grabbing Ben from behind to help slow and control his collapse. Despite everyone's best efforts, the four of them tumbled to the ground in an awkward pile of arms and legs. Undeterred, Callie held onto Ben with all her might, refusing to let her tight grasp of his hands go, even to brace her fall. Her right elbow hit the pavement hard, despite Taylor's quick intervention, and a stream of blood began to flow down her arm.

"Callie!" Taylor gasped as he righted himself and began tugging Ben off her. "Are you alright?"

"I can't let go. I must keep ahold of him until the transfer is complete," she said frantically, tears forming in her eyes.

Taylor and Lee worked to shift Ben so he lay alongside her. Then, Taylor quickly began feeling Ben's neck, moving his fingers several times as his face grew pale. "I can't find a pulse, and I don't think he's breathing either."

"It'll be alright," Callie comforted. "Just wait. Give it a minute." Though there was an inexplicable calm in her voice, tears began sliding down her cheeks. All she knew for sure was that she had to hang on. An uncompromising voice inside her commanded this. If Ben was gone, she wouldn't still be breathing, so as long as she was, hope remained.

"Cal." Lee spoke as he shifted to sit next to her, placing a hand on her arm. "Are you sure about this? What if you're making it worse by—"

"I'm sure. Absolutely sure. I love you, Lee, and I'm sorry, but right now it's important that you don't touch me. Everything I have needs to be going straight to him."

Lee withdrew his hand but stayed close beside her.

Callie closed her eyes, wishing she could feel something, feel the Succouri leaving her and flowing into Ben. However, in contrast to the draw Ben experienced when helping others, the only proof of her offerings came by visually observing the results. In this case, there was nothing at all to see. All she had was faith.

"Ben! Please. Please," she whispered, not sure if she was pleading with him or their Succouri or both. She put her mouth near his ear. "Please, please wake up. Breathe, my love, please breathe." Softly, she kissed his face as her tears dripped into his hair.

She couldn't help remembering when he'd done the same with her. The night Ruiz had shot her on her porch, Ben had leaned over her, keeping both hands over her wounds, begging her to hold on and fight to stay with him. His warm tears had dripped onto her cheeks and rolled into her hair. His touch had cured her blindness, and in that moment, she'd stared for the first time into his deep blue eyes and fallen irrevocably in love with him.

"It's your turn. You have to fight. You promised me you would. You promised you'd use all your strength to stay with me. Please fight for us, Ben. Don't give up! Never give up!"

As Lee and Taylor knelt beside them, watching helplessly, their own desperate tears began to flow.

Callie pressed her cheek to Ben's. "We can have every dream we ever wanted, my beloved. You're not going to die young, you won't have to give up your Succouri, and you'll keep your strength. We're going to have an entire lifetime together, our own wonderful forever. Do you hear me? Your transformation wasn't a mistake. It was a gift, a beautiful, wondrous gift from our Succouri. It chose you and me and changed you so you could live out your life and do amazing things. But you must wake up." She shook him as panic began to rise in her chest. "Wake up! Please, Ben," she cried in desperation.

Gripping his fingers more tightly, she hovered just inches from his face, watching, waiting. As another minute passed and there was still no sign of life, a sob shook her whole body. "No!" she shouted. "Ben Sawyer, it isn't too late. You're not gone. You're mine forever, so you fight your way back to me, right now! You wouldn't let me give up. Don't you dare give up on me! Remember our deal? I'll be there so you be there."

Her whole body began to tremble, and she felt her consciousness slipping away. "Ben, please, stay with me. Don't leave me. Please, please!"

She collapsed against his shoulder weeping uncontrollably as the fear that she may have arrived too late to save him overtook her. She knew what she was doing was the right thing, his only chance to pull through, but she didn't know whether or not the damage caused by the missing portion of his Succouri had progressed to a critical point already, beyond what it could repair. She shouldn't have gone to Philly. She should never have left his side. She had what he needed, but maybe she was too late.

"Dear one." Taylor put a hand on her back, being careful not to contact her skin, as he tried to comfort her even through his own sorrow, but she was barely aware of anyone else around her.

As darkness pushed its way into her mind and the world around her faded away, she lay down, covering him with her body and bathing him in her tears. The urging in her chest abruptly ceased and a soothing warmth filled the space. And then, Ben was there: his beautiful heart, his adoring smile, and his matchless love returning to reside in her chest, but this time in the exact spot where her heartbeat pulsed life through her veins.

She closed her eyes, breathed in the scent of his neck, and whispered one last time. "Alright, then, you'll get your wish, my love. From heaven to heaven." She exhaled, blissfully content to follow him wherever he would go.

. . .

As Lee and Taylor knelt over the silent pair, shouting their names and shaking them frantically, Ethan Devereaux watched from a distance. Though he'd been sure his irredeemably shattered heart had long ago rendered him calloused and cold, as he watched the familiar scene of pure love, mingled with agonizing despair, a steady stream of unchecked tears wet his face and soaked into his beard. "No! Not again. Please, don't let it happen to them, too," his desperate soul begged.

Ben blinked, disoriented as he stared at an image of his own face. Unsure of where he was, he shifted his gaze to search his surroundings. He appeared to be standing in the midst of a forest, but in every direction, a dense fog hovered, allowing only a few feet of visibility. Squatting, he reached out to touch what he thought was a large mirror, but when his hand breached the wet surface, he realized it was water.

"Ben! Fight! Come back to me." Callie's voice echoed around him. Alarmed, he stood and turned in a circle, but he saw nothing through the mist.

"Callie? Where are you?"

"I'll be there, so you be there, remember?" Her sweet, desperate cry tore at his heart.

"Sweetheart! I can't find you. I can't see you!"

"Alright then. As you wish. From heaven to heaven."

"No!" he shouted, twisting around again and squinting as he frantically searched.

"You'd better hurry and make up your mind, Ben Sawyer," a familiar voice interjected from the direction of the reflecting pool. Once more, he squatted and stared at his own face. As he leaned in closer, a strand of hair fell into his eyes and he pushed it to the side, but the reflection didn't mimic the action. It remained static, like a captured photograph.

"Hello?" he inquired, wondering who had spoken to him.

"There's not much time. You must decide."

Though the image didn't change or move, Ben was now sure that the voice he heard was coming from it.

"I want to go back to her. I need to go back to her," Ben pleaded.

"She already understands and believes. She'll explain it to you, but you still might not accept it."

"Accept what?"

Though the blue eyes of his reflection didn't blink, they became shadowed with deep sorrow as they held Ben in their gaze.

"You still might not believe that, long ago, I chose you. There was no mistake."

All at once, Ben recognized the familiar voice. It was the one that was missing from his consciousness, much like his, but speaking distinctively.

"You're... You're my Succouri!" Ben whispered.

"I am of you and of her." The face didn't change, but the voice chuckled sending small ripples through the water. "Though she already knows me far better than you do."

Dazed by the reality of at last coming face-to-face with the being who had shared his mind and body for fifteen years, he struggled to speak. "I... I have so many questions. There's so much I don't understand."

"Choose wisely, for time is very short. If you don't return soon, this will be the end of our story."

"Why me, and why the confusion for so many years?"

"From the beginning, I knew you. You have a rare, pure heart, but a diamond can't emerge without pressure and heat. Pain and hardship produce humility, compassion, and courage. There's no shortcut to acquiring these virtues, and without them, there's no true greatness. You first had to learn the lessons you will teach, and it was necessary for you to taste the darkness so you would never be tempted to stray from the light. The rugged path you traveled was the only one that would bring you to her and to your destiny. Would you have chosen differently?"

"No," Ben answered easily. "I would not." He spoke the truth, recognizing that he would have gladly and freely chosen any road, no matter how treacherous, that ultimately led him to her.

"Though you closed your ears to my voice, you've never walked alone. I took great care to prevent you from sinking too deep or running too far."

"Do you mean... Are you saying you're the reason I never lost my mind through all the years without a bond, and that it was your influence that kept my heart open enough to accept Callie's love?" Though he asked the question, deep in his heart he already knew the answer.

The eyes of his reflection stared straight into him, down to the deepest recesses of his soul. "I am for you, Ben Sawyer, not against you. I discern well what is in your heart, for your heart is also mine."

Ben dropped his head, humbled by how shamefully wrong he'd been. Through the difficult years of his childhood, he'd thought of his Succouri as an invader, a bully, an enemy of his human dreams and desires. Even though he'd recently come to view its gifts in a more positive light, he remained prejudiced in his attitude toward the giver, clinging to the resentment of being altered against his will.

Regardless of the results of the change, he perceived the act itself as a violation, and the bitterness of that perspective tainted every thought and experience he had with it. Somehow, in his mind and heart, he'd drawn an invisible line of separation, embracing his Succouri abilities and the life they offered him and Callie, but not the one who provided the gifts. When Callie had told him about her vision on the beach, he couldn't accept the idea that his Succouri had actually warned her because he didn't believe it was capable of that kind of altruism. Perhaps that was why it chose to speak to her rather than him. It knew he wouldn't believe its words.

But now, as he stared into his own image, confronting a part of him he'd spent years loathing, he at last understood that the gifts and the giver were the same. He couldn't love one and despise the other or embrace one and reject the other. The heart, the character of his Succouri was revealed in what it offered: his priceless bond with Callie, his healing touch, and the promptings to offer compassion whenever someone was suffering. He could no longer continue to believe that the tree was poisonous while freely plucking and devouring its sweet fruits. It was unfair.

His biases had developed when he was young, immature, and afraid, but he wasn't that vulnerable boy anymore. His Succouri had saved his life and brought him Callie, and those blessings were more than enough to pay back whatever debt he felt was owed.

"What is my... our destiny? What are we supposed to do?" he asked softly, his heart chastened by his short-sightedness.

"First, choose who you will be."

"I don't understand. Are you... Are you leaving?" Ben

asked, suddenly fearing that this unprecedented face-to-face encounter was some kind of farewell.

"That is entirely up to you. When you were a child, I gave you no option. But I won't be your master as I desire companions, not servants. Choose your life, Ben Sawyer, and I will stay or go at your bidding. But know this, whatever path you set your feet on this day will determine your direction for the rest of your life. There is no going back."

This was what he'd always wanted, the denied opportunity that had embittered him for fifteen years. Though he knew full well what his decision would cost them both, there wasn't a single reservation in his immediate answer. "Please, stay with me. I choose to be Succouri."

As he spoke the words, a healing heat began moving through him, and the voice from the pool returned to its rightful place in his mind. For the first time, the image shifted its expression. Its eyes lit up with pure joy and a warm smile lifted the corners of its mouth. It gazed at him with such sincere affection that Ben could barely breathe from the intensity of the emotion. His Succouri was no tyrant. It knew him, the bad and the good, even better than Callie did, but it regarded him with such lavish favor that all Ben could do was stare in awestruck gratitude.

Then, Callie was there, inside his heart again, filling the aching hole that had been the worst of his agonies. Every muscle in his body strengthened and his thoughts became clear.

"Very well. As Callie has also made her choice, the three of us will journey together toward our destiny. At last, you are ready. It can now begin."

"What can begin? What do I need to do?"

"Henceforth, you will know my voice and your ears will

be inclined to hear it, so I will speak to you. But for now, hurry! You must return, or it will be too late."

"One more question, please." Ben wished he had more time, but the fog was rapidly overtaking him.

"Quickly."

"Why did we become ill? What was the reason for the suffering of the last few weeks?"

"To give you a gift."

"What gift?"

"There's no time. You will know soon enough. Go!"

"What do I do? How do I get back?" Ben stood as the fog closed in around him, so thick that he could no longer see his reflection in the pool.

"Breathe, Ben Sawyer. Just breathe."

"That's it, son! Breathe," Taylor shouted as he paused the chest compressions he was administering to see if Ben would continue to revive on his own.

Ben's eyes opened, and he smiled as he gazed at his father's tear-streaked face. "It's alright, Dad. It's over. I've made my choice."

Taylor lifted his son off the ground, embracing him as a relieved breath flowed from his lungs. "I thought I lost you. I couldn't bear it if—"

"It's alright, Dad. It's alright now." Ben returned his embrace.

"Ben! Callie!" Lee cried out, as he sat cradling his sister in his arms.

Quickly, Ben released his father and turned, his heart contracting at the sight of her pale face. He grabbed her hand, noticing that the scabs on his knuckles had vanished. "Not so fast, sweetheart. It's not quite time for heaven yet."

Slowly, as they all held their breath, color began to return to her cheeks. Lee gently placed Callie in Ben's arms, but kept his eyes locked on her face.

"Come on. Now you breathe." Ben leaned down to kiss her, and when his lips brushed hers, she sucked in a deep breath.

Lee put his face in his hands. "Thank God," he whispered, as his shoulders sank in relief.

Smiling, Ben lovingly watched Callie as she revived, breathing in and out several times before her eyelids fluttered. "That's it. Come all the way back to me. Everything's alright now. Once again, you saved my life by believing when I couldn't. Thank you. I love you my beautiful, courageous, gracious wife. I love you."

After blinking several times, her face lit up with the most radiant smile Ben had ever seen. "I can see the peace in your eyes, beloved. You made the right choice."

As Taylor and Lee watched, mesmerized by their display of pure love, yet confused about what had transpired, Ben softly kissed her once more, caught up in the pleasure of a second chance, a new beginning, a sacred moment in time they'd never forget.

CHAPTER 7

THE DILEMMA

By the time the five of them arrived back at the Navarro home, Ben and Callie had done their best to explain to Lee and Taylor what had happened during the few moments when they'd both stopped breathing, though the experience was hard to put into words. Once Ben had made his choice and their Succouri had returned to him, reigniting their bond, Callie had silently witnessed their exchange.

In addition, through the connection to his heart and her clear view of his eyes provided by his returned healing touch, Callie innately understood much of what Ben had experienced and the profound difference it made in his outlook. No longer a victim of circumstance, Ben had voluntarily chosen his future. Like chains had broken and prison doors flung wide, Ben walked like a free man, and Callie rejoiced greatly at the new optimism and peace that flowed from his heart to hers.

Overwhelmed by all that had happened, Lee, Taylor, and Ethan spoke very little during the drive. Their relative silence was also a courtesy as they recognized that she and

Ben would want to talk about what happened that day privately before freely discussing it with everyone.

As they pulled into the driveway, however, Lee put the car in park and turned to look at Ben. "So, it's over then? No more sickness or catching you when your off button suddenly gets flipped?"

Ben laughed. "It's all over, Lee. I promise. And, thank you for that, by the way."

Lee nodded but then crinkled his brow in confusion. "So, what was the point? I mean, what was this all about?"

Before answering, Ben glanced at Callie, and she smiled and nodded. "Our Succouri said it wanted to give us a gift. I don't know what that means, but it promised that we'd figure it out soon enough."

Lee blew out a breath and shrugged. "Alright then. But it had better be a nice gift, not some cheap little trinket. We've all been through hell and—"

"Lee!" Callie scolded, but she put her hand on his shoulder. "I don't know how to thank you for all you've done for us." Callie looked over at Taylor. "Both of you. I'm sorry for putting you through this."

Lee placed his hand on top of hers. "That wasn't a complaint, sis. Apart from four or five minutes of stark terror, I always believed it would work out."

"Yes, you did," Ben confirmed.

"I suppose it's just hard to believe it's suddenly over, just like that, especially when we don't understand why it started in the first place. It's like whiplash or something."

"I understand," Callie agreed with a sigh. "But it is. Whatever our Succouri was up to, it's done, and everything's back where it belongs. We'll just have to be patient and wait for the answers to come."

"And in the meantime," Taylor spoke up. "We all need

to rest and eat. Let's check in with the doctor, relieve that poor man's anxiety, and then I'll go and get us some dinner."

At the same time, everyone in the car looked at Ethan Devereaux, who sat still and silent in his seat. He hadn't said a word since before they'd arrived at the airport, but his eyes were red, and Callie wondered if he'd witnessed the dramatic scene behind the hanger.

When Ben turned his eyes to her, Callie smiled, still soaring from the joy of being able to read his heart once again. "Why don't the three of us head inside and let you two talk?"

Lee and Taylor exited the car, but Callie lingered for a moment, holding her smile as she enjoyed a few more seconds of gazing into his eyes. He softly kissed her forehead and ran his fingertips down her cheek before releasing her hand. "Be sure to get the doc to clean that scrape on your elbow," Ben reminded. Then, he leaned in to whisper the rest into her ear. "Though I doubt it will be around for long."

Offering him one last smile, she exited the car, taking Lee's arm as they headed for the house.

Ben allowed a few moments of silence after everyone had gone as he listened, with new ears, for his Succouri's voice. Now that he'd had the chance to speak with it directly and had released all obstructing animosity, it was significantly easier to locate and recognize.

"Will you walk with me?" he finally asked.

Dusk had fallen, making the tall trees of the surrounding forest appear as dark, hovering statues.

Ethan sighed, but he at last nodded and exited the car

as Ben did the same. Side by side they strolled at a leisurely pace down the dirt road, watching the stiff arms of the shadowy statues dip and sway above them.

"You saw everything," Ben finally said, certain enough of the fact to state it rather than ask it.

Ethan took a deep breath before responding. "I've been Succouri for forty years, Mr. Sawyer, but I have no idea how to even begin to understand what I witnessed today. You and your wife are no ordinary Succouri, and your bond is unlike any bond I've ever heard of or seen."

"Please, just call me Ben. I think we've been through way too much today to hold on to formalities."

Reluctantly, Ethan nodded. "Alright, Ben. Then, I'm Ethan."

Ben smiled, glad for the small expression of warmth and cooperation. "I wish I could explain it." He paused to chuckle. "It seems that my wife knows a lot more than I do, so she'll have to fill me in when we get a chance to talk, but I can tell you this: there's a lot more to being Succouri than any of us realized."

"Perhaps so, but I for one am glad that my time as one is ending."

Ben halted and turned to face Ethan. "I can understand that. There's no way to get around the truth that this life, this calling was meant for three. Without her, you and your Succouri are incomplete, so you carry a double portion of grief in your heart." Ben lowered his head. "We are extraordinarily privileged to love and connect with another soul in a way that the rest of humanity can't comprehend, but that also means we have the potential to suffer unfathomable loss that's much too heavy to carry alone."

Momentarily, Ethan allowed his pain to surface as tears

glistened in his eyes. "Do you... Do you think it will get better when its gone, when I'm not Succouri anymore?"

"Truthfully, I don't know," Ben admitted in a compassionate whisper. "I'm not sure one can ever entirely shed his Succouri identity once he's possessed it. It becomes a part of who we are. Though I was barely Succouri for the last twenty-four hours, the agony of missing my bond with Callie was crushing, even though she wasn't really gone. But I think there is a way to ease your grief, Ethan."

His eyes asked the unspoken question.

"Use your gift to help your daughter and granddaughter."

Ethan shook his head. "I don't have much power left in my touch anymore and—"

"Not that part of your gift," Ben clarified. "Use your compassion, your empathy, your love. They need you. Your daughter is alone, and she's in a lot of pain."

Ethan threw up his hands. "She's got Gordon and she doesn't need my—"

Ben put a hand on Ethan's shoulder. "Ethan! Her husband died from cancer a little over a year ago. She has no other family. She and Allie are struggling alone."

After staring in stunned silence for several heartbeats, Ethan abruptly turned away from Ben, putting his hand to his forehead.

Ben allowed time for the truth to sink in before continuing. "You can't possibly believe that your presence, the arms of her father, would be unwelcome. You don't need to say anything; just be there for her and Allie. That young girl's got a radiant heart. I'm betting that her name's not the only attribute she shares with your wife."

Speaking into the forest, Ethan's voice shook with emotion. "You don't understand. I left her. After the accident, I got out of the car and ran. I left Jes alone to deal with everything: the funeral, the grief, even the house and finances. I just disappeared."

Ben inhaled slowly before responding. "I did the exact same thing six years ago when my mother took her own life. At the time, she was the only family I had and the pain of losing her, mingled with the confusion and isolation brought on by what I believed to be my curse, caused me to run and keep running until the day I met Callie. There were other people who cared about me; one of them is the man whose life you now have the chance to save, but I was too broken to reach out and accept any help. That was a mistake, Ethan. Healing couldn't begin until I allowed my heart to open again and until I forgave myself for the blame I'd placed exclusively and entirely on my shoulders."

Slowly, Ethan turned back toward Ben, his face a mask of shame and guilt. "I've never even met her; I didn't even know she was a girl. My daughter will never forgive me for walking out of her life, but I couldn't help her then. I don't know if I can help her now either. I don't know if I can bear seeing Lexi's spirit living on in my granddaughter or hearing the echo of her in Jessica's laugh."

"Trust me when I tell you they need you to heal. Jessica is angry, bitter toward the Succouri. She nearly prevented me from helping Allie. But bitterness has its roots in pain and loss. It may take time, especially for Jessica. The sorrow of her mother's death, the void left by the absence of her father, the grief of the recent loss of her husband, and the fear over Allie's health scare is likely all jumbled together and may come hurtling at you as one large boulder of displaced resentment. But she needs to let it out, and you're her father. You may be the one safe place she can go to release it. If you're prepared, in it for the long haul, and willing to help her carry her burdens, eventually she'll be able to do the same for you. As for Allie"—Ben smiled—"she has an open, generous heart. She's enamored by the Succouri, despite her mother's distrust and negativity. Before I helped her, she looked into my eyes and knew I was one. I've only ever experienced that with young children. I think you'll find her accepting and quite ready and willing to forgive."

A slight smile lifted one corner of Ethan's mouth. "Then she does possess Lexi's spirit."

Ben nodded as his grin grew. "I don't know how long they'll need to remain in Baltimore for Allie's recovery, but Lee is keeping in touch with Allie. When we return home, you're more than welcome to come and stay with us so you can be nearby and start the process of reuniting with them. Callie, Lee, and I will help you however we can."

Ethan looked at the ground. "I don't know. I appreciate the offer. I'll think about it." After a breath, he looked back up into Ben's eyes. "Why are you doing this? I mean, I'll help your friend. I want rid of this, this burden so... You don't have to—"

"Ethan," Ben interrupted, his voice gentle. "I've been where you are. Actually, just about an hour ago, but also for years before I met Callie. I understand our circumstances were a little different, but I know the emptiness; I understand all too well. I don't believe a Succouri who loses his partner is irredeemable," Ben said with strong conviction. "It appears that so many things we thought we knew for certain are erroneous. It's true that I don't know exactly how to help you, how to heal that open wound in your heart, but if you're willing, I'm sincerely offering to walk this path with you and see if, together, we can find a way out of the darkness."

A long silence lingered as the emotions in Ethan's eyes shifted, cycling fear, hope, sorrow, and desperation. Remaining quiet, Ben gave him the time and space he needed to sort through his options and choose his own course.

At long last, as the black curtain of night descended around them, Ethan offered his outstretched hand and nodded at Ben. "You are indeed no ordinary Succouri, Ben Sawyer."

When Ben grasped Ethan's hand, he felt an odd sensation, something he'd never experienced before. He knew his touch was uniquely capable of offering strength to other Succouri, as it had done with Louis, but this wasn't a draw. It felt more like a stirring, like his Succouri had shifted inside him. The only other Succouri he'd ever touched were Louis, who no longer possessed the gift, and Raul, who wasn't in the ripening stage. He'd felt a draw from Louis but nothing whatsoever from Raul. Ethan was in the ripening stage, an in-between phase where he still possessed the gift, but its power was waning.

As he walked beside Ethan back to the house, he decided it must be this transitional state of being that prompted the experience.

Yet, deep within him he heard his Succouri's voice softly whisper, *"Teach what you learn, give what only you can give, and—with one mind—restore what's been lost."*

When Ethan and Ben entered Doctor Navarro's lab, they found Maggie, Doctor Navarro, Taylor, Lee, and Grace circled around Callie as she sat on a hospital bed.

"Is everything alright?" Ben asked with concern as he swiftly approached the group, Ethan remaining several steps behind him. Immediately, Maggie, Grace and Doctor Navarro shifted their stunned gazes to him.

Callie laughed. "Everything's fine. We're just, once again, bewildering the good doctor here. I've been doing my best to explain what happened today but..."

"While you're at it," Ben chuckled and put up his hands. "Maybe you can explain it to me. I'm still confused by what you told me before I collapsed."

Doctor Navarro slowly approached Ben, staring at him like he didn't recognize him. "You... You're completely recovered? No different from before this all started?" As he asked the question, he put his hand to Ben's forehead, checking for a fever.

Seeing the exhaustion and stress in the doctor's eyes, Ben's heart was moved by the obvious affection he held for them and the tireless efforts he'd made in the last twenty-four hours to save their lives. "I am," he answered with a smile. "Better than ever."

After holding Ben's gaze for a moment, the doctor shook his head and turned back toward the bed. Ben went to Callie's side and took her hand.

"Maybe we should start by filling Ben in on what the doctor discovered in my blood work from this morning," Callie said with a sly smile.

Raising his eyebrows, Ben looked at the doctor.

Still shaken from watching Ben walk through the door, perfectly healthy and fully recovered, the doctor didn't respond immediately, but at last he sighed resolutely and answered. "I... I found Succouri additive. Just a trace, but unmistakable."

"So, you were right," Ben said, perplexed as he looked at Callie. "You did feel a draw because you had some of my... my gift."

She smiled satisfactorily, though Ben had a feeling she'd never had any doubts.

"Though the fact that my wife was, once again, correct in her assessment doesn't surprise me in the least, I still don't understand how that's possible," Ben said, scratching his head. "No blood was transferred between us."

Taylor and Callie smiled at one another, then Taylor looked at Maggie. "During our visit, Ben brought up a very interesting question."

"I remember," Maggie responded. "He wondered about how the Succouri gift was transferred before modern medicine, before blood transfusions and transplants. None of us knew the answer."

"Right," Taylor said putting up a finger. "But Carozza did." Briefly, Taylor looked at Callie for approval to continue and she nodded, so he went on. "Carozza believes that the Succouri of old, the Antico as he calls them, sought a perfect match, a specific human soul to unite with, whose heart and character were like its own. The terminal triad, made up of the Succouri, the host, and his partner—called a Datouri—had a special destiny, a mission to carry out for the good of humanity. It often took hundreds of years to meet up with him, but the Succouri was determined and strategic, moving from host to host, each transfer bringing it one step closer to the chosen one. Because the Succouri knew the route, but the host did not, Carozza asserts that it was the prerogative of the Antico, not the host, to select the recipients."

Seven confused faces stared at Taylor.

"But if the host didn't know who was next in line"—Lee spoke up—"how did he know who to give blood to?"

"There was no need for a blood transfer," Callie explained. "At the time and place of the Antico's choosing, it moved to the next host in the same way it transfers healing, through touch."

Baffled and skeptical faces stared back at Callie.

"Are you saying that, in the last couple of weeks, my Succouri was trying to transfer itself to you?" Ben asked, crinkling his brow as none of this was making sense to him.

"No," Callie said, offering a brief laugh. "It's still true that a woman can't be Succouri, only Datouri. Why a portion of your Succouri moved into me is still a complete mystery. What we're telling you is the way that small portion transferred to me was by touch. According to Carozza, that's the only way an Antico should ever be transferred."

"But," Doctor Navarro objected, "In all my years of working with the Succouri, I've never heard of the gift transferring that way. And if it were truly that simple, why does the host enter the ripening stage at all?"

"To alert him, let him know that his time as Succouri is ending, and to begin the process of returning his body to its pre-Succouri state," Taylor explained. "According to Carozza, originally, a host's term was much shorter than what we see nowadays, typically only ten to twenty years. Because of that, the cumulative damaging effects of the draw weren't as severe or permanent. After the Antico departed, the host could go on and live out a normal lifespan without significant weakening."

"But that's not what happens," Doctor Navarro argued, looking increasingly distressed as their explanation unfolded. "I've never known anyone who's had the gift for such a short period of time, nor have I known one who hasn't weakened after the transfer." He shook his head. "I'm not sure this source offered you anything of value; just a lot of unsubstantiated myths."

Looking directly into the doctor's eyes, Taylor answered his objection with a tone of empathy. "I would agree with you, save for one thing." He paused and shifted his gaze. "Ben."

All eyes focused on Ben as another silent moment lingered.

"I don't understand," Maggie at last spoke. "At this point I think we all know that Ben is different than other Succouri, but Owen wasn't, and Ben possesses his... his gift."

Once more, Taylor and Callie exchanged a quick glance. "I think I'd like to speak to Ben privately about his specific situation before saying more," Callie said apologetically. "But"—she turned back to Maggie—"we will tell you what we can as we sort through all of this. I promise."

Maggie nodded in understanding.

"Alright," the doctor said with a sigh. "If whatever this man told you about Ben convinced you that he was more than a misguided quack, why don't his assertions align with the experiences and observations of anyone I know who presently works with the Succouri?"

For several awkward seconds, neither Taylor nor Callie answered, but at last, Taylor cleared his throat and spoke softly. "Because Carozza passionately believes that our modern imposition, our immoral meddling in the way the gift is transferred, has permanently altered the phenomenon."

Doctor Navarro stepped back and his eyes grew wide. "How?"

"When an Antico undergoes a forced transfer of the host's choosing, it knocks it off course, making it impossible for the Antico to ever meet up with its intended terminal match. As a result, the spirit or will of the Antico essentially dies. It becomes… inanimate, no longer active in plotting its own destiny. Consequently, the gifts it's able to offer its hosts are diminished. In addition, as the Succouri has withdrawn from the transfer process completely and therefore no longer monitors or modifies it, a longer and thus more damaging term plagues the hosts who carry it. And, as if all that weren't bad enough, perhaps the worst consequence of them all is the unfortunate foregoing of the impactful blessing that the destined triad was meant to bestow on mankind."

Though every face in the group expressed alarm, the doctor's look of dismay was particularly acute. "Are you saying that the blood transfers we've been performing for decades have destroyed the Succouri?"

Though Ben was confused about how much of what Callie and his father were describing applied to his specific situation, his heart dropped in unison with every-one's in the room, as they all cared deeply about the Succouri and had dedicated their lives to protecting the secret treasure.

Callie's eyes filled with tears as she answered, trying to take some of the misdirected heat off Taylor. "That's what Carozza believes," she said softly.

Ethan came up beside Ben. "So, if I give my blood to your friend, save his life, I'm killing the Succouri in me?"

"No!" Callie exclaimed, turning her eyes to Ethan. "This happened long ago, likely many transfers before you received your Succouri. What's done is done. It's no one's fault. If all of this is true, no one knew. No one, at least no one alive today, did this on purpose."

"And the gift is still beautiful," Grace softly reminded them, her high, lilting voice soothing everyone's raw nerves. "It still saves people, helps people."

Reaching out her hand to pat Grace's arm, Callie offered a weak smile. "It certainly does."

Each of them wrestled with doubts, fears, and questions. Ben tightened his grip on Callie's hand, and she turned her eyes back to him, just as a tear slipped down her cheek. He felt her eagerness to share what she knew about his specific situation, and Ben hoped that the information was far more optimistic.

Finally, the doctor blew out a breath and lifted his eyes to Taylor. "How many are left?"

"I don't know," Taylor admitted. "I don't think Carozza knew for sure either, but not many. Perhaps only one." Every eye turned to Ben once more, but no one asked the question, respecting Callie's request.

"And there's no way to right the wrong, revive and restore the original… Antico?" There was a desperate plea in the doctor's question.

"Carozza doesn't believe there is, but he was… severe in his judgments, and I'm not sure his mind was open to the possibility."

"If he knew about this, why didn't he tell anyone, warn the network about the consequences?" Maggie asked.

"I'm not exactly sure," Taylor admitted. "It appears Carozza's been mistreated and outright rejected by most who've heard his theories. Even his own family doesn't believe him. Those experiences have made him guarded and distrusting of people generally and of talking about the Succouri specifically. His attitude is decisively harsh, which is a barrier to hearing him out and accepting his theories."

"But you both believe all of it?" Lee asked, glancing between Callie and Taylor.

When Taylor nodded, all eyes shifted to Callie.

Callie closed her eyes, sobered by the impact she knew

her answer would have. "Because of what he knew about Ben," Callie said softly, "yes, I do."

"Where does this leave our situation?" Ethan interjected, looking toward Donovan's bed in the back corner of the room. Due to the shock of Ben's miraculous recovery and the subsequent questions that it had provoked, Ben hadn't had the chance to introduce Ethan to Maggie and Grace yet, but, as they seemed to know exactly who he was, Ben guessed Callie or Taylor had filled them in on Ethan's decision to help Donovan.

"Donovan doesn't have much longer," the doctor said, his voice tight with stress. "Maybe a couple of days, if that."

Ben sighed and looked around at each person in the group. "We're not going to solve this dilemma in that short period of time. We need more information, much more. I'd like to talk with Carozza myself, see what else he might know. But Donovan can't wait for us to get the answers." He turned to Ethan. "If you're still willing, I'd like to introduce the two of you and give you a chance to get acquainted with him and with Grace."

"That's not really necessary."

"Please," Ben gently encouraged, and Ethan reluctantly nodded.

Letting go of Callie's hand, Ben turned to grip the doctor's shoulder. "Doc, you need some rest. If you think he'll be alright to wait until tomorrow for the transfer, then why don't you go get some sleep? Callie and I will stay close by to make sure Donovan remains stable. The rest of you are more than welcome to head to our place in Cape Cod for a full night's sleep as well."

"Callie needs to rest," the doctor insisted. "She's hardly slept at all since you got here."

"I'll make sure that happens," Ben promised.

Before anyone left for the evening, Silvia graciously treated them to a home-cooked meal she'd prepared. Smiling, Ben watched Callie eat heartily as did he. As everyone was exhausted and occupied with their own thoughts, the meal was quiet, but the doctor, in particular, continued to look troubled, and he excused himself to retire to his bedroom after just a few bites of dinner. As Silvia hadn't been present for the conversation in the lab, she watched her husband with confused concern, and after they'd all made quick work of the dishes, she headed upstairs as well.

Maggie agreed to stay, resting nearby on the couch in the front room between regular checks of Donovan's vitals. Though they all tried to convince Grace to go with Lee, Ethan, and Taylor, she refused to leave Donovan, though she did agree to trade off shifts with Callie and Ben throughout the night.

Before the group of three departed, Grace, Ethan, Ben, and Callie returned to the lab and stepped to Donovan's bedside. His friend's face was pale, and though he was still sedated, his expression wasn't restful.

Ben placed his hand on Donovan's arm and Callie placed hers on top of his. As they waited for the healing to circulate through Donovan's body and revive him, Ben smiled contentedly at her. Just a few hours before, they weren't sure they'd survive another day, much less regain what they'd lost. Joy and gratitude at returning to their collaborative mission, once again working side by side to dispel pain and suffering, filled their hearts.

"Hey, Ben." Donovan's weak, raspy voice shifted Ben's attention. Grace rushed up on the opposite side of the bed with a cup of water and a straw.

After a long, steady drink, his brown eyes moved to take in the room, as he tried to figure out where he was.

"Welcome to Doctor Navarro's Succouri hospital," Ben said with a chuckle.

Donovan squinted his eyes. "We made it. Did Allie make it alright?"

Callie put her free hand on Donovan's shoulder. "Everyone is just fine, including you."

Looking intently at each of them, particularly Grace, Donovan considered Callie's words of reassurance. "How long have I been out? You all look warn out."

"A little more than a day," Ben answered, slightly out of breath as the force of the draw required to counteract the sedative in Donovan's system was nearly overtaking the benefits of Callie's touch.

Frustratedly, Donovan huffed and shook his head, as he focused on Grace. "Not exactly how I would have chosen to spend my last days."

"Not your last days," Grace declared with delight, smiling as her eyes lifted from Donovan's to Ethan Devereaux's. Remaining partially hidden behind Ben, Ethan shifted uncomfortably.

Continuing to smile sweetly at him, Grace beckoned with her hand, inviting Ethan to come and stand next to her, and he reluctantly complied as Donovan watched with curiosity.

"My friend," Ben began with a grin. "I want you to meet Ethan Devereaux. Ethan, this is Donovan Bradshaw."

Donovan's expression gradually shifted from confusion to understanding, and he handed the cup of water back to Grace so he could extend his hand. When Ethan took it, Ben felt a shift in the sensation of the draw. Though Ethan's Succouri power was waning, his contribution eased Ben's burden slightly, but there was more. Once again, he felt the strange shifting inside him, though less intense than when he'd made direct contact with Ethan. Callie briefly glanced over at him looking concerned, but then she shifted her gaze to the handshake between the two men, relaxing as she drew the same conclusion. As he'd never healed in cooperation with another Succouri before, he hadn't known what to expect from the experience.

The two men studied each other in silence for another breath before Ethan let go and stepped back.

"Ethan has agreed to offer you his gift," Ben explained with a smile. "If that's still something you and Grace wish to accept."

Donovan kept his eyes on Ethan. "How long have you been Succouri, Mr. Devereaux?"

"Forty years," he answered stiffly. "Fifteen years longer than I wanted to be."

"Forgive me, Ben is the only one I've ever known, and I've only known about him for a few weeks. You don't like being Succouri?" Donovan asked with genuine interest.

Ethan looked at the floor. "Not without... Not alone."

Gradually, understanding dawned in Donovan's eyes. "What was her name?" he asked gingerly.

Surprised by the question, Ethan lifted his eyes to Ben, and Ben nodded, acknowledging that Donovan had been told about his wife's death. "Lexi," he answered, sorrow mixing with annoyance in his tone.

Sensing his discomfort at the topic, Donovan changed the subject but kept his eyes focused on Ethan. "Before... Did you like being Succouri? Did you find the life it offered you meaningful, worth the costs?"

Caught off guard once again by Donovan's sincere, yet direct question, Ethan shifted his weight and cleared his throat. "I... Well, I..." He let out a long, slow sigh. "Yes, Lexi and I were honored by the gift."

Inwardly, Ben applauded Donovan's approach. Though he knew his questions were motivated by his own genuine need to understand the gift he would soon possess, they afforded Ethan the beneficial opportunity to recall the positive aspects of his Succouri life, the one he'd shared with Lexi, which was likely something he hadn't done in quite some time.

"And the costs?" he inquired, his tone gentle. "Giving up the chance to be a father and all the rest: was it worth it for you and Lexi?"

Ben glanced over at Callie, wondering if he should intervene, but the look in her eyes and the slight shake of her head persuaded him to remain silent. This was an important conversation that needed to be as private as possible between the giver and the receiver.

"Well, we... we already had a daughter before... before I was changed so we were fortunate in that way."

Surprised, Donovan shifted in bed, and Ben had to hang on tightly to him as he rose to a sitting position. "I see. And what does your daughter think about the Succouri and the lifestyle that comes with it?"

Ethan's eyes dropped again to the floor. "As a child, she loved everything about it." Gesturing toward Callie, Ethan chuckled, momentarily forgetting his pain as he got lost in a sweet memory. "When Lexi would help me like that, Jes would put her tiny hand on top of her mother's pretending to offer her own Succouri power. She would kneel by her bed at night and pray that God would send her a Succouri husband someday, so she could love him like Lexi loved..." His voice trailed off as the reality of the present returned to his mind.

"That's beautiful," Grace whispered.

"Did she?" Donovan asked.

Confused, Ethan looked up at Donovan.

"Did she marry a Succouri?"

"No. But her husband was a good man. I know they were happy, and Lexi and I were glad she didn't give up the ability to have children of her own."

"So, you have grandchildren?"

Again, Ethan looked to Ben, and Ben shook his head, answering his unasked question.

"Mr. Bradshaw, Jessica Hughes is my daughter. I believe you traveled with her and my granddaughter, Allie."

Donovan, Callie, and Grace turned stunned, questioning eyes to Ben and he smiled in confirmation.

"That delightful, spunky girl is your granddaughter?" Donovan asked with a chuckle that communicated both joy at the fact and wonder at the coincidence.

As she gasped, Ben observed a new understanding alight in Callie's eyes as she put all the pieces together.

When Ethan didn't smile or answer, Donovan's enthusiasm faded. "You've never met her, have you?"

Ethan's silence and diverted gaze were answer enough.

As they all waited, unsure what to say next, Ben's hands began to subtly shake, and Callie noticed, pressing down on his hand to try to boost the inflow coming from her, but there wasn't much of a change. He couldn't keep Donovan awake and healthy for much longer.

"Until a few days ago," Donovan said, "I hadn't spoken with my parents in many years. They didn't approve of my choice to serve in the military, and they took my decision to go against their wishes as a rejection of them personally. I didn't want to die and leave anything unsaid, so"—he paused to smile at Grace —"at the kind nudging of Miss Sophia, I reached out. It was... awkward, difficult, but I'm glad I did it. I said what I needed to say, opened the door, and the rest is up to them. It's worth it, Mr. Devereaux, taking the chance. Whoever's right or wrong; it doesn't really matter. If you're going to help me get my life back, I'd like to help you get your family back, if I can."

Though his walls rose quickly, Ben caught Ethan's fleeting expression of appreciation.

"I haven't made up my mind yet. Right now, I just want free of this. Perhaps without it, I'll be able to offer them something worthwhile, rather than just hurting them all over again."

Remaining still and quiet, Donovan considered Ethan for a moment before responding. "Alright then," he at last said with a nod. "If, as Ben suggested, this is a situation where we both stand to benefit, I'll accept your gift of life with gratitude, Mr. Devereaux. Thank you. But please, consider my offer. And I'll gladly accept any guidance you can give me about my new life as Succouri. I have much to learn."

"I'm sure Ben can help you. I wouldn't be a good teacher as I haven't used my gift in years and my perspective is biased. I'll return in the morning and, if you still want this burden, you can have it. But I warn you, Mr. Bradshaw, though it might seem like a blessing, if it all goes wrong, it will trap you in a kind of death much worse than what you're facing right now. No one ever warned me how relentless the suffering could be, so I'm warning you. Consider that my contribution to your Succouri education."

At that, he turned on his heels and rushed from the room, as they all stared after him.

CHAPTER 8

THE RENEWAL

After Ethan left the room, Grace placed her hand over her heart and whispered softly, "That poor man!"

Ben's hands were trembling furiously, but he couldn't let Donovan slip back under the effects of the sedatives without explaining Ethan's outburst.

"He reminds me of you," Donovan said, "before you met Callie."

Nodding, Ben sighed in sad agreement. "The pain of a missing bond is severe and perhaps permanent for a Succouri, much more so than the ordinary grief suffered by typical human loss. It doesn't lessen with time. The emptiness is consuming, growing from a deep gaping hole inside." Ben took a deep breath and Donovan looked down at his hand. "I'm hoping I can help him fill the void with the love of his daughter and granddaughter. Truthfully, I don't know if that will be enough, but I have to try. Though ill-timed, his warning was valid, Donovan. There are grave risks to this life in addition to the benefits."

Donovan offered a weak smile. "If I were afraid of risks,

I never would have joined the Navy SEALS, my friend. And let me correct you. *We* have to try. I want to be a part of this, helping him find healing."

"Me too," Grace said.

"But"—Donovan put his hand on top of Callie's—"the two of you need to let go now. Thank you for working a miracle, getting me here, convincing Ethan to give me his gift, and saving my life. I'm indebted to you both. Please, go and get some rest. I know I will," he said with a half grimace, half grin.

"I wish I could give you and Grace a few more minutes, but I promised the doc that we'd be ready in case you need us during the night, so..."

"Conserve your strength. I understand." Donovan lay back down. "I'll see you in a few hours, and when I do"—he grinned at Ben once more—"we really will be like brothers."

Ben patted his shoulder with his free hand. "Indeed, we will."

Twenty minutes later, the lights in the lab had been dimmed and Ben and Callie reclined together in an over-sized chair near Donovan's bed while Grace slept in one of the spare bedrooms upstairs. She had argued with them, wanting to take the first watch and let them sleep, but Callie was eager to talk with Ben about what she'd learned earlier in the day from Carozza, and she knew she wouldn't sleep until she did, so she at last convinced Grace to rest first.

"I can't believe Jessica Hughes is Ethan's daughter and Allie is his granddaughter," Callie said, tucking her head deeper into his neck as he softly stroked her arm. "I understand much better now why she reacted to us the way she did. Her father's shattered heart drove him away. That had to be devastating, especially after she'd just lost her mother."

Ben didn't respond, so Callie lifted her head and looked into his eyes. It seemed as if his mind were a million miles away. "Are you alright?"

"Callie, I... I hope you truly know how much I love you."

She smiled at the tenderness in his voice, but she also raised her eyebrows in confusion. "Of course. Ben, what is it?"

"I made a choice today, a choice that impacts both of us for the rest of our lives. I don't know exactly what the alternative was, but truthfully, I didn't ask or care. I chose to return to my Succouri life and all that comes with it: the shortened lifespan, the inability to have children, all of it. And you weren't there: you didn't get a vote. I obligated you to it without your consent. I know you agree with the choice, but I still feel badly for making it without you. The freedom to choose my own destiny is something I've always wanted; it's changed my entire perspective, and I'd never want to take that from you, but—"

She pressed her lips to his, halting his explanation. "You gave me a choice," she reminded him. "As I watched my very first brilliant sunrise break over a Massachusetts horizon, you knelt on one knee and offered me a proposal, and I said yes." She smiled and kissed him again. "It's still a yes, Ben Sawyer, to all of it, but..." She sat back and grinned at him, her heart pounding as it could no longer contain the excitement of the news she had to share.

"Callie?" He returned her smile, picking up on her enthusiasm. "What did you learn today, about me, about our Succouri?"

"You... You..." The words tumbled around in her head, but she couldn't figure out exactly where to start.

"It's an Antico, isn't it?" Ben asked as he also sat up. "Our Succouri, it's not... not lifeless like the others. There's no way it could have spoken with me like it did if it were."

"It is! It's an ancient, spirited Succouri, full of wisdom," she exclaimed as she laughed and threw her arms around his neck. "That's how it spoke to me on the beach, how it communicated with Louis, and why our bond is so different; so much stronger. It may very well be the last of its kind."

Though he returned her embrace and smiled at her excitement, he was hesitant to express his own. "But I don't understand, Callie. Doesn't that mean my time is nearly over? I've had it for fifteen years. If it moves more frequently from host to host, that could mean it may depart anytime now. Since I can't survive without it, doesn't that leave us with less time together than what we'd already reluctantly accepted?"

She put her hands on the sides of his face and looked into his eyes, shaking her head as she continued to laugh with joy. "Just the opposite, my love. It isn't going to leave at all. It's going to stay with us for our entire lives, until you and I are very, very old."

Perplexed, he blinked blankly at her. "How... What makes you so sure of that?"

"Because that's why it changed you. Ben, that was intentional! It strengthened and fortified your body so you could survive a lifetime of the draw and everything else that comes with being Succouri. The changes it made in your physiology were all for your good. Your transformation was a gift, a generous provision from our Antico. It offered us the blessing of a long, full life."

Ben gaped, unable to speak for a time as he took in her words. "But.. but why? he stammered, his eyes wide. "Why me? Why not Owen or Dad or—"

"Because you're the one it was looking for!" she exclaimed, exuberance bubbling out with every word. "Perhaps for a thousand years. You're this Antico's chosen one, its destined match. You are the last host it will in-dwell, and someday, far into the future, it will perish when we perish. Because it found its intended and will never pass to another, its fate is tied to ours, just as our fates are tied to each other's. None of it was a mistake, Ben! Do you understand? Not your acquisition nor your transformation. It pursued you specifically. Waited, moved, and strategized. Its one goal, from the beginning of its existence, was to reach you."

Ben froze, not breathing or blinking. She could see the struggle in his eyes, the inability to accept what she had told him. Abruptly, he stood and turned away, putting his hands over his face, hiding from a truth he couldn't take in or comprehend.

Giving him time to process her words, she remained where she was until she heard him begin to breathe again, though unsteadily. Then, she rose and approached, standing just behind him.

Slowly, he turned to face her, his eyes full of doubt and his voice shaky. "Why? I mean, I'm... I'm nobody! I wasn't even intentionally conceived or wanted by my parents. I've spent all but the last few months hating the gift, fighting it. It can't be true! I can't be the one, Callie. You must be mistaken."

Brokenhearted by the way he still saw himself, Callie took his hands in hers. "You still can't see it, still can't understand or believe it when I tell you how extraordinary you are. But perhaps that's the precise reason it chose you. Your humility makes you who you are, makes you the only person who can do what you're meant to do. But it still breaks my heart. I promise you, I'm not mistaken, my love. You *are* the one."

When she lowered her head, he let go of one of her hands to lift her chin with his finger and look into her eyes. "Then, if you are that confident, though I don't understand it, I believe you. But, Callie, please help me understand. How does Carozza know this? He hasn't even met me."

"Because the Antico would only alter the final host, as it would have no intention of staying with anyone else for a lifetime. Because your touch heals all, even other Succouri. And because only the chosen one and his Datouri share a tight enough bond that their fates become intertwined as ours are."

"And Carozza knew about these things, even before you offered the information?"

She laughed. "He did. Believe me, I was nearly as stunned as you are right now when he asked me if you could heal other Succouri with your touch. Ben, it is true! Listen to the voice of our Succouri. It will confirm that what I'm telling you is exactly right."

Ben continued to wrestle with his doubts as silence lingered for a long moment.

"'She understands and believes. She'll explain it to you, but you still might not accept it'," he whispered to himself, looking off to the side. "'Long ago, I chose you. There was no mistake. I am of you and of her. I know your heart, for it is also mine'," he continued, mumbling almost inaudibly.

"Ben?"

He looked back down into her eyes. "It already did. In my vision, it told me you knew the truth and would tell me, and it predicted I would have a hard time believing it, just as I am right now."

Like a light had suddenly been turned on, his entire countenance lifted as the truth registered deep in his soul. Then he laughed. "It also told me you knew it far better than I did and have already accepted the life, made your choice."

She stepped to him and put her arms around his neck. "Because I know you, chose you, and love you." She smiled playfully at him. "I hope you're alright with a few more years with me than you anticipated when you said I do, Mr. Sawyer. I'm afraid your stuck with me for a very, very long time."

"Callie!" The word flowed out with a breath, the sound of a heart bursting forth with a spring of pure joy it can't contain. He lifted her off the ground and swung her around in circles as they laughed and cried, sweet tears of relief and happiness. And then, he kissed her, so passionately that when he finally relented, remembering their promise to keep a watchful eye on Donovan, Callie's knees were weak, and her head dizzy.

"Do you remember when I told you that loving you for a thousand years wouldn't be long enough?" he asked breathlessly near her ear.

She clung to him, her smile filling her face and lighting up her eyes.

"That day, I greatly underestimated the ecstasy of loving you, Mrs. Sawyer. Forever, an eternity, won't be nearly long enough."

Though Callie slept soundly in his arms during their periodic two-hour respites in the Navarro home's spare bedroom, Ben's mind and heart were too overwhelmed to settle. The information Callie had learned about them from Carozza— confirmed by the proclamations from their Succouri—as well as the free choice he'd made to wholeheartedly embrace his destiny, had radically changed his view of himself and his and Callie's future.

Though only twenty-seven, ever since Ms. Essie told him about the average term for a Succouri, he'd felt more like a man in his forties, the clock rapidly ticking down the days until he'd inevitably burden her with his deteriorating condition. Now, it was as if someone had reversed time, given him back his youth. Because his Succouri had changed him, enabling him to live out a full lifespan, he and Callie could set and accomplish long-term goals, build a home together, perhaps even consider adopting children someday, as he'd now be able to watch them grow up and have children of their own. It was very possible he could live to be a grandfather, all the while caring for his family with the added benefits of his Succouri gift.

As he had been when he looked at his reflection in the pool, he was once again humbled by his unfair prejudices. From the moment it had come into his life, he'd assigned nothing but negative motives to its every action toward him. He assumed it left him in confusion on purpose because it didn't care about him, when, in truth, it had sought him out for the entirety of its existence. He'd believed it had no particular deference or concern for him but, though he still struggled to understand why, he was, in fact, the object of its greatest affection. He'd viewed his transformation as a violation, a malicious mutilation of his humanity. Now he knew that his Succouri had altered him to protect him from the ravages of the draw and, thereby, give Callie and him an unabridged lifetime together. He'd been wrong about everything, yet it had still chosen him, still saved his life, and still offered him an autonomous choice.

Though unworthy of it all, somehow Ben had been abundantly blessed: first by his Succouri, then by Callie. He couldn't change the past, but in the silence stillness of the new dawn, he made a vow to his lifelong partner to never again harshly judge its actions, and to offer himself as a willing partner in whatever destiny lay ahead for the three of them. In response, he felt a wave of warm affection wash over him, a tangible gesture of compassion, appreciation, and forgiveness. Though he would never be able to comprehend it, his Succouri saw him like Callie saw him, through generous, loving eyes of grace.

As he thought about their future, he marveled at how, in a few short months, his and Callie's bond had developed far beyond what other Succouri couples enjoyed. He could only imagine what wonders and depths of intimacy awaited them in the years to come. Since there didn't appear to be another Succouri couple like them, there was no way of knowing what the future might bring, but the possibilities were thrilling.

As he held Callie close, pleasuring in the warmth of her body and the renewing strength pouring into him from her touch, he watched the light in the window brighten as morning dawned. Just a day before, he'd made her a promise, desperate to make up for the endless tears she'd cried since meeting him. He'd vowed to change that, fill her life with joy, laughter, and love so profuse that it would overshadow the pain and sorrow they'd endured, leaving even the memory of it faded and distant. Now, for the first time since he'd met her, he thought he just might be capable of giving her that kind of life.

As his finger lovingly traced the soft features of her angelic face, he swore to himself that even if, from this moment forward, their lives were nothing but pure bliss, he would never forget that she'd steadfastly stood by his side through the bleakest night. When hope was scarce and her own life endangered, her love and faithfulness never wavered. She had no regrets about binding her heart and future to his.

So many times, when he'd lost all faith, she'd stood firm, anchoring him through the fiercest storms. If not for her, he would have never embraced his father or his Succouri life. Flinging wide the locked doors of his heart, she taught him to trust and forgive himself and others. She'd given him the strength to face his past and to heal the wounds he'd acquired there. There wasn't a doubt in his mind that had it not been for her, Ben would still be running and hiding, forever doomed to a life of isolation and fear. He owed her everything, more than he could ever repay, but that wouldn't stop him from trying.

"Good morning." She startled him with her soft greeting. He looked down to see her smiling at him, her eyes shining.

"I'm sorry. Did I wake you?"

Pressing up against him, she sighed contentedly. "No, I think the sun did. Do we need to relieve Grace?"

"We've got a few minutes. The doc will probably be up soon as well. Today's a big day after all."

Though Ben was relieved to finally complete their mission and get Donovan back to full health, since hearing about the devastation caused by the blood transfers, his enthusiasm for witnessing the procedure had diminished considerably.

Hearing the conflicting emotions in his voice, Callie looked up at him. "Are you alright?"

"I have so many questions. I wish there was time to pay Carozza another visit before the blood transfer, but I can't put Donovan at any further risk. But a part of me feels uncomfortable with the procedure now that we know what we do, and I'm confident the doctor feels the same way."

"That's understandable." She placed her hand over his heart. "Ultimately though, I believe, the answers are in here, in you. I don't think Carozza has much to offer in solving the problem with the dispirited Succouri. He believes there hasn't been a terminal matchup like ours for hundreds, if not thousands of years, so knowledge about this special relationship and what's involved in it has largely been lost. And unfortunately, his heart is too embittered to be open to considering solutions. Unfairly, he's vilified those in the network, so he can't recognize the value of the experience, knowledge, and skill they bring to the table in potentially helping to remedy the situation. I hope, when we go back to see him, we can prove to him that everyone involved has risked their livelihoods, and perhaps much more, to protect the Succouri. No one wanted to harm them, certainly not destroy them. Realistically though, I think it will be you, my love, who discovers the answer, the solution. If there's any way to revive the spirit of the Succouri, surely our Antico knows how."

As always, her logic was flawless. The Succouri he carried was old, ancient even. It had existed long before blood transfusions. And that thought brought him to another question he'd been pondering all night.

"Callie, how did our Antico evade the same fate as the others? Granted, we don't know for sure about Owen's reception, but it definitely moved to my dad and then to me through blood.”

She smiled. “Your father asked Carozza the same question. Maybe it transferred through blood, then again, maybe it didn’t. Carozza believes it may have moved through touch but then hidden itself until it was safe to manifest. Years of strategizing, doing whatever it needed to do to stay on course, undoubtedly made it resourceful.”

“But I didn’t meet my dad until the day he shot Ruiz and saved our lives.”

Her smile became crooked and she tilted her head. Ben sat up, holding her gaze. “Callie?”

“Um… I think he’d enjoy the opportunity to share that story with you himself, so I won’t rob him of that pleasure, but let’s just say, there was one opportunity for a touch transfer in your case and likely many opportunities for one between he and Owen.”

Though she’d assuredly piqued his curiosity, he appreciated her thoughtfulness regarding his father, so he didn’t press further.

“The other possibility Carozza proposed,” Callie continued, “was that, in this unusual case, what the Antico wanted matched what the host wanted. Since the transfer didn’t disrupt its path to you, it willingly went along with it.”

“So, it isn’t the blood transfer specifically that’s the main cause of the problem; it’s the selection of the recipient.” Ben stated, and Callie nodded in confirmation. He paused to stroke his chin for a moment before continuing. “You said ten to twenty years was the average term for an interim host, but what about Owen? He served a full forty years, and he weakened afterward, just like those who carry a dispirited Succouri?”

"Carozza did say that the term was indeterminate. I took that to mean it could vary significantly, but ten to twenty years was average. In retrospect, since we know it wanted to reach you, staying with Owen for that long may have been the only way to accomplish that, but..." Closing her eyes, she considered her next words. "Carozza told Owen about all of this, but he didn't believe it. If he had, I don't think he could have kept it from Maggie, and I don't think he would have gone through with a blood transfer. Carozza told us Owen didn't black out and didn't forget what happened after he was attacked; he just refused to accept Carozza's explanation, so he convinced himself that he couldn't recall the blood transfer because he was unconscious. The man who passed the Antico to Owen via touch did believe. He was joyful, excited to see it move on because he thought Owen was the chosen one. If..." She focused on his eyes again before continuing. "If the Antico's goal was to transfer to your father, I wonder why it didn't do so when Owen originally rescued Taylor. That would have been a shorter term for Owen, saving him from the weakening."

"Maybe that would have disrupted my father's path to me. He wasn't the same man back then. He needed to change, go through detox, and put enough years between his new life and his old one before he was stable, and his heart had softened enough to want contact with me."

"You're probably right," she conceded. "But I also wonder if some level of cooperation or permission from the host is required for the touch transfer to work. Perhaps the host has to... let go, consent, or in some way release the Antico for it to move on by touch. If Owen never believed it could happen that way, maybe that's why it never did."

"'I desire companions, not servants'," Ben mumbled, closing his eyes as he recalled his Succouri's words.

"Exactly." She nodded, following his thoughts. "At every level, this is a partnership. The Antico chose you when you were too young to understand what it all meant, and it had to save your life or there would have been no opportunity for the matchup and it would have been too late to transform your body. But yesterday, it made sure you had a chance to choose for yourself. It chose me for you, but so did you, the human part of you. And I had a chance to choose both of you. Part of the beauty and power of the gift is that three become one, working together in a voluntary collaboration that yields blessings beyond what any one of us could do alone. But"—she lowered her head—"maybe its greatest strength is also its greatest vulnerability. If any of the three are lost or choose not to cooperate in the partnership, the whole thing breaks down, bringing dysfunction and misery to all."

Ben sighed. "I am certainly a poignant example in support of that hypothesis. I didn't hear its voice for fifteen years because I didn't want to, didn't care about what it had to say. During my vision, when I asked it about my destiny, it requested that I first make a choice. Come to think of it, at the very beginning, when it first spoke, it urged me to decide. I believe that was the whole purpose of the vision."

With compassion in her eyes, she looked back up at Ben. "I agree. I don't think the Succouri can accomplish its ultimate purpose without the host's full support. Owen's lack of cooperation wasn't malicious; he simply didn't have the same evidence we have. It's a fortuitous blessing that in our rare case, though Owen wasn't aware of it, his choice for a recipient did align with our Succouri's plan, but perhaps he could have spared himself and Maggie many lost years if he'd trusted his experience and Carozza's words and worked in cooperation with our Antico."

"Perhaps. I don't know if we'll ever know for sure what could have been. I don't fault Owen Briggs though. As far as we know, Carozza is the only one that knows anything about the Antico and the original method of transference. Everyone else's experience and knowledge is exclusively with the Succouri phenomenon as it exists today. If it weren't for the fact that I'm so different, changed in such an undeniably drastic way, and my experiences weren't so contrary to other Succouri's, frankly, I doubt I'd believe Carozza either."

"Isn't that what Louis said?" Callie asked, a mix of excitement and wonder in her voice. "Didn't he say that your mission, your purpose was something that only you could do? Maybe this is part of it, Ben. Maybe you're meant to be living proof, undeniable evidence of the Antico and the Succouri's original ways. The doctor, for example, has been baffled since the first day he met us. Without meeting us and performing all his tests, he wouldn't have considered these theories, as they counter most of what he'd been absolutely certain of for at least a decade."

"But, Callie, what's the point in persuading people if we can't change anything? I mean, why wake people up to what being Succouri used to involve, if there's no hope of ever regaining what's been lost? The touch transfers are null and void if the Succouri aren't willing or able to be involved in them anymore."

"That's why I think... I'm sure there must be a way!" Her optimistic declaration made her entire face glow.

Shaking his head, he searched his mind, but came up empty. "But I don't know how, sweetheart. If our Antico has the answer, it's not sharing."

"Not yet," she answered as she continued smiling.

CHAPTER 9
THE OUTBURST

After showering and dressing, Ben and Callie headed downstairs. Silvia was already up, working in the kitchen to prepare another meal for the group, and Ben lent her a hand while Callie headed for the lab to check on Grace and Donovan.

Though they were more rested than they'd been the day before, the rotating shifts during the night hadn't allowed them much deep sleep, which meant they faced the new day still somewhat sleep deprived. Simultaneously, Callie and Grace yawned as they stood together at Donovan's bedside.

Giggling at their mutual action, Callie put an arm around Grace's shoulders. "Tonight, we can get some real sleep, Gracie. Donovan should be strong enough by then to not need constant supervision, and I know we'll all be able to relax knowing he's on the mend."

"How long until he's... changed?"

"It seems to be different for each person. Sometimes it happens in a few days, other times weeks. But he'll be healthy nearly immediately."

Grace fidgeted with her sleeve as her smile wilted, and Callie squeezed her shoulder. "He's going to be alright. It's extremely rare for the transfer not to take and—"

Grace waved her hand in the air. "It's not that."

"Then, what is it?"

Turning back toward Donovan, Grace sighed. "He's going to need a bond soon, right? I mean to be fulfilled and healthy as Succouri."

"He will?" Callie's answer was spoken as a question as she still didn't understand what was causing Grace to be so anxious.

"How do I know that... that I'll be the one? What if his Succouri chooses someone else?"

"Oh, Gracie!" Callie exclaimed. "That's not how it works. I mean, yes, the Succouri initiates the bonding process, but it won't select someone randomly. Donovan already has a bond with you and you with him. As far as I know, in every case where there's been a pre-existing relationship, the change has served to deepen that connection by adding the benefits of the Succouri bond. Ethan and his wife, for example, were married and had already had Jessica when he became Succouri. The change won't alter his feelings about you. Not in the least. It will only enhance them and offer the two of you an even deeper connection."

Grace's shoulders relaxed and she smiled at Callie. "What's it really like, Cal?"

"Like nothing you could ever imagine, my sweet friend. Quite literally, Ben is part of me, in my heart and soul. I know him as well as I know myself and we share a... a place, a sacred, intangible space where our thoughts and feelings are known and experienced by the other." She lowered her gaze, feeling somewhat awkward about sharing something so personal, even with her dearest friend, but she knew

Grace needed to understand. "It may take you and Donovan a bit longer than Ben and me to develop that but you will."

"And we'll be..." Grace shifted, looking shy about her inquiry. "We'll be even more attracted to one another? Physically, I mean?"

Callie laughed dispelling some of the unease. "That definitely is part of it. You'll be drawn together in every way, heart, mind, and body. It's a package deal. Physical closeness is an essential part of the bond because that's how you use your Succouri gift, how he benefits from it. But there's more to it than that. It's difficult to explain." She patted Grace's hand. "You'll see. It's a wonderful adventure, Gracie, and the blessings of what you'll share with him will far outweigh any costs."

Nodding, Grace resumed her smile. "I watch you and Ben, and despite all the two of you have been through, I see something I've never seen before. I didn't know that kind of love existed, except in fairytales. My parents weren't in love, at least not by the time I was old enough to understand what that meant and to notice how they treated one another. When they divorced, I stopped believing in happily ever after, even though deep down, I craved that kind of love story. But then I saw how Ben looked at you the first day I met him when he came to your father's hospital room, before you were even dating. I'd never seen that look before. He barely knew you, but he already loved you. He would have laid down his life for you, that very day, Cal, before your first kiss. That's why I called him a knight in shining armor, because of what I observed in his eyes. Though I didn't understand how he did it, I wasn't a bit surprised when he saved your life the night you were shot, and when you told me you had to leave and you'd be safe with him, I had no doubts that was true. Of course he took a bullet for you, stepped in to save the day!" She shrugged. "I expected nothing less. When you told me about his... his superpower, I was shocked, but at least I finally had an explanation. Because Ben possessed an exceptional gift, he could offer you an exceptional love. It made sense, and though I was a little jealous, it set my world back in order. It was still true that that kind of love didn't exist for the average, ordinary person." She paused to take a deep breath. "And then, I met Donovan. It didn't happen all at once, but when I met him that day in your living room, he looked at me like... like he knew me, and I looked at him the same way. Talking to him was like talking to a lifelong friend; easy and natural. When he pulled away because of his health issues, the loneliness I felt at his absence surprised me." Laughing, she gently stroked Donovan's sleeping face. "I thought I was ridiculous. I mean, I'd only known him for a week. I scolded myself, remembering that I didn't really believe in love anyway. But..."

Enthralled by her friend's story, which she'd never heard in full, Callie reached out for Grace's arm, nearly begging her to finish. "But what?"

Grace's girlish giggle brightened the room. "When I picked him up at the airport—when we locked eyes as he walked toward me..."

"Grace!" Callie exclaimed as her friend left her in suspense again.

"I saw the same look in Donovan's eyes, the one I'd seen in Ben's. It turned my world upside down. He wasn't Succouri, had nothing unusual inside him drawing him to me, but he loved me with that... that forever kind of love. We had a lot to work out, still do really, but I believe in it now—the happily ever after thing—with or without the bond. The look in Ben's eyes that day, Cal; I don't think it had anything to do with him being Succouri. His heart loved you before his Succouri chose you."

Embracing her friend, Callie's profound happiness for her raised the pitch of her voice. "And it is the same with you. There's no need to worry about being chosen for the bonding. There's no doubt at all that it will be you. If Donovan already loves you and you love him, nothing will ever change that."

IT WAS easy to see that Silvia hadn't slept well, and when Doctor Navarro joined them in the kitchen, Ben noted with concern that the exhaustion in the doctor's posture and eyes hadn't improved much despite his night off.

"Maggie tells me that all was quiet overnight," the doctor said, pulling a coffee mug from the cabinet. I hope you and Callie were able to get some rest."

"Callie slept, but I had a lot on my mind." Ben picked up his own mug and followed the doctor to the small table in the corner, sitting across from him as Ben watched Silvia quietly slip out of the room.

Doctor Navarro chuckled. "I can well imagine. When this situation with Donovan is resolved, I hope you will consider sharing what you've learned about your unique situation, but if I may, can I ask you, after hearing about what Callie learned from this... Carozza concerning you specifically, are you convinced that the rest of it is true? Do you think what we've been doing with the blood transfers has destroyed the Succouri?"

"Doc," Ben said with a sigh, hearing the unwarranted guilt this kind man was carrying. "Since the moment I met you, you've worked tirelessly and passionately to help Callie and me. Despite a woeful lack of information, you didn't hesitate for a second to take us on as patients and as friends as you sought answers and tried to save our lives. Your motives, intentions, and dedication to the Succouri aren't in question."

"I appreciate that, Ben, but" —he leaned forward, locking Ben in his gaze—"you didn't answer my question. Do you accept Carozza's theories?"

Hesitantly, as his heart ached for the regret he knew his answer would cause, Ben nodded his head. "Not just because of what Carozza knew about me, but also because of what my Antico itself told me yesterday."

Rubbing his palms together as he leaned on his elbows, the doctor blew out a long breath through his lips. "So, you *do* possess perhaps the last of the spirited Succouri, one that still seeks its intended match." Though the doctor's words weren't spoken as a question, Ben nodded once, then shook his head.

A few seconds of confusion wrinkled the doctor's brow, but it didn't take his keen intellect long to understand. "You *are* the intended match!" he exclaimed, dropping his hands and sitting back in his chair as his eyes grew wide.

Smiling, Ben watched the doctor's expression as he wordlessly processed the revelation, each mental checkmark yielding new questions he wanted to ask, yet fearing the answers.

"Astounding! What does this mean for you and Callie?"

Stroking his chin, Ben continued to grin. "As a result of my physical transformation and our Antico reaching the end of its journey, we won't need to worry about the lifespan issue. And I suppose that from now on, drawing blood from me will, unfortunately, involve enduring your very inventive torture device, but other than that, your guess is as good as ours. In some ways, we're not that far off from where we were two days ago. We'll still have to learn by living it out and seeing what happens."

Massaging his temples, Doctor Navarro's expression fell. "Perhaps it's true that not much will change in regard to our approach to your care, but what we've learned in the last twenty-four hours certainly alters our perspective and likely our practices relating to the rest of the modern Succouri. How can I possibly continue to assist with the transfer of the gift? I vowed to do no harm. I believed my work was noble, helping to save lives; not just the lives of those who received the gift, but also those who would subsequently benefit from the new Succouri. By passing it on, I thought I was preserving it, preventing it from becoming extinct."

He paused to lean on his elbows and lower his head into his hands. Helplessly, Ben pained at his distress. "I can't abide the thought that, in reality, my actions are responsible for all but killing it."

Rising, Ben went to sit beside the doctor, desperate to relieve his sorrow and displaced blame. "That's not fair. You had no way of knowing. Don't take the burden of this on yourself. I possess an Antico, a Succouri full of wisdom and spirit, yet I sense no hint of animosity toward anyone who has acted in good faith, risking everything to help in the only way they knew how. If there's any blame to be had, it would be on those who knew about the touch transfers and chose to usurp them, perhaps for their own gain. As those responsible are all long dead and buried and we will probably never know their rationale, all we can do is move forward, Doc, and do the right things from here on out to the best of our ability."

"But what are those right things?" he asked, looking somewhat comforted by Ben's assurances but still overwrought. "How do I take blood from Mr. Devereaux and transfer the gift to your friend, knowing that I might be worsening the problem, sealing the Antico's fate?"

"Doc, it's not like that," Ben refuted. "This happened long ago. Ethan's Succouri is already silenced."

"Are you sure?" Are you absolutely sure there's no trace of will or spirit left?"

Intentionally softening his tone, Ben lowered his gaze. "I can't be one hundred percent sure, but if it still had a will of its own, it probably wouldn't have stayed in Ethan for this long and—"

"But he's lived in a cabin in the woods, Ben. There's been no opportunity for him to pass it."

"But he would have entered the ripening stage and..." Ben sighed. "I can't give you all the answers. I don't understand everything myself yet. We need time to sort this out, to gather more information."

The doctor rose and crossed to a nearby window, folding his arms as he stared blankly out of it. Ben also stood, but he didn't approach.

"I don't have the luxury of time. I must make a choice today, this morning. If I go ahead with the blood transfusion, it's possible I'll be dealing the final blow to an extraordinary being, wiping out its irredeemable potential to benefit others and perhaps all of mankind. But if I don't perform the transfer, Donovan will die, and his death will be on my conscience." He put a hand to his head. "I can't live with that either."

Ben understood the doctor's miserable predicament, and how, no matter what he did, he'd be left with some measure of guilt.

"It's a terrible situation, but consider this: we don't know for certain about the Succouri, but it is likely already dispirited. We absolutely do know about Donovan. We know he will die if we don't do this."

The doctor dropped his hand to his side, but raised his eyes, looking up into the sky. "I need more than that. Sacrificing one life for another isn't acceptable to me."

Hesitating, Ben thought carefully before he spoke again, listening for the voice inside that had the answers they both needed. "Callie believes," he began, speaking softly, "and I'm inclined to agree, that part of my destiny, the reason I was chosen, changed, and tested is to right this wrong. My differences from other Succouri prove Carozza's theories. Without that evidence, no one would listen to the man. If I'm a testament to the truth, intentionally designed and placed in this very moment, then that must mean something, mean there's a solution, an answer, a way to revive the Antico." Stepping forward, Ben shook his head. "Right now, I don't know what that solution is, and no matter how much I try, I can't presently coax my inner partner into showing me its hand, but if the possibility exists, then even if the transfer today silences Ethan's Succouri, that may not be permanent. But if Donovan dies, that most definitely is."

"Your wife has been consistently correct in her predictions, so I take her words very much to heart, but how can an Antico's spirit be reborn if it has lost its opportunity to unite with its destined match and thus accomplish its purpose? If that goal is what fuels it, keeps it motivated and involved in the transfer process, I don't see how that can be redeemed."

"Maybe there's a way to reset its course, inspire it to select a new final host and an equally impactful mission. I honestly don't know yet, but if it's possible, do you at least agree that this alters the parameters of our current dilemma?"

The doctor continued to stare out the window as he considered Ben's question. At last, he turned his eyes to Ben. "Yes, if we were reasonably sure that was possible, then the nature of the choice changes significantly."

"Then, I suppose it comes down to whether you trust Callie and me and our instincts about our mission. If saving Donovan was the wrong thing to do, I'm confident my Antico would alert me. I understand and appreciate the struggle with your conscience, but sometimes we just don't have all the information, and we must act on faith."

"And there's no way you could persuade that inner voice to hurry it up a bit with a direct answer?" he asked, offering Ben a weak smile.

Ben chuckled. "I'll do my best, but as we now know, this one has a will of its own. I am learning to trust its timing. It will give us the answers precisely when we need them."

With a resigned sigh, Doctor Navarro approached Ben and set a hand on his shoulder. "You've changed, my friend. There's a new confidence and peace in you that's quite gratifying to see as it suits you well."

"Yesterday, I was given the chance to choose or reject this life and the calling that comes with it. My decision to remain Succouri has, at last, resolved an inner conflict that's weighed me down for fifteen years. The offering of an autonomous choice has laid a new foundation of trust, making it possible for me to engage as a cooperative rather than combative partner with the voice in my head. I finally understand and have embraced who I am, and that opens the door to some intriguing possibilities."

At his words, the doctor's smile became full, erasing some

of the lines of exhaustion on his face. "What a privilege it has been to witness your and Callie's journey thus far! Though I don't know if I'll have much to offer you as a physician going forward, I hope you'll allow Silvia and me to remain your friends, supporting the two of you however we can."

Doctor Navarro offered Ben his hand, and Ben gripped it firmly. "We wouldn't have it any other way, Doc."

As everyone had enjoyed a more restful night's sleep, breakfast was significantly livelier than the meal the night before.

Before Taylor, Lee, and Ethan arrived at the house, the doctor had performed a thorough check of Donovan's vitals and had withdrawn the sedatives, wanting him awake and alert for the blood transfusion. During that examination, Ben had pulled Callie aside and relayed the gist of his conversation with the doctor.

"I can understand the moral dilemma," Callie had empathized. "He's a good man and has devoted his life to healing, not harming."

"I'm relieved he's decided to proceed with the transfer, but I wish I could do more to ease his mind and conscience."

"No answers from our resident expert?" she asked with a hopeful smile.

Frowning, he shook his head. "Not yet. But I'm listening."

As the group sat eating together, Lee paused his chewing to point his fork at Ben. "Your place in Cape Cod is awesome, Ben. Fantastic views of the water."

He reached for the bowl of eggs, scooping another large

heap onto his plate. Callie was glad to see that his appetite hadn't suffered, despite the stress of the last few days.

"I haven't been there in years," Ben admitted, looking pleased by Lee's assessment. "But I remember it being very comfortable."

"That's an understatement," Lee teased. "Just how many fancy houses do you own, brother?"

"Lee!" Callie scolded, but Ben took her hand and smiled, accustomed to her brother's frankness by now.

"Callie and I own a few," he answered. "And you're welcome to stay at any of them anytime you'd like, Lee, as they're family properties now."

Taking a bite, he drummed his fingers on the table as he chewed. "Sweet! I'm already picturing some memorable LeVray-Sawyer vacations in the near future. Maybe when Allie's better, she could join us."

"What did you say?"

All eyes turned to Ethan Devereaux who was staring at Lee with a look of shock.

Lee squinted in confusion. "Um... I said I'm planning some vacations..."

"The names. What names did you say?" he interrogated; his jaw tight.

"I... I..." Lee stammered, caught completely off guard by Ethan's question and his intense expression.

Callie cleared her throat. "LeVray is my maiden name," she explained in a soft voice.

Ethan turned angry eyes to her, and his face contorted in a look she couldn't define, but it almost looked like hate. Ben gripped her hand more tightly and shifted closer, as he focused on Ethan. No one moved or breathed as confusion hovered.

"Is your mother Molly LeVray?" He confronted her as his face turned red with fury.

Bewildered, Callie nodded. "Yes. But she died many years ago."

"Ethan," Ben interjected gently but firmly as he put his arm protectively around her. "What's this all about?"

Abruptly rising, Ethan began advancing toward Callie, but Ben swiftly moved to block his path. Taylor also stood, coming up just behind Ben. "Hold on, Ethan." Ben put up his hands. "What's going on?"

"She killed her!" he shouted. "Molly LeVray killed my wife!"

Gasping, Callie put her hands over her mouth as her heart dropped and tears filled her eyes. Ben sharply inhaled sensing her pain, but he held his ground, never looking away from the enraged man's eyes. Taylor took a step back, keeping his eyes on Ethan, but placing a comforting hand on Callie's shoulder.

Everyone around the table sat frozen in place, confused about what was happening.

"I see." Ben exhaled sorrowfully as he continued to speak softly, trying to bring calm to the situation. "I understand your anger, but Ethan, that wasn't Callie or Lee. They were children and—"

"It doesn't matter," he fumed. "Their mother drove drunk and rammed her car right into my beautiful wife, crushing her body so forcefully that I couldn't recognize her face. Molly LeVray took everything from me, my heart, my life, my daughter, my granddaughter, everything! For fifteen years, all I've wanted is to go and be with her, but because I'm cursed, I can't manage to die."

Holding his hands out, Ben stepped forward. "Please, Ethan, let's step outside and—"

Balling his hands into tight fists, Ethan backed away from the table. "I can't help you, Ben Sawyer, or your friend. I can't give anything to those who took everything from me."

With that, he turned and rushed from the room, leaving everyone stunned and shaken.

Instantly, Ben folded Callie into his arms, stroking her hair as her tears began to flow. How could this be happening? Just when the light was breaking through, the darkness threatened to overtake it once more.

Callie knew her mother's addiction had killed a wife and mother. The sorrow of that truth had tormented her for years. But now, to find out that the woman was a Datouri, like herself, an essential part of a rare union that couldn't survive without her, was unbearable. What if it had been Ben who lost her like that? She knew he'd never recover, just as Ethan hadn't.

And now, not only had her mother's tragic choice cost Ethan his wife, Jessica her mother and father, and Allie her grandfather, but it would also cost Donovan his life and Grace her chance at happily ever after. She couldn't bear the heavy load of guilt.

"Sweetheart, please," Ben begged, his own tears audible in his hoarse voice. "This isn't your fault, just as my mother's choices weren't mine."

Rationally, she knew his words were true, but fault didn't matter much right now when the consequences were falling like a ton of bricks right on top of them. For a long while, she continued to weep, and Ben patiently held her, doing what he could to sooth her aching heart. Stronger than it had been before Ben's strange illness had temporarily severed the connection, their bond transmitted Callie's sorrow directly into Ben's heart and he struggled to control his emotions as he shared her pain but couldn't find the words to ease it.

When at last she'd cried herself dry, Ben released her and put his hands on the sides of her face. He kissed her forehead and wiped the streaks of tears from her cheeks. Taylor offered her a tissue as he watched them with concern. Without her noticing, Lee had moved, and now sat beside Ben, looking distraught, but not as mournful as Callie. Everyone else had left the room, giving them privacy.

"Dear one," Taylor comforted, looking into her red eyes. "Ben's absolutely right. This isn't your fault. You must not put any blame on your shoulders, you or Lee. I'm a parent who made more mistakes than I can count. Ben should never own a single one. If he tried, I wouldn't allow it and I know you wouldn't either."

Sniffling, she nodded. "But regardless of who's to blame, how do I live with the shame of what she's done and all the lives that have been destroyed as a result? And what are we going to do about Donovan?" A lingering tear slid down her cheek. "Ben, we can't let him—"

"It will be alright," Ben consoled, catching the tear before it dripped from her chin. "He has no choice but to pass the gift on, and he doesn't have any other prospects. If he walks away from this, he'll only be prolonging his suffering. He can't leave anyway as he doesn't have a vehicle here. Let's give him a chance to cool off, catch his breath, allow rationality to return, and then I'll go and speak with him."

"I'm coming with you," she declared.

"So am I," Lee added.

"I don't think that's a good idea," he said, shaking his head as he looked between them. "I don't want him attacking either of you again. You don't deserve that."

Callie put her hand on his. "I appreciate your desire to

protect my heart, but remember what I told you before our wedding when we sat looking at the photo of my parents?"

Sighing, he nodded, recalling how she'd told him that, if she ever got the chance, she wanted to offer an apology on behalf of her mother.

"I have to say the words, Ben. She's not here to do it, so I have to. Ethan deserves an apology, even though I know it won't bring back his wife or mend his broken heart. If he shouts at me again, I'll walk away and let you talk with him alone, but I feel I must do this, even more so now that I know the people who were hurt and the extent of the devastation caused by my mother's recklessness."

"I'm not sure I feel obligated to do all that," Lee said with a frown. "I mean, this was fifteen years ago, and I was like... three. But I'm damn well gonna be there in case he threatens my family again. That guy's crazy."

"Lee." Callie stretched to pat his hand. "You don't need to do or say anything. Ben won't let anything happen to me; you know that. I think it would be best if just the two of us go."

Ben put up a hand. "Let's wait it out for a bit, give everyone's heart and mind a chance to settle, and give Ethan time to cool off. We don't have to decide anything right now."

Callie lowered her head. "But Donovan may not have much time left, Ben. If we can't change Ethan's mind soon, even your miraculous touch won't be enough to save him."

CHAPTER 10

THE OFFERING

When they left the dining room, Ben and Callie met up with Doctor Navarro as he was exiting the lab. Sympathetically, he offered them a slight grimace as he approached.

"Is Donovan alright?" Ben inquired, privately pondering what, if anything, he should tell his friend about Ethan's change of heart.

"He's awake and in pain. If we're not going to do this soon, I need to put him back under. Grace is trying to get him to eat, and I'd like him to try to sit up for a bit."

"Has he been told?"

"No," the doctor answered. "Until we have a solid answer either way, it's best to avoid putting him through any unnecessary emotional turmoil. He needs his strength and energy focused on staying with us right now."

Nodding, Ben momentarily lowered his eyes. "Understood. How much time before you need to sedate him again?"

"An hour. Maybe less. There's no justification for allowing him to suffer any longer than that."

Glancing at Callie and then back to the doctor, Ben sighed in frustration. "I guess I'd better go find Ethan then. I wish we could give him more time to come around, but we don't have that luxury."

Sad resignation shadowed the doctor's eyes. "If this doesn't work out, don't blame yourselves. Frankly, Ben, I was amazed that you made as much progress as you did with him. Ethan's lost much more than just his wife and family. The ability to reason, interact in a healthy way with others, and find healing by grabbing onto a new purpose or even a new love relationship seems to be impossible for him. This option was a long shot from the beginning, and you nearly accomplished it."

Pondering, Ben crossed his arms and closed his eyes. "He's not much different from our dispirited Succouri. When they lose their path, their purpose, they give up and shut down." He opened his eyes and straightened his posture. "But I refuse to accept that fate for either of them, Doc. I won't believe that anyone, human or Succouri, is irredeemable. Hopelessness is a condition worse than death. I've been there, existed there for years, but love brought me back to life again." He smiled at Callie. "If we can connect Ethan to his family, he'll have a new purpose. They need him and he needs them. This... tragedy from the past has set us back, but I'm not giving up."

Smiling, the doctor patted Ben's arm. "If anyone can do it, I still unquestionably believe it is you."

"Keep him alive, Doc. We'll be back."

With another pat and a nod, the doctor retreated to the lab.

Ben turned and took Callie's hand, honored by the pride in him shining in her eyes. "I still think it would be best if I went alone, but if you feel you need to speak your piece, I won't argue with you."

"Let's ask your father to accompany us. His presence shouldn't provoke strong reactions from Ethan. When I'm finished saying what I need to say, he can walk me back to the house while you stay with Ethan."

"Alright." Though he still wished Callie didn't feel the need to apologize for something that wasn't her responsibility, he knew her heart wouldn't rest until she did her best to reconcile the situation.

When the three of them stepped outside, there was no sign of Ethan anywhere.

"Are you sure he didn't figure a way out of here?" Taylor queried. "He certainly seemed determined to leave."

"He's around," Ben assured him. "I think I might know where he is."

Following the same route his own desperate heart had taken him, they eventually reached the gurgling stream. As they cautiously approached, the hunched form of a man, sitting on a familiar log with his head in his hands came into view, and Taylor fell back as Callie and Ben approached.

The sound of the rushing water muted their footsteps, helping Ben understand how Lee had managed to sneak up behind him without his awareness. When they were still ten feet away, Ben squeezed Callie's hand and turned to face her. He could feel her heart pounding. Though she was determined to follow through with what she felt she had to do, Ethan Devereaux frightened her, and that triggered his protective instincts. If he was going to be of any help to the man, he needed to stay calm, speak gently, and remain clear-headed, but until Callie was at peace and on her way back to the house, Ben would have to fight to control his conflicting emotions.

"Are you sure?" he whispered near her ear. "This really isn't necessary, sweetheart. I hate that you're putting yourself through this."

She took a slow, deep breath and tried to smile, but it looked forced and unnatural. "I'm sure, but thank you for being beside me."

"Always." He bent down to softly kiss her lips before turning toward the stream. "Ethan," he announced, loud enough to be heard.

Ethan twisted around, then stood, raising both hands. "Don't bother, Ben. I have nothing else to say."

Releasing Callie's hand, Ben stepped forward. Listening carefully to his Succouri's guidance, he inhaled and let his compassionate stare capture Ethan's attention and focus. "That's fine. I understand. But would you consider listening for just one minute? Callie has something she needs to say; has wanted to say for fifteen years. If, after hearing her out, you still have nothing to say to us, I promise we'll leave you be. I'll make sure you get a ride back to your cabin, and no one will bother you again. Do we have a deal?"

Ben watched Ethan's shoulders rise and fall as he breathed heavily, confusion, fear, and pain emanating from his whole being. Before he answered, he shifted his gaze to Callie, softening slightly as he took in the tears on her cheeks.

At last, Ethan nodded his consent, and Ben stepped back to take Callie's hand. He guided her forward, maintaining a safe distance from Ethan, yet ensuring she was close enough that she wouldn't need to shout to be heard. Then, he took up a position just behind her, letting her have the floor while still making his supportive and protective presence known. He kept contact with her, gently touching her arm so she could see into Ethan's eyes.

His anger somewhat tempered now, Ethan avoided eye contact with her, even as she did her best to hold his gaze.

"My mother was a terrible alcoholic," she began, and Ben was astonished at how steady, yet gentle her voice was, despite the intense pounding of her heart. "My dad tried his best to help her, but she wouldn't help herself. She neglected Lee and me, resulting in my brother getting hit by a car when he was just a toddler. After that, my dad separated from her, hoping the distance would sober her up, but it never did. My father was a good man, the best kind of man, and he protected us, even from our own mother." Momentarily, she lowered her head, and Ben stroked her arm with his thumb, trying to offer her some comfort amid the painful memories.

"When the accident happened, it had been over a year since I'd seen her. In the fog of her addiction and destructive behavior, she'd forgotten her own children. If it hadn't been for my father and his love and dedication, Lee and I would have suffered the loss much more than we did. Lee was so young and the memories I carried of her were few and not warm or pleasant, so we never really grieved for her, not like my father did. The fact that her own folly killed her—"

"Your mother also died in the accident?" Ethan interrupted, surprised by the revelation.

"She did," Callie confirmed with a sigh. "She was in the hospital for two days but ultimately succumbed to her injuries."

"I... I didn't know that," he admitted. "When I saw the

news story about the accident, it said she was injured. I assumed she survived."

Continuing to watch Ethan's eyes, Ben was surprised to observe that the anger had vanished completely now. Though tragic, finding out that the accident had also cost Callie's family loss seemed to dispel his outrage.

Callie took a step forward as did Ben. "Mr. Devereaux, my mother's death was a direct result of her bad choices, the consequence of her behavior. But your wife was innocent and didn't deserve to pay for my mother's sins, and neither did you nor your daughter. Though I was young and my father hid most of the details about the accident from us, from the moment I found out that a wife and mother was killed, I've wanted to say these words, though I know they won't bring her back or mend anyone's broken heart. I'm so desperately sorry," she cried, folding her hands over her heart. "The sin was hers, but the shame remains on my family and in my heart. What she did was unfair and unforgivable. She took from you an irreplaceable treasure, a one-of-a-kind soul that was meant to stay by your side until your last breath." As she cried softly, her body trembled, and Ben wrapped his arms around her shoulders.

"Callie, please," Ben begged. "That's enough, more than enough. Please, I can't bear to watch you hurt like this. Let it go now. You've done all you can do."

When she nodded, submitting to his plea, he let out a relieved sigh and held her tightly against him for a long moment, before turning her around and walking back toward his father. But after taking a step, Ben felt a hand grip his arm, and he looked up into the tear-filled eyes of Ethan Devereaux.

"Please, Ben, may I speak with her, just for a moment?" His voice was gentle, with not a trace of the rage he'd previously expressed. But more than that, as Ben scrutinized the man before him, he almost didn't recognize him. His eyes were warm, gleaming with a soft kindness that calmed Ben's soul. He looked younger, stronger, as if the Ethan Devereaux of fifteen years ago had stepped into a time portal and exited right in front of Ben.

Callie had demolished this man's walls and ground to pieces the hard exterior shell that protected the tender-hearted man inside. All Ben's efforts had barely scratched the surface of that armor, but in just minutes, she'd utterly destroyed it. Of course she had! She'd done the same thing to him. There was something magical, unexplainably powerful about his wife's gracious heart, and he once again marveled at how blessed he was to have her love and part-nership.

When Ben turned questioning eyes to Callie, she nodded, no hint of fear or hesitation in her expression. Cautiously, he scanned his senses, searching for any hint of dread or danger, but he felt nothing except an unmistak-able, reassuring nudge from his hidden companion.

"Alright," he agreed, stepping back. "If you don't have enough healing power in your touch, she'll need to take your arm."

Ethan offered Callie his hand, and when she took it, she smiled, providing an answer.

"I'll be close by," Ben promised before turning to join his father.

CALLIE WALKED with Ethan to the fallen log, and he steadied her as she stepped over it and sat. The sound of the water was peaceful, quieting her heart after the storm of powerful emotions she'd experienced in the last hour. Ethan sat beside her and released her hand. Rubbing his hands on his knees nervously, he lowered his head, contemplating how to begin.

"My anger was terribly misplaced, Mrs. Sawyer. I'm sincerely sorry," he said just above a whisper.

"Please, I'm just Callie, Ethan. I do understand."

"Does your father still grieve for her?" Ethan asked hesitantly.

Closing her eyes, she shook her head. "My father's in heaven now. He died from a stroke a couple of months ago. Ben and I actually met through circumstances related to that tragedy." She turned her face toward him. "But I think a part of his heart always grieved for her. He loved her, despite her shortcomings, and her inability to be a wife and mother broke his heart long before her death did."

"Did he... Did he ever find love again?"

"He was dedicated to Lee and me, and between that and his busy job, I don't know that he had much time for romance, but even if he had, I don't think his heart was ever ready to take the chance again." She put a hand on his arm. "But, Ethan, he had us. He filled the empty place inside him with our love, and you can do the same thing. Your granddaughter"—she paused to beam—"is beautiful, charming, and open-hearted. She'll want to hear all about your life as Succouri, and she'll want to know about her grandmother."

Wiping his eyes, he took a shaky breath. "Lexi was thrilled about being a grandmother. She loved children, but of course, we weren't able to have more after the change. Just before... before the accident she was gushing with excitement about the new baby, telling me how she already loved the little one, even though she hadn't met her yet." He smiled. "She was making plans for decorating the nursery, as if the baby were hers, not Jessica's and Gordon's. The last thing she said to me was how happy she was, and how she didn't regret our lives as Succouri, even though we couldn't have any more children. As always, she'd been reading my mind, sensing my regret at not being able to offer her that. Despite her words of encouragement, I knew this grandchild would fill a void in her heart. If"—he pressed his fingertips to his forehead, covering his eyes with his hands—"If Lexi knew I ran away, that I never met her, I… I think she'd be heartbroken. In a way, I separated Lexi from the granddaughter she desperately wanted and loved. If I'd been in Allie's life, told her stories, showed her pictures, it would have been a way of keeping her memory alive and fulfilling her dream."

Wiping her own eyes now, Callie felt the ache of the loss for Ethan and his wife deep in her heart. At last, she understood. The anger he'd expressed wasn't just about her mother's sin. Ethan carried an unbearable load of guilt about his own behavior as well. His irreconcilable grief forced him to run and isolate himself from his family, which was exactly what he knew Lexi wouldn't have wanted for him or for Jessica and Allie. Trapped in an unending loop of grief and regret, Ethan's frustration and hopelessness had caused him to lash out.

Overcome with compassion and sorrow for the helplessness he felt, Callie looked at Ethan Devereaux with new eyes. "Ethan, what are the odds that our path would cross with yours, your daughter's, and your granddaughter's all in the span of a couple of days? What are the odds that Ben would save your granddaughter's life just twenty-four hours before meeting you? What are the odds that the one person capable of saving Donovan just so happens to be the husband and father whose heart was broken by my mother's tragic choice fifteen years ago?" Repeatedly, she shook her head before finishing. "This entire thing is not a coincidence. I believe we were meant to help heal each other's broken hearts, bring closure to the past, and walk together into a much brighter tomorrow. Ben and I genuinely want to help you, and not just because we're trying to save Donovan's life. I spoke privately to Jessica on the plane. Her heart needs mending. She needs to understand why you left and stayed away. She needs to know that it's because of grief, not because you rejected her or Allie. And you need them just as much as they need you. It's not too late to tell Allie about her grandmother."

Ethan didn't speak for a long moment as he considered her words. When at last he did, his voice cracked. "Callie, you're Ben's partner. You share the bond with him, understand how deep it runs, and, from what Ben told me, you both know how devastating the emptiness of losing it is."

He paused and Callie nodded, encouraging him to go on. "Do you... Do you think Lexi could ever forgive me for what I've done, for abandoning our daughter and granddaughter?" The abiding torment this unanswered question brought him was evident in his voice.

As she answered, she spoke as gently as she could. "If Ben lost me tragically, I would certainly understand his grief and pain. I wouldn't fault him for running, hiding away for a time or wanting to shed his Succouri burden since it can't function properly without a partner." She sighed, hoping he'd hear her heart as she continued. "But, Ethan, if we had a daughter, or grandchildren, I'd want him to take care of them. I would hope his love for me, even in my absence, would drive him on, motivate him to cling to the family we created together, and keep them safe and well. I would forgive, but I'd mourn the brokenness and want it healed."

Ethan stared straight ahead, unblinking as her words registered in his heart.

A blinding beam of bright sunlight suddenly broke through the thick trees on the opposite side of the stream, bathing them in warmth and spotlighting them, as if they were leading actors on a stage. Callie smiled, as the timing of its appearance supported her assertion that none of this was coincidental.

Squinting into the light, Ethan shook his head in wonder. "I think I have my answer. Thank you, Mrs… Callie." He paused for a pensive inhale. "Please don't carry the shame of what your mother did in your heart any longer. Though your words brought me healing, you didn't need to apologize, as the fault wasn't yours. Lexi wouldn't want you to carry that burden. She'd have forgiven your mother long ago, and she'd want you and me to do the same."

"Alright," Callie said, his words bringing the healing full circle, back to her own heart. "On one condition. Please let us help you, walk beside you, be your friends, and support you and your family as you work to heal."

Patting her hand, he nodded and smiled. "Ben Sawyer is very fortunate. It's easy to understand how you've inspired him to be a better man. I'm sure he's told you this, but just in case; don't ever forget how much your love means to him. You're his heart, the reason he has the will and strength to give each day." Once again, he looked off into the distance, wishing he could speak the words to his wife one last time. "In his eyes, you're beautiful, perfect in every way. There's nothing he would change about you; you're exactly what he needs. He'd win you every prize on earth if it would make you smile, and he'd valiantly take on a thousand giants to keep you safe. There's no luxury he'd deny you or piece of himself he would hesitate to offer you. After all, he cares nothing about his life if you're not beside him. It's a selfless love, Callie, one that finds happiness in your joy and heartache in your pain."

"And I love him in exactly the same way," she whispered. "And, Ethan, I know for certain, Lexi did too."

With an appreciative smile, Ethan stood and turned toward the road. For a breath, Callie remained seated, letting the warmth of the sunlight dispel the last of the chill that lingered in her heart.

When she at last stood and turned, Ben was there, smiling and offering his hand. She stepped back over the log and came up alongside him.

"Thank you for allowing me a moment to talk with your lovely wife," Ethan said. "Truly, she is an inspiration, and she was able to answer a question I've carried for a long time; one that only a Datouri could answer. As I did with her, I want to offer you an apology for my inappropriate outburst. It was out of line. I've never thanked you for saving my granddaughter's life, Ben. I know you used your gift at great risk to you and to Callie. Because of you, I have a second chance to do the right thing. I want to return the favor. Your friend is obviously a good man. I'm sure he'll honor and enhance the gift with his generous spirit."

"Alright, then." Ben smiled, glancing at Callie with awe. "We'd better head back. The doctor didn't want to keep him awake for more than an hour. Thank you, my friend."

Nodding, Ethan looked between the two of them. "I'm going to hold both of you to your promises to help me reunite with my family. It's what Lexi would want, and it's what I want, too."

"You got it," Ben assured him enthusiastically.

When Ethan moved out of earshot, Ben put his arm

around Callie's shoulders and whispered into her ear. "Your superpower puts mine to shame, Callie Sawyer."

Puzzled, she smiled crookedly as she looked up at him.

"The grace and kindness in your heart is like dynamite, shattering everyone's walls into pieces. My touch may bring healing to the body, but you bring healing to the soul. It happened to me, then Jessica, and now Ethan. I don't think he ever needed what I had to offer, more what you did."

Tenderly, she reached to brush a strand of dark hair away from his eyes. "He needed both of us." She smiled and put one finger to the side of her mouth. "Well, actually, all three of us, partnering together. That *is* how this works, after all."

Chuckling, he retook her hand, and they began to walk back toward the house. "Gracious, wise, and breathtakingly beautiful," he charmed with a wink. "I'm indeed the luckiest man alive."

CHAPTER 11

THE STIRRING

When they stepped back inside the Navarro home, relieved faces greeted them. Everyone's eyes registered surprise, then delight at the marked softening in Ethan's expression. Discreetly, Lee, Maggie, and Silvia sent Ben questioning looks, and he nodded in response, confirming Ethan's decision to proceed with the transfer.

Before they entered the lab, Ethan approached Lee and offered him a sincere apology for the way he'd treated him and Callie.

After seeing the satisfied smile on his sister's face, Lee readily extended his hand. "Don't sweat it. Though this was all before my time so I don't feel much connection to it, not like Callie does anyway, I do remember the pain it caused my dad, and I can only imagine it was much worse for you and your family. What a crazy coincidence though! I mean, what are the odds?" He smirked and Callie put her hand on his arm.

"Not a coincidence, Lee. A tremendous opportunity."

He considered her statement carefully before finally

flashing a full grin. "I like that." He tossed Callie's curls playfully. "As usual, my sister's right. That's the best way to look at it."

Ben smiled at the exchange, never having doubted that his big-hearted brother-in-law would easily forgive and forget.

When they all entered the lab, Grace and Doctor Navarro turned hopeful eyes to them. Callie let go of Ben's hand and rushed to her friend, who looked as if she'd been crying. Donovan's eyes were closed, and Ben worried that perhaps the doctor had already sedated him.

Warily, Ethan stepped forward. "I'm sorry about earlier," he said, shifting his gaze between Grace and Doctor Navarro. "I'm ready to proceed if..." He looked at Donovan.

The doctor's expression relaxed. "I think it's important that the two of you talk before we move forward with this. Ben, you might want to..."

"Understood, Doc," Ben interjected, already heading for Donovan's bed, but before he reached it, Ethan intercepted him. "Ben, let me. I think I still have enough to at least keep him out of pain briefly while we talk. But it would probably be wise for you to stay close by, just in case."

Ben was about to protest, to argue that there was no reason for him to weaken himself right before donating blood and especially without the aid of a partner, but the look in Ethan's eyes changed his mind. This was something he needed to do; his last chance, and perhaps the only opportunity he'd had in many years, to use his gift.

Gesturing for Ethan to proceed ahead of him, Ben fell back, staying close enough to watch both men carefully. Everyone else moved away, granting them a private moment.

When Ethan stepped up beside Donovan, he opened his

eyes, confusion slightly altering his look of resignation. It appeared that, regrettably, either Grace or the doctor had informed him about what had transpired with Ethan earlier. Thanks to his advanced investigation skills, it was difficult to hide anything from his friend, so perhaps they'd had no choice but to tell him the truth. He had the look of a man who'd given up, was at peace with his fate.

Ethan set his hand on Donovan's wrist, and Ben watched as the strong draw hit him hard. Slumping his shoulders, he used the edge of the bed to brace himself with his free hand.

"Ethan?" Ben questioned, taking a step forward.

"I'll be alright for a few minutes," he insisted, though he sounded out of breath.

Ben nodded but stayed where he was.

A little color returned to Donovan's face, but he remained silent, and Ben could still see pain in his eyes.

"Donovan, I'm ready to help you now. I'm sorry I caused confusion."

Glancing at Ben, Donovan squinted, perplexed by the change of heart. Ben smiled and nodded reassuringly.

"I don't understand," Donovan said. "I thought you changed your mind."

"It's a long story. I learned something that upset me, but it wasn't related to you or the transfer of my gift. Unjustifiably, I became angry and said something I shouldn't have. But I do want to give you my gift. I need to..." The strain of the draw cut off his explanation. Fighting hard against his instincts, Ben restrained himself from stepping in. Ethan deserved to do this his way.

Donovan took a deep breath, and Ben saw Ethan cringe, though he tried to hide it. "Ethan, I'm at peace with dying. If you have any doubts, any questions about passing the gift to me, it's alright. No hard feelings or resentment." He looked at Ben, holding his gaze for a breath before returning his eyes to Ethan. "When I signed up to serve my country, I knew this was a possibility. I don't regret anything, except for the broken heart I'll leave behind." He directed his mournful gaze toward Grace, who stood on the other side of the room with Callie's arm around her shoulders.

Ethan vigorously shook his head. "I haven't changed my mind. I need to move on from this, shed my Succouri identity. It's the only potential path to healing for me."

Ethan's hand trembled. Despite his desire to do this on his own, he simply didn't have enough strength to keep this up much longer.

"I promise you, Donovan. This is what I want. No doubts, no hesitations."

As the trembling spread to his arm, Donovan studied him. "If that's your final decision, then I have one more question before we proceed."

Though Ethan could barely lift his head, he did his best to nod, encouraging Donovan to continue.

"When it's over, and the gift is gone, do I have your word that you won't do anything... rash? I know you miss your wife terribly, but I won't be involved in enabling you to... to harm yourself once that becomes possible."

Again, he tried for a nod, but his body was shaking, making it hard to complete the motion.

Ben stepped forward. "Ethan, you need to let go. You won't be strong enough for the transfer. Please."

Sighing, Ethan released Donovan and briefly grasped Ben's arm to steady himself as he tried to straighten his posture. Upon contact, Ben felt a draw from him, but once again, stronger this time, he also experienced the strange sensation of shifting he'd felt before, like everything inside him was rearranging. When Ethan looked up at him in surprise, Ben knew he felt something, too.

"Are you... Do you feel that?" Ben stammered, just as Callie came up beside him.

Momentarily, Ethan pressed down harder on Ben's arm, looking bewildered. "I... I can feel strength from you," he stuttered. "How is that possible?"

Callie smiled. "Ben has a unique gift that permits him to help anyone in need. This has happened before."

"She's right," Ben acknowledged. "But there's something else there too. Do you also feel... I don't know exactly how to describe it: a stirring?"

"Maybe... I don't know. I've never been on the receiving end of the gift, so I don't know what's normal and what's not." Ethan withdrew his hand, and, though he continued to be puzzled by the experience, Ben returned his focus to Donovan, taking over where Ethan left off as Callie assisted him.

After several slow inhales, Ethan's breathing settled enough for him to answer Donovan's question. "Thanks to everyone's patience and kindness, I have decided to return to my daughter and granddaughter and do my best to repair the damage I caused by the years of separation. Without the consuming emptiness of the absent bond, I'm hopeful that I'll finally begin to heal. I give you my word that my intention is to honor my wife by taking care of our family and passing along her legacy of love." He locked eyes with Callie. "That's what she would want me to do."

Donovan searched Ethan's eyes for confirmation that his words were sincere. Despite his weariness, Ethan didn't look away or drop his head.

Gradually, a smile lifted the corners of Donovan's

mouth, the expression revealing the restoration of hope taking place in his soul. "Good enough, Ethan. Let's do this."

DOCTOR NAVARRO TOOK his time preparing for the transfusion as he wanted to give Ethan's body a chance to recover from the draw. After the conversation between Ethan and Donovan concluded, Ben released Donovan, knowing that it wouldn't be long before his suffering ceased for good. Though they all watched the progress of the doctor's preparations with eager anticipation, everyone, except Maggie who assisted him, stayed out of his way.

Smiles and light laughter accompanied their conversations as, for the first time in days, everyone breathed easy. Callie stood with Grace and Donovan, and Ben smiled at the way renewed hope had brightened his friend's eyes and improved the color in his face, even without the assistance of Ben's Succouri touch.

Though he enjoyed the celebratory scene before him, Ben retreated from the group and leaned on a nearby wall. Maybe it was the overwhelming emotions of the past few days or perhaps it was nerves over the impending transfer, he wasn't sure, but his heart felt oddly unsettled.

"Son?" Taylor came up beside him, frowning as he took in Ben's contemplative expression. "Everything okay?"

"Just fine." Ben weakly smiled.

Not buying his answer, Taylor put a hand on Ben's shoulder. "What's on your mind?"

Ben softly chuckled. "I know I can't hide anything from Callie, but now, that seems to apply to you as well."

"We're a lot alike, in more ways than just our appearances. I recognize that pensive look."

"To tell you the truth, I'm not sure what's bothering me." He lowered his voice to just above a whisper. "This is what I wanted, what we've worked and sacrificed for, but now that it's happening, I don't know, Dad. I feel… uneasy about it." Ben shook his head. "Just a few hours ago I talked the doctor off the ledge when he was in the exact same place, questioning the morality of the blood transfers now that we know what we do. The arguments I presented were sound and still apply, but suddenly…"

Taylor stepped back so he could look Ben squarely in the eyes. "Suddenly?"

Ben rubbed his forehead. "It feels all wrong somehow. I want Donovan saved, and I'm not going to put him through any more turmoil, but I think…" Ben gritted his teeth. "I don't know, Dad. I just think I'm supposed to do something, but I don't know what."

Glancing over at the group surrounding Donovan's bed, Taylor sighed. "Is this the human in you talking or your Succouri?"

Looking off to the side, Ben deliberated. "After my face-to-face encounter with it, it's easier than it used to be to distinguish its voice from mine, but it's still not always straightforward. Since I don't know why the human part of me would be bothered by this, I think I can be reasonably sure this is coming from my Succouri, but it's not offering clear reasons or instructions."

Crossing his arms, Taylor's forehead wrinkled as he concentrated. "When I asked Carozza about your illness and what I should do to help you, he told me to ask your Datouri. Callie has been right about everything. She seems to have a special connection with your Antico, a way of discerning its intentions. My best advice is to seek her counsel and take her suggestions very seriously."

Ben nodded, smiling at the unarguable truth in his words. As he glanced her way, Callie suddenly turned, and, though he knew she couldn't see his eyes from that distance, she patted Grace's arm and headed straight for him. Taylor chuckled, squeezed Ben's shoulder, and walked away.

"Ben?" Callie questioned with raised eyebrows as she reached for his hands.

"Let's go for a walk, shall we?" he invited, shaking his head at the wondrous connection of their bond.

"Do we have time?" she asked, looking toward the doctor.

"Let's make the time. I'm sure we'll be back before it begins."

She nodded, and they quietly slipped away.

As they walked down the driveway and on to the dirt road, Ben could feel Callie probing his thoughts and heart, and he did his best to hold the door wide open for her.

Abruptly halting, she turned surprised eyes to him. "You don't want the transfer to happen? I don't understand. This is what we planned, what we've gone through all this hardship and risk to accomplish." There was no accusation in her voice, just confusion.

Repeatedly, he shook his head. "I don't understand either, Callie. I need your help figuring this out. Why do I suddenly feel upset about the transfer? Dad thinks it's our Succouri warning me, and I think he's right. It's trying to communicate something, but I can't hear it clearly, can't quite grasp ahold of it. You know its heart better than I do because, from the beginning, you believed in its goodness. I need your insight, please."

Relaxing at his explanation, she smiled lovingly at him. "We'll figure it out together."

She turned back to the road, and they walked for a time in silence as they each sorted through their thoughts and instincts and tuned in to the heart of the other, trying to find an answer.

"Now that you've been offered a choice and you've freely chosen to remain Succouri, do you feel different in any way? I mean, I know you're at peace with your calling and your Succouri, but has anything else changed?"

He laughed. "Well, I think our bond is getting stronger by the minute, and the voice of our Antico is noticeably louder than before, but otherwise..."

"What has it said to you since your restoration to health that you're absolutely sure of?"

Ben thought for a moment. "When I talked with Ethan, the first time after we returned from the airport, I definitely heard it speak to me. It said, 'Teach what you learn, give what only you can give, and—with one mind—restore what's been lost'." He wrinkled his brow. "I wasn't really sure what that meant but..."

"Ben! Of course!" she exclaimed with excitement. "That's our mission. It was defining our calling!"

Ben looked at her in confusion.

She stopped walking and turned to face him. "What do you have to give that's unlike any other Succouri?"

"Um... I can help other Succouri with my touch."

"Exactly. And what needs restoring? What's been lost that we ourselves just learned about and have now begun to teach to others?" Her voice bubbled with unrestrained delight.

Understanding dawned as Ben recognized that when he'd originally heard those words from his Succouri, he hadn't been told yet about the Antico and the devastation of the blood transfers, so he hadn't made the connection.

"So, our mission, our calling *is* indeed to bring back the dispirited Succouri, to restore what was lost," he exclaimed in a breathy voice filled with awe. "Just as you suspected. Once again, my wife's wisdom, like her beauty, is unmatched." He smiled and caressed her cheek.

She grinned at him as her eyes danced.

"But that still doesn't explain how. How exactly do I do that, Callie?"

Again, she pondered silently before answering. "Tell me what happened when Ethan touched your arm."

Unconsciously, Ben rubbed at the spot where the contact had been made. "It felt as if... as if my blood suddenly rushed to the spot where he touched me—like everything inside me moved around, reorganized." He threw up his hands. "Sorry. That's the best I can do."

"And have you ever felt anything like that before?"

"Never."

"But," she considered. "Before Ethan, you hadn't touched another Succouri for longer than a quick hand-shake. Right?"

"Except perhaps Louis."

"But he didn't possess a Succouri."

"True. So what are you saying?" he asked, squinting his eyes.

"Perhaps you haven't felt that odd shifting before because you never had the opportunity to or..." Her eyes grew wide, like she'd at last found a lost treasure she'd been searching for. "Is it possible, now that you've made the choice to be a fully cooperative partner and you've learned the truth about yourself and the Succouri, something new has been unlocked? Since you trust one another now and no longer resent it, maybe our Succouri's been... unleashed, so to speak, freed to offer all its bountiful gifts."

Practically jumping with uncontainable excitement, the pitch of her voice rose. "What if, just as you believed its presence was restricting your human life and freedom, your distrust and rebellion toward it similarly restricted its ability to do what it was meant to do, carry out its destined purpose? Just as Owen's disbelief impacted his experience with it, up until now, maybe the same was true for you. Perhaps, as we also hypothesized about the touch transfers, the free and full cooperation of each member of the triad is required in order to accomplish the determined task, and without that, it can't happen."

"So, you're saying that the new sensation I experienced when I made contact with Ethan is some kind of newly unleashed ability related to our calling to restore what's been lost?"

"That's exactly what I'm saying." Her eyes glowed, no hint of doubt in them, and Ben couldn't help but get caught up in her giddiness. As he did, he mentally prodded the corner of his mind inhabited by the elusive third member of their unique triad. If this was a partnership, it was time for its contribution.

All at once, familiar words resounded through his mind, almost as loudly as Callie's physical voice. "'The three of us will journey together toward our destiny'," Ben mumbled, looking at the ground as he repeated the words his Succouri had spoken during his vision.

Callie reached for his hands, speaking the next sentence with him. "'At last, you are ready. It can now begin'."

The reason his Succouri wasn't presently speaking to him wasn't because it didn't have anything to say; it was because it had already spoken, already told them what to do.

Simultaneously, they looked up into each other's eyes.

"Those were the words it spoke right after I made the free choice to remain Succouri for the rest of my life."

"I remember," she said in a barely audible whisper. "Ben, I think we should hurry back to the house."

Feeling the same acute urgency, Ben nodded, already turning them around.

CHAPTER 12

THE WAKENING

When Ben and Callie reentered the lab, Ethan was lying on one of the hospital beds, arm outstretched as the doctor wiped the injection site with a sterile cloth. Donovan's bed had been moved, now situated alongside Ethan's with a few yards of space between them.

"Hold up, Doc," Ben said, raising a hand as he and Callie stepped to the end of Ethan's bed.

Startled, the doctor took a step back and turned questioning eyes to them.

"There's another way."

"Did... Did you receive an answer?" The doctor's voice was hopeful as, even in his preparations, he'd continued to look uncomfortable with his decision to proceed with the blood transfer.

"Not step by step instructions. More like an arrow, pointing us in a general direction, but I'd like to try if Ethan and Donovan are willing."

"Ben, what's going on?" Donovan questioned, his voice weak and hoarse. Because of his condition and constant sedation, Donovan had largely been excluded from the chaotic happenings of the last few days. Though he wanted to be open and honest, there wasn't sufficient time to catch him up on every detail, but Ben and Callie did their best to quickly give him the basics of their discoveries about the Antico and the ancient way of transferring the gift.

"And you possess one of the originals, the kind that still has a will of its own?" Donovan asked, struggling to focus through his pain.

"I do," Ben answered.

"And that's why you're... different?"

"It's a big part of the reason."

"So..." Donovan took a deep breath and grimaced, and Ben felt the urgency to move forward with the transfer as he hated watching his friend in pain. "You have no idea how much longer your Succouri will stay with you?"

Ben cleared his throat. "Well, in my case, I'll remain Succouri all my life. I won't ever pass the gift."

Maggie gasped at the revelation. Though he struggled to do so, Donovan raised himself to a sitting position and locked eyes with Ben. "You're the one it was seeking," he stated.

Still intimidated by the notion himself, Ben was unsure how to respond to the stunned reactions of others. He offered a weak smile and a nod.

Donovan whistled in amazement. "Weeks ago, I told Callie I always thought you had a uniquely courageous heart. I guess I'm not the only one who noticed that fact."

Humbled by the compliment, Ben bowed his head.

Breaking the silence in the room, Donovan's monitor suddenly began beeping and Doctor Navarro responded. He silenced the alarm, but as he took in the information on the screen and rechecked Donovan's pulse, the panic on his face was just as jarring as the piercing noise. "We need to hurry," he urged.

Immediately, Ben turned to his father. "Let's push their beds closer together."

Taylor came to assist him and they rolled Ethan's bed directly alongside Donovan's as Doctor Navarro pushed unnecessary medical equipment out of Ben's way. Then, with Callie by his side, Ben took a deep breath and stepped to the open side of Ethan's bed.

"I'm not exactly sure what's going to happen here." Ben paused to smile at Lee, who was standing at the foot of the adjoining beds. "How's your back, brother? Can I count on you if my world goes black again?"

"Strong as an ox," Lee answered confidently. "I got your back." Lee grinned as he and Taylor took up positions a few feet behind Ben and Callie.

Ben turned his focus to Ethan. "If my Succouri can make contact with yours and wake it up, I'm not sure what you'll experience. I do believe that, for it to leave you and transfer to Donovan, you—the human part of you—must consent. If you resist or refuse to relinquish it, I don't think it can go."

"Ben." Donovan spoke in a barely audible whisper as he struggled to breathe. "If Ethan's Succouri becomes sentient, doesn't that mean it gets to decide who the next host is? How do you know it will choose me?"

"It's my firm belief that you are the intended recipient. The timing of my illness, my loss and then subsequent restoration of healing power is too coincidental. If it wasn't fated for you to be saved by the reception of the gift, why did my Antico work everything out so perfectly, even down to the amazing coincidence of being on the same transport flight with Jessica and Allie?"

Briefly, Ben looked over at Callie and she nodded emphatically, her eyes shining with joy and understanding. "You and Donovan are meant to be the first, the initiation of a new beginning for the Succouri." He chuckled. "Or actually, more like a rebirth. Though I don't know exactly how it's all going to happen, this feels, this is right. My Antico's telling me this is the way it should be." Ben held out his hands as if ready to receive a gift. "I can't explain why I'm so certain of this but I am... we are," he corrected himself, again glancing at Callie as she nodded repeatedly. "We're humbly asking for your trust."

Donovan smiled and relaxed back into his pillows. Briefly, he lifted his eyes to Grace, whose full smile provided all the assurance Donovan needed. "I couldn't be in better hands," he declared, with no hint of reservation.

Every eye in the room turned to Ethan, who looked puzzled.

"This must be done of your free will, Ethan," Ben reemphasized. "It won't work otherwise."

"I don't know if I believe in all of this," Ethan admitted. "We're all putting a lot of faith in this... Carozza and his unorthodox views. I've been a Succouri for forty years and besides you, Ben, there's nothing in my experience to support these wild ideas. But..."

Everyone held their breath and the doctor tightened his jaw as he continued to watch Donovan's monitor.

"I can't deny that what I've witnessed in the last twenty-four hours has been extraordinary, inexplicable by our conventional wisdom." His eyes met Ben's, then shifted to Callie's. "I don't trust Carozza, but I trust the two of you. You've risked a lot to help me. You saved my granddaughter's life, and I believe you genuinely care about my family. When we met, you didn't flatter me or offer me false hope,

Ben. You were honest and straightforward about what you could and couldn't do." He grinned and glanced at Lee. "You and your brother-in-law. Callie's like my Lexi, strong, yet kind and infinitely generous. It's evident the two of you are sincerely persuaded of the correctness of this course of action." He raised his hands in surrender. "If we're all being duped here, so be it." He smiled and nodded at Ben. "I'll cast my lot with yours."

CALLIE'S HEART swelled with pride in her husband as he confidently, yet humbly won the full support and trust of everyone in the room, including Ethan Devereaux.

After his offer of full confidence, Ben patted Ethan's shoulder and turned to her. He took her hands in his and leaned his forehead against hers.

"As always, I need you, sweetheart. 'With one mind,' it said; that means this requires all three of us. I won't be able to communicate while it's happening, so you'll need to keep everybody calm and informed of our progress."

Though she felt a little nervous about the unknowns, she wasn't afraid. Like him, she was fully convinced this was the right path, what they were meant to do. She closed her eyes and breathed in and out in rhythm with him as their thoughts united.

A small gasp caught in her throat when she felt the powerful urging of Ben's Succouri compelling him to make contact with Ethan. Perhaps its instructions had been somewhat obscure before, but now, there was nothing at all subtle in its directive. How he'd managed to speak so calmly and patiently with this impulse pushing at him, she couldn't comprehend, but it gave her all the more reason to admire the man she loved.

When the connection was complete and pulsing strong, Ben leaned away and looked into her eyes. "*Ready?*" he asked, speaking to her inside their bond.

"*Absolutely,*" she responded in kind. "*I'm so proud of you, and I love you, Ben Sawyer.*"

He smiled at her.

No one blinked as Ben turned and gripped Ethan's wrist tightly with both hands. A few seconds passed before Callie felt the shifting Ben had described, like everything inside him was coming undone, being dislodged from its assigned place. It wasn't exactly painful, but it wasn't comfortable either. She was certain that, if it weren't for his distinctive physiology, Ben wouldn't be able to endure it. This was another reason he'd been changed. It wasn't just about tolerating years of the draw. His transformation enabled him to survive what had to happen inside his body to accomplish their calling. Without these modifications, he wouldn't live through what came next.

Acute disorientation gripped him, and Ben physically winced and softly moaned as his thoughts groped for solid ground.

"*I'm here, beloved. Hold on to me.*" Callie spoke directly to his heart, and she felt his mind cling desperately to her like a drowning man gripping a lifeline.

Though her central focus remained on the drama playing out in their invisible world, she was able to maintain a vague awareness of the happenings in the lab as well. Ben, however, had lost all connection to reality.

Lee stepped forward, responding to Ben's vocalized distress, but Callie put a hand on his arm. "He's okay. It's dizzying and uncomfortable, but, so far, not excessively painful."

Lee stepped back, but his eyes stayed locked on Ben.

Ethan closed his eyes and his body stiffened.

A few minutes later, the stirring intensified, becoming a rushing torrent, like the wild rapids of a churning river. Ben lowered his head and clenched his teeth as the sensation morphed into something resembling the draw he'd experienced when he'd revived Callie's father.

Inside their bond, Callie saw an ominous black hole open behind Ben, and the sudden, forceful suction of the resulting whirlwind knocked him off his feet. Instantly, Callie grabbed his hand as the opposing pull attempted to rip him from her grasp. Though she could feel his desperate struggle, she wasn't being sucked in herself, so she tightened her grip and dug in her heels, determined to win the tug-of-war.

In the doctor's lab, everyone watched in confusion and concern as, in a parallel action, Callie set her jaw and gripped the back of Ben's shirt in a tight fist, breathing unevenly.

"Callie!" Taylor's anxious cry momentarily broke through her consciousness.

"It's okay," she panted. "I've got him. I won't let go no matter what. I promise." Though those in the laboratory heard her words, they were primarily intended for Ben.

As she closed her eyes, she saw him, suspended in deep darkness; his only anchor the tight grip on her hand.

"*I can't hold on, Callie,*" Ben screamed. "*It's going to take me.*"

As she held out her free hand to him, he stretched, his face contorting with the effort as he fought the rival pull to extend his hand and firmly latch onto her. Now, she had a double grip, both of his hands in hers, and she smiled at him, confident she could win this fight.

"*You don't have to, my love. Don't fight it. I've got you. Trust me. I'll never let go, never let you disappear."* Looking into her eyes, Ben ceased his struggle, relaxing his body even as the pull intensified.

"It's left me, Callie. Our Succouri's gone," he shouted, panicked and confused.

Though Ben was surrounded by thick darkness, Callie could see clearly. In her mind's eye, she saw a closed door gradually open and behind it stood Ethan Devereaux. He held out his hand and the starlit image of Ben, the one she'd seen on the beach, approached and grasped hold of it. As they held the handshake, flashes of light surrounded Ethan and his image began to glow like Ben's. At once, Callie understood exactly what was happening.

"I can see it, Ben! Don't be afraid. It will return. It moved to Ethan, just for a moment, to awaken his Succouri. The ripening opened the door. And we were right. Your cooperation released the power of rebirth. It's... It's beautiful! When it's done, it will come back to you. Just hang on a little longer."

"I can't see anything, except you."

"That's all you need to see," she answered with a tender smile. *"Keep your eyes on me."*

His frantic eyes locked on hers, the stare nearly as binding as his grip on her hands.

"You're the bridge," he cried out, as understanding dawned. *"You're filling the gap left by its absence, keeping me from"*—his eyes briefly glanced behind him—*"falling in there and vanishing forever. Without you, my Succouri couldn't do this because I wouldn't survive it. It wasn't just my choice that changed everything, Callie. It was also you."*

She didn't argue with his conclusions. Instead, she smiled a little broader as she also understood why it had been so essential for them to quickly develop a deep enough bond to enable their thoughts to unite. Without that special connection, she wouldn't be able to anchor him, keeping him safe from harm.

For what felt like hours, they remained there, Callie's unyielding hold Ben's only lifeline. As time passed, the whirlwind pulled harder, but her determination also grew, and she countered its force.

Callie agonized at the strain he endured as his body was yanked in opposing directions, but he never looked away from her, and that unwavering focus tilted the scales ever so slightly in her favor.

Just when the strain on both of them reached a critical point, the tugging abruptly ceased. For a split second, she lost sight of him as the textures and colors around them transfigured. But when she blinked, Ben reappeared, this time kneeling in front of her on the ocean floor as rays of shimmering sunlight and schools of playful fish danced around them.

Ben released her hands, but she still felt no need to breathe.

"It's alright now. Thank you, sweetheart. Once again, you saved my life."

She cupped his cheek with her hand. *"Just returning the favor, beloved. Didn't I tell you I'd never let go, never give up on our happily ever after?"*

His hypnotizing blue eyes sparkled. *"And I promised I'd use my last ounce of strength to hang on to you."* He leaned forward taking her in his arms as his soft lips met hers, sending a healing wave of strength through them both. With a smile that held a promise to continue the kiss later, he leaned away and sighed contentedly. *"You'd better let the others know we're alright."*

Glancing up, she frowned in concern. *"Aren't you coming?"*

"I can't go quite yet, but you can."

She hesitated. *"But you are coming, right?"*

He grinned playfully at her. *"Mrs. Sawyer, don't you know by now? You can't get rid of me that easily. I'll be right behind you. I promise."*

One last time, he leaned forward and kissed her, and she could taste the salt on his lips.

"Callie, what's going on?"

Doctor Navarro's frantic voice shot her to the surface, and she opened her eyes and gulped a mouthful of oxygen as she lifted her head.

She looked around the room, the real world strange and foreign as if she hadn't existed there in years.

"Everything's alright. The worst is over now."

Hunched over but still in contact with Ethan's arm, Ben's eyes were closed and his hands trembled fiercely, but the expression on his face was placid and so was Ethan's. As she watched carefully, Ethan mouthed something and then sighed.

"Callie!" The doctor came up beside her, grasping her arm, and pointed toward Donovan's monitor. "We're losing him."

Grace put one hand to her mouth as she held on to Donovan with the other. "What do we do?" she asked in a desperate cry.

Callie closed her eyes again, but she couldn't get back to Ben. "It'll be alright," she encouraged.

She let go of Ben's shirt, and started to reach out to touch his hand, but then thought better of it.

For an unbearable moment, no one moved, unsure

what to do or say as Donovan's monitor ominously signaled his faltering heartbeat.

"Please," Grace pleaded, leaning over Donovan. "Hold on, just another minute. Don't give up." A sob shook her, and Maggie put an arm around her shoulders.

"Ben!" Callie whispered near his ear. "He's dying. Please hurry."

Inhaling deeply at the sound of her voice, Ben blinked and slowly straightened. Callie put her arm around his waist, and he released Ethan and moved closer to her.

"It's up to Ethan now," Ben panted, beads of sweat on his forehead. "He has to choose to let go."

"Did you... Did you wake it up?" Doctor Navarro asked.

Ben smiled at Callie before nodding his response. He accepted a bottle of water from Taylor and took a long sip before speaking. "My Succouri did. My only job was to hold on for dear life while it did what it needed to do inside Ethan. And that would have been impossible if it weren't for Callie. She held on to me, tethered me to reality. Without question, she saved my life."

Every face in the room held the same perplexed expression, and Ben chuckled as he knew there was no way to explain what they'd been through in the last few minutes.

"Let's just say we now understand why this life, this calling requires the full engagement of all three partners."

Callie's emphatic nod confirmed Ben's statement, but she also could find no words to describe their experience.

The beeps that accompanied Donovan's heartbeat momentarily sped up and then slowed, nearly to a stop. Grace sharply inhaled and lowered her head into her hands.

Ben started toward his bed, but suddenly halted as the voice in his head directed him to stop. "I can't help him,"

Ben explained, mourning the truth. "His only chance now is the transfer."

He stepped back and leaned over Ethan. "Ethan, come on," Ben whispered. "You have to let go."

Donovan's heart monitor beeped, then ceased for five seconds. As everyone froze, suspended in terror, one last heartbeat echoed through the tiled room, and then, silence.

"Come on, Ethan. Come on." Ben gritted his teeth. Grace collapsed into Maggie's shoulder, sobbing inconsolably.

At that moment, Ethan opened his eyes and looked at Ben. A profound peace emanated from him. For the first time, Callie noticed a striking resemblance to his granddaughter.

"Ethan!" Ben pointed with urgency. "Donovan."

Shaking off the disorientation of the last few minutes, Ethan nodded and looked over at Donovan's pale face. Then, he reached out his hand and touched him. Callie put a hand to her heart, hoping it wasn't too late.

Sitting up, Ethan twisted his whole body so he could place both hands firmly around Donovan's arm. Every eye stared unblinking at the monitor, willing it to sound. Doctor Navarro wrung his hands and wiped at his forehead, mentally tracking the time since Donovan's last heartbeat.

When the beep resounded, loud and clear, sweeter than the most beautiful music any of them had ever heard, the room erupted into shouts and claps of joy and relief.

Callie threw her arms around Ben's neck, and he returned her embrace as they shed happy tears. Soon, everyone gathered around Grace, embracing her and laughing gleefully as Donovan's heartbeat grew stronger and steadier by the second. Doctor Navarro put his head in his hands, shaking it repeatedly, overwhelmed by the intense emotions of the last hour.

Ethan kept contact with Donovan for a while, but eventually, he let go and sat sipping from a bottle of water as he too pleasured in the second-by-second improvements in Donovan's condition.

When the celebrating settled, Ethan jumped down from the hospital bed and he and Taylor moved it out of the way so the whole group could circle around Donovan's bed.

Within minutes, normal color was restored to his face, reminding Callie of how he'd looked the first time she'd met him. His breathing evened out, sounding easy and strong, and the dark lines of pain around his eyes faded away. Though she thought it might just be her imagination, as Callie watched him from the shelter of Ben's arms, she thought he looked several years younger.

Grace took his hand, kissing it excitedly and laughing as she witnessed the man she loved coming to life again. Tears flowed freely down her cheeks, but these were beautiful ones, sourced in pure happiness.

As everyone shifted to make room for him, Doctor Navarro performed a full check of Donovan's vitals, his smile broadening with each completed test. When he was finished and satisfied with the results, he began removing sensors, concluding with the withdrawal of Donovan's IV.

Callie watched Ben shake his head in wonder and relief as he stared at his friend's restored condition.

"You did it," she whispered, kissing his cheek.

"Oh no," he countered. "*We* did this. All three of us." He thought for a moment. "Well, actually the five of us as Ethan and his Succouri were important participants in this undertaking, too."

She laughed and nodded at the truth. It had indeed

taken all of them, partnering together in unity and single-mindedness to accomplish the feat. If any of them hadn't been on board or had withheld even the smallest portion of what they had to give, the endeavor would have failed miserably and Donovan would have died.

As for her, Ben, and their Antico, they were, at last, a team, no bitterness, confusion, or reluctance between them, blocking their potential. With the new knowledge of their calling and the ability to carry it out, they stood at the beginning of an untraveled road. But the three of them stood there together, and because of that, she wasn't afraid.

A few minutes later, Donovan opened his eyes. His gaze immediately focused on Grace, and Ben subtly signaled to the group, bidding them to give the two a private moment. As they left the laboratory, Ben smiled, reminiscing about his and Callie's first moments of bonding when the inexplicable heat had moved through their hands. Having no idea what the bonding was at that time, it had bewildered them both.

When they'd relocated outside the lab, Ben led Callie away from the others in response to Ethan's subtle beckoning gesture. They stepped outside and settled in the chairs on the front porch. As Ben took a seat next to Callie, fatigue hit him hard, and Callie squeezed his hand in concern when she heard him sigh.

"Well, you've certainly made a believer out of me now," Ethan said with a chuckle after a moment of silence. "How could we have gotten it so wrong all these years? It's a shame, a terrible shame."

Though his voice held distress for the unfortunate truth, which was now unquestioningly proven, it was calm and happy, conveying a sense of wholeness that he'd sorely lacked before.

Leaning forward, Ben looked inquisitively into Ethan's eyes. "How are you, my friend?"

Meeting Ben's gaze, Ethan smiled and held out his hands. "It's gone, Ben. Totally gone."

"Your Succouri? Yes, of course, but didn't you—"

"No, not that. The hole, the emptiness. It's healed!"

Ben straightened. "You... You can't feel it at all anymore?"

"I cannot. I still miss her, and I'll always love her, but"—he inhaled slowly—"at last, I can breathe. It erased it, took away the agony, like removing a burdensome weight off my back."

"Your Succouri?" Though Ben was thrilled by Ethan's statement, he was surprised by his description of complete restoration.

Ethan emphatically shook his head. "Not mine. Yours."

Confused, Ben stared blankly at Ethan.

"Ben's Succouri healed your heart?" Callie sought clarification, her voice high with excitement.

"It did. After it revived my Succouri but before it returned to Ben, it... it touched me, in a manner of speaking." He placed his palm over his heart. "It gave me—the human me—a priceless gift. There wasn't any reason or obligation for it to do so, and it put Donovan at risk by delaying the process, but it genuinely wanted to help me out of pure kindness." He looked straight into Ben's eyes. "Precisely like you. Though your initial motivation was to convince me to donate to Donovan, you extended sincere compassion, wanting me to find a way out of my personal prison and back to my family. Your Succouri did the same. It came to me because it needed to revive my Succouri, but it lingered when it saw my misery, and it repaired it because"—his eyes moistened, and he blinked hard—" because it is you. I know that sounds strange, but I don't know how else to explain it. Your Succouri's heart—if you can call it that—is a reflection of yours." He leaned back in his chair, looking a bit frustrated at his inability to find the right words to communicate his experience.

Callie laughed lightly. "Having had a face-to-face encounter with it myself, I know exactly what you mean, Ethan. The two of them indeed match perfectly. Now you understand why it wasn't difficult to accept the truth that Ben was the one it had sought out for all those years."

Ethan smiled and nodded at Callie.

Ben pressed his palms together, ironically the only one in the circle confused about what exactly had occurred. "But I don't understand. Once awakened, why didn't your Succouri offer you that gift?"

"I don't think it could. There was a moment, after mine was revived, when they both whispered in my head. Though there was a remarkable distinction between the manner of my Succouri before and after the rebirth, there was also a stark contrast between your Succouri and mine. It was like..." He tapped his finger on his knee as he thought of a comparison. "Like a child versus an adult: mine inexperienced, innocent, and a little naïve and yours mature, perceptive, and reasoned."

"Carozza said Ben's Succouri was extremely clever," Callie explained. "To evade domestication, as he called it, for so long, it had to be. Plus, it's been around for a very long time, seen a lot through its hosts' eyes and experiences."

"And I suppose it makes sense that, in a way, yours *is*

like a child as it just reemerged from decades of dormancy," Ben added.

Ethan wrinkled his brow. "All of that is part of it, but there's more to it than that. It's more about"—he leaned forward again and gestured toward Ben—"finding you, Ben. It changed, or maybe, realized its full potential when it united with you. Just as we suffered the emptiness of a missing partner and bond, I think a Succouri suffers in much the same way. Until it reaches its final host, I don't think it can be what it's meant to be, just as you couldn't until you met Callie."

Callie's face lit up. "Yes!" she exclaimed. "Carozza said that the bond mimics the relationship the Succouri desires to have with its final host and his Datouri. Until it finds them, the bonds it has with its interim hosts are lesser, not as tight."

"That's exactly right. Your Succouri recognized the painful emptiness inside me because it knew the feeling well, had endured the same for centuries. It was a pure offering of empathetic compassion, and I'll never forget it. Since it's back inside you and thus I can accomplish this with one simple offering"—Ethan extended his hand to Ben—"I want to say thank you for giving me back my life, a chance to move forward, and love my family once more. I may not have many years left, but I'm going to take full advantage of whatever time remains."

As he witnessed the tears of gratitude in Ethan's eyes, Ben grasped his offered hand, feeling no sensation of stirring this time. "Trust me when I tell you that it has been a pleasure to walk with you thus far, Ethan, and it will continue to be as we see you reunite with your family."

Once again, he felt the sting of deep regret for the time

he'd wasted distrusting and mischaracterizing his Succouri. Yet it had been patient, waiting for him to mature and realize the power and comfort available through their partnership before presenting him with the ultimate choice. If it had offered him the option before he'd met Ms. Essie and Callie, he undoubtedly would have made the wrong decision, forfeiting the benefits of the bond and the fulfillment of their extraordinary destiny. Love, not indifference or scorn, was the motivation behind its silence all those years. Through that time of confusion, Ben learned and grew, and the temporary discomfort of it saved him from a lifetime of profound regret.

CHAPTER 13

THE PLAN

When Ben and Callie reentered the house, Grace was already chatting with Lee and Taylor but Donovan was just rounding the corner into the front room. As he locked eyes with Ben and moved to intercept him, Ben rejoiced at the sight of his friend in full health, and wearing normal clothes rather than a hospital gown. Grace pulled Callie aside, and the two women laughed and hugged as Ben advanced toward Donovan.

Enthusiastically, Donovan embraced him, and Ben returned the affection. Even when he leaned away, Donovan maintained a firm grip on Ben's shoulders as he gazed at him with moist eyes. Then, seeing Ethan just behind Ben, he beckoned for him to join them. He put one hand on each man's shoulder, allowing his emotions free rein as he smiled at them.

"There's nothing I can say or do to express my gratitude to the two of you. You saved my life at great personal cost, and I'm forever in your debt."

Ben patted his arm and sent him a teasing smile. "Alright then. Your penance is to be my lifelong friend."

Donovan laughed. "That was already a given, but"—he stepped back and offered his hand—"I accept your terms."

After the handshake, Donovan turned to Ethan, who said, "I want nothing from you. As I was just explaining to Ben, I've already been compensated far beyond my wildest hopes." He looked down for a moment, contemplating before refocusing on them. "I'd like to help you, Donovan. I don't know how much I can offer since this is an entirely new thing with your awakened Succouri, but I'd like to at least share what I know and be there to answer questions you might have. If that's alright with both of you?"

Ben patted Ethan's back. "That's more than alright, Ethan. That's the way it should be."

"Grace and I will rely on you both. We have much to learn. You look like a different man," Donovan noted as he studied Ethan's clear eyes and confident posture.

"So do you," Ethan returned with a low chuckle.

"How do you feel?" Ben inquired of Donovan.

"Let's see…" Donovan grinned but raised his eyebrows and folded his arms. "Here are the things I *can* describe: I feel strong, free from pain, and ten years younger than I've felt in… well, in the last ten years I suppose. But there are also an assortment of new sensations I'm struggling to define. It's a little disorienting, maybe even unsettling."

Ben and Ethan nodded empathetically.

"Be patient with yourself," Ethan encouraged, "and give it time. It will be interesting to find out what's different about your experience as a result of your Succouri being revived." They both turned their eyes to Ben.

Ben sighed. "I was very young, and my memories are tainted by the confusion and fear I experienced. As I am the last recipient of this Succouri, that sets me apart in some ways. I'm hoping you and Grace will agree to travel with us when we go to see Carozza as he may have more answers to offer us, but according to Callie, the biggest difference will be the indeterminant length of the term you will serve as Succouri. It could be five years or thirty. There's no way to know. The good news is, assuming the term of service is significantly shorter than the previous norm, your body won't suffer the same debilitating effects, so even after your Succouri departs, you'll live a long full life. As I'm also doing, you'll need to learn to listen for your Succouri's voice, as it now has a much louder one to hear. When you enter the ripening, your only duty will be to keep an eye out for those who might be candidates for the transfer, but ultimately, you'll need to submit to your Succouri's will for the selected inheritor. Assuming you've learned to tune in to its voice by then, I'm guessing it will communicate with you regarding its choice. When the recipient is identified, you won't need a blood transfer. Simple touch contact will be all that's necessary for the exchange, just as Ethan did with you. Besides that, there's not much else we know for certain yet. You're a pioneer, my friend."

"Then, I'm in very good company," Donovan noted with amusement. "The doctor took some blood samples. Until we can determine more, I guess I just wait it out and see what happens. How will I know when... when it all kicks in and I can heal like you can?"

As he asked the question, Grace and Callie joined them, and Ben put his arm around Callie's shoulders.

"It should be at least a week or two, but..." Ben smiled down at Callie. "There's an easy way to test it right now if you wish."

Picking up on his suggestion, Callie grinned and extended her hand, and Ben momentarily released his hold on her. "Donovan?" she offered.

After a second of confusion, Donovan nodded his understanding and took Callie's hand, hopeful anticipation in his eyes.

Everyone watched Callie as she blinked and stared straight ahead. "Sorry," she said at last, shaking her head. "Not quite yet. But I'm sure it won't be long."

When Donovan released her hand, Ben patted his shoulder. "In my case, it took almost a month before I started manifesting signs of being Succouri. We'll be nearby whenever you want to test it out."

Content to wait, Donovan sighed and took Grace's hand. "In the meantime, from the looks of it, everyone in this room could use some sleep. I think I'm the only one here who's had ample rest over the last few days."

"We're planning to head to our place in Cape Cod within the hour. Whoever wants to join us is more than welcome. I want to check on the doc, though, make sure he's alright. Is he still in the lab?"

Donovan nodded. "Running his tests. He seemed shaken up by everything that happened today, so I think that's a good plan."

After exchanging one last celebratory embrace with his friend, Ben left Callie in the company of the others and headed for the lab. He found Doctor Navarro in the back corner, leaning over a microscope.

"Doc," he announced as he approached.

When the doctor straightened and turned to Ben, Ben's heart twisted at the storm of confusion and anguish in his eyes.

"Today was a good day," Ben said, encouragingly, putting out his hands. "Everyone's healthy and whole."

"Indeed. What we all witnessed was revolutionary." The doctor's eyes softened with genuine affection. "From the moment I met you and Callie, I knew the two of you were special. It's now abundantly clear that that impression was a significant underestimation. I can't begin to comprehend everything that occurred, nor can I grasp the extent of the dramatic consequences that will follow. Nevertheless, it's the unmistakable truth that you, Callie, and your Succouri saved the day. I'm gratified, but..." Wearily he sat on a nearby stool and Ben pulled one over and sat facing him.

"But it means it's all true." Ben finished the doctor's thought.

"Precisely. Carozza was correct. We've... I've been doing immeasurable harm, which has resulted in unfathomable loss and destruction."

Lowering his head, Ben ached for the doctor as his kind heart, which passionately wanted to heal others, couldn't bear the thought, even though there wasn't a hint of malice in his actions.

"Do you know why I left regular practice to work with the Succouri?"

Ben shook his head.

"Twelve years ago, a young woman stopped at a gas station on her way home from an exhausting day of teaching a pack of wild third graders. After filling her tank, she felt the urge for a hot cup of coffee, so she grabbed her purse and headed inside. As she approached the counter to pay, a man in a ski mask burst in and started shouting and waving a gun in the air. Everyone in the store hid, except for the young woman and the teenage clerk as they had nowhere to hide and the gunman had already set his sights on them. Calmly, the woman set her purse on the counter and backed away with her hands up, but the scared kid behind the counter panicked. He turned his back and ran for the back room, unsettling the gunman, which resulted in a reckless spray of bullets, fired in the general direction of the retreating clerk. The teenager was killed instantly as five bullets ripped through his back and skull. The young teacher ducked but it was too late. Two bullets struck her, one in her arm and the other in her chest. She crumpled to the floor in a pool of blood, gasping for air as fluid filled her punctured lungs. Realizing what he'd done, the gunman fled in cowardice."

The doctor paused to take a shaky breath, as Ben's heart pounded at the terrifying story.

"As she lay dying, struggling for her final breath, an older man rushed out of the restroom, and when he took in the scene, he hurried to her side and placed his warm hands on her bleeding arm. Immediately, all pain ceased, and she took a deep, refreshing breath. The man instructed an onlooker to call 911, and he stayed with her, holding firmly to her arm until the paramedics arrived. She asked who he was and how he was relieving her pain, but he only chuckled and said, 'It's simple. Today's your day for a miracle.'"

Despite his present distress, the doctor smiled.

"Doc, that girl... That was your daughter, Elena. Wasn't it?"

"It was. Her recovery was long and difficult, and we almost lost her several times, but she made it, thanks to the healing touch of a kind stranger. Elena is our only child. We struggled for years to conceive; truthfully, I thought we never would. She was our miracle baby. When she recounted the events of that dreadful night, I became obsessed with discovering who saved her and how." He sighed. "It's a long story, but suffice it to say, eventually I found Elena's savior, and he and his wife became close family friends. Two years later, he entered the ripening and the young man he chose to save with his gift was—"

"Raul." Ben concluded the doctor's sentence.

"Indeed. So, you see, Ben, the Succouri saved the life of my only daughter and brought her a husband who loves and protects her better than we could have dreamed possible. It's true, we missed out on grandchildren, but my work with the Succouri has brought wonderful people into our lives, who have become family, so we suffer no loss or regret. Leaving my practice was a decision I made because I wanted to give back, to repay the debt I owed for the blessings the Succouri bestowed on me and my family."

Falling silent, the doctor lowered his head into his hands. The crisis of conscience brought about by Carozza's shocking revelations, now proven to be legitimate, was unavoidable. Discovering that the established procedures, believed to be noble endeavors, were actually detrimental practices felt like a punch straight to the gut.

"But don't you see, Doc? We can turn this around. More than simply knowing the truth, we have a solution now, a way to repair and redeem what was lost. The damage that's been done is not permanent, not the end of the story."

Though he nodded, the doctor's shoulders remained slumped. "It does seem that you and Callie will bear the burden of righting this wrong, which is patently unfair. However, I am grateful you are able and willing to do so."

He started to turn back to his microscope, but Ben leaned forward and captured his gaze.

"We can't do this alone. We only know a handful of Succouri, and without your medical analysis of my unique physiology and your testimony as a witness to prove Carozza's theories, no one will listen or take our assertions seriously. Your extensive connections in the network and your solid reputation will be crucial in affecting real change. Doc, your work with the Succouri is far from over. I'm asking for your help, your partnership. We can't do this without you."

Hesitantly, but with a glimmer of hope in his eyes, he turned back to Ben. "What exactly is your plan?"

"We need to cease the blood transfers once and for all. But to do that, we have to educate everyone in the network about what we've discovered and convince them of its validity. When people hear that you've changed your mind, discontinued the transfusions, they will take notice and want to know more."

"I can certainly put you in contact with people and—"

Ben shook his head. "I don't have your widespread and well-established reputation and credibility. They don't know me. Plus, if I spend all my time meeting with individuals in the network, building a rapport, educating them on the truth, and persuading them to give up the old ways, I'll never have time to do what I'm meant to do: wake up the slumbering Succouri. I need partners, and"—Ben smiled—"I'm sincerely hoping you'll be one of them."

Closing his eyes, the doctor stroked the side of his chin with his thumb as he considered Ben's offer. As a result of his misplaced guilt, his initial instinct to withdraw from the Succouri and everything related to it was evident, but from personal experience, Ben knew that wouldn't ultimately bring him healing or resolution. Being directly involved in fixing the problem he'd inadvertently helped to create would be a much more productive way of coping with his guilt.

At last, he opened his eyes, but his expression was still tentative. "Big picture, how do you see this playing out,

Ben? How does every Succouri that exists today become reborn?"

"One Succouri at a time. As my Succouri can only enter the host and awaken it during the ripening phase, we should begin by convincing those who are in or close to that stage. Once we've revived a few and they've successfully transferred via touch, I'm guessing word will spread fast, making the task significantly easier. Since I'm twenty-seven and my gift has no expiration date, even if someone receives the gift today, I should live long enough to awaken every Succouri in existence; assuming we can find them all and convince them to participate. It will be a lifelong endeavor, but this is my and Callie's destiny. It's what we were meant to do."

The doctor's expression shifted to alarm. "Do you know what you're giving up, Ben? Since you are the only one who can perform this miraculous feat, you'll be infamous. In no time at all, every person in the network will know your name and though most of them are trustworthy, I'm all too aware of Succouri who have come under suspicion and worse, even without the kind of notoriety you'll possess. There will be people who will disagree with you, perhaps even outright oppose your efforts. In their misguided passion, they may be willing to expose you, which could put you and Callie in great danger. Anonymity and direct control over the revelation of one's name and identity are crucial in this life. You'll lose that control. The two of you will have no privacy, and you'll need security for yourself, Callie, Lee; anyone and everyone who's close to you."

As it had been mere hours since the revelation of their calling, he hadn't had time to think through the ramifications yet, but it didn't matter. Though that level of risk, especially to Callie's safety, made Ben's stomach churn, he was solidly convinced of their calling. Therefore, he had no other choice but to move forward in faith, trusting that the rest of it would work itself out.

"I do have a best friend who was a Navy SEAL and specializes in protection, and a father in the FBI," Ben reminded himself as much as the doctor. "We will certainly avail ourselves of their wisdom and assistance, but other than that, Callie and I will take it one day at a time and try not to let worry overshadow the joy of what we've been called to do. If you help us, you'll likely suffer much the same, so I won't hold it against you if you refuse my request."

This time, the answer appeared quickly in the doctor's eyes. "I've already offered you whatever assistance you require. As I figure it, bearing the risk is fair punishment for the damage I've inflicted. From the start, your character and courage have impressed and inspired me, but you now additionally manifest a clarity and confidence of purpose that will make you an exceptional leader; one well worth following." He held out his hand to Ben. "I'm honored to work alongside you and Callie and thank you for the opportunity to right my mistakes."

A SHORT WHILE LATER, Taylor, Ethan, Lee, Callie, and Ben made the drive to Ben and Callie's house in Cape Cod. Out of an abundance of caution, the doctor requested that Donovan and Grace remain at his home overnight so he could continue to monitor Donovan's restoration to full health.

Callie instantly fell in love with the white, seaside cottage with its nautical decor and bold color themes.

Unlike Ben's childhood home, the furniture was comfortable and cozy, and though the house was spacious, it wasn't enormous, which made Callie feel much more at home. As Lee had pointed out, the views of the cape were indeed breathtaking.

The master bedroom had a private deck that overlooked the water, and, that evening, after they bid everyone goodnight, she and Ben sat side by side in matching rocking chairs sharing a heavy blanket as they sipped cups of chai tea and enjoyed the beauty of the setting sun. They were beyond exhausted, but as they'd had very little time alone in the last few days, they were eager to indulge in a private moment together before heading to bed.

They began by catching each other up on the private conversations they'd had that day. Callie told Ben about her talk with Grace and how she believed that she and Donovan were already experiencing the earliest signs of the bonding, including a heightened sense of magnetism. Ben softly chuckled and shook his head.

"Since he hasn't yet manifested any of the other gifts, I'm skeptical that the source of their experiences is Donovan's Succouri. The fact that he's finally healthy and strong, the ecstatic emotions of the day, and the near guarantee of a wonderful future together are much more likely culprits for these feelings," Ben conjectured.

"You're probably right," Callie replied, attempting to smile through a yawn.

Ben recounted his conversation with the doctor, as Callie listened with concern. "He's right about the loss of privacy and anonymity, sweetheart. Being widely known within the network will undoubtedly increase the risk of exposure significantly, for all of us."

She reached over and took his hand. "It can't be helped. I'm betting our astute Antico will suggest some strategies to evade danger as well as provide clear warnings to keep us safe, just as it warned you when I was at risk."

"I don't doubt it will. Additionally, as soon as Donovan's settled in his new identity, I'll seek his counsel on the matter. It can't hurt to be prepared for any eventuality."

Yawning again, she nodded. "Now that we're clear on our calling, what should we do, Ben? Do you think we need to remain here so we can be close to the doctor and be more accessible to those in the network?"

Leaning his head wearily against the back of his chair, Ben turned to look at her. "Unless you feel strongly about that being the right course of action, I hadn't planned on relocating permanently. I think we should stay here for a while, be sure Donovan's off to a good start, and give the doctor the opportunity to run whatever tests he'd like, but, Callie, I want to provide you with a home and some semblance of a normal life, not to mention a close relationship with your, our brother. As those we seek to help will be from various places around the country, even around the world, we can just as easily meet with them back home as we can here."

As she smiled in obvious agreement, her eyelids drooped, and Ben stroked her hand as he watched her struggle to stay in the conversation.

"Agreed, but let's keep this place. I love it here."

Ben lifted her hand to his lips, kissing it softly. "Whatever you wish. If I'm with you, I have everything I need."

Kissing her hand again, he let his lips linger on her skin, feeling the gentle pulse of strength flowing into him. Sheltering her hand over his heart, he closed his eyes for what he thought was a few seconds, but when he opened them again, the sky was black, a smattering of stars filling the expanses between the clouds.

He sat back to admire his new bride, soundly asleep, a contented smile still lifting the corners of her mouth. She was beautiful, the perfect features of her face softly glowing in the moonlight. In mesmerized silence, he lingered for a long moment before tucking the blanket around her, rising, and lifting her into his arms.

There were so many things he wanted to say to her. She'd saved his life today, kept him sane and anchored when his Succouri left him, and helped him discover their mutual mission. Without a second of hesitation, she'd jumped in with both feet, accepting and embracing a new destiny that forever abolished any real chance at a normal life. Her loyalty and faithfulness to him and their Succouri was unparalleled, and somehow, he wanted to express the depths of his gratitude. But now was not the time. The greatest gift he could presently give her was to let her rest, catch up on the many nights of sleep she'd forgone to save him and Donovan.

Carrying her back inside the bedroom, he delicately lowered her onto the bed. Though she didn't speak and barely acknowledged what was happening with an occasional sleepy smile, she cooperated with him as he helped her out of her clothes, then tucked her under the covers. After he undressed, he joined her, sighing at the incomparable pleasure and wholeness they enjoyed exclusively in each other's arms.

With warm nostalgia, Ben remembered their first night together after leaving home for Boston. After the traumatic shooting into her bedroom and the revelation about their inability to have children, she'd confronted him in the park, pledging her heart to him and assuring him that the sad news hadn't changed her desire to build a life with him. Following that emotional encounter, she'd fallen fast asleep in the car, and he'd carried her to their hotel room.

Though he'd left her fully dressed that night, he'd allowed himself the pleasure of pressing against her as they slept and from that night forward, he'd fervently craved her presence whenever he'd slept alone.

The countless trials they'd endured had, at last, brought them here, to a place of acceptance and confidence in their future. Though much of their time together thus far had been fraught with hardship, Ben wouldn't go back and change a thing. The trials had permanently bound them together and taught them to trust in their love.

That love had radically changed him, little by little bringing him closer to becoming the man he'd always wanted to be. She gave him wings to fly while also anchoring him to solid ground. Together, they'd found the answers to his past, his present, and their future, save for one remaining quandary.

He still didn't understand why their Succouri had withdrawn from him and moved into her, bringing them both to death's door, only to suddenly reverse course and inexplicably return them to normal. Despite his confusion over this mystery, he no longer impulsively attributed it to malicious or indifferent motives on the part of his invisible consort. He was fully assured that, whatever the reason, it would prove to be for his and Callie's good, and he relaxed in his Succouri's promise that, in due time, they would understand.

As he pulled Callie closer, he brushed his lips across

hers before sinking back into his pillow and joining her in blissful, undisturbed sleep.

THE FOLLOWING week passed quickly as each day they delighted in watching Donovan strengthen and gradually become more aware and connected to his thriving Succouri partner.

"I'm starting to hear its whispers, faintly, like the second or third echo of someone's voice off a canyon wall," he explained the following Sunday morning as the group sat eating breakfast together around the dining room table.

Ben grinned at the apt description. "It won't take much time before it more closely resembles a first echo, or perhaps even the voice itself. My shortsightedness delayed my progress in this regard, but that won't be the case with you. Has Doc approved your travel with us tomorrow?"

"He has, though reluctantly." Donovan crossed his arms and sighed frustratedly.

Though Taylor had gone back with Maggie to Boston a few days prior, he was scheduled to return late that evening and travel back to Philly with Ben, Callie, Ethan, Grace, and Donovan the following morning. They were surprised by how much they missed Taylor's presence, and they were glad he'd vowed to visit as often as possible. Already, they'd discussed designating Callie's former bedroom back home as permanently his, encouraging him to leave some clothes and supplies in the closet for his use whenever he came to town.

As Taylor and Callie had hoped, Carozza had been moved to a local nursing home after the anonymous report of elder neglect. Within the last twenty-four hours, Taylor had learned that his condition was deteriorating rapidly, despite the improved conditions. Each of them wished to offer the man their heartfelt gratitude, as well as some well-deserved vindication after the ridicule he'd suffered because of his unorthodox theories.

"The good doctor worries too much," Donovan continued. "Even as a teenager, I never felt this strong. He wants to keep me under observation until my gift fully manifests. I suppose, out of profound respect for him, I'll tolerate his torturous tests until then, but after that, Grace and I are anxious to move on and begin our journey."

"What does that look like for the two of you?" Callie asked hesitantly, hoping they planned to stay nearby.

Grace's unabashed grin put Callie's heart at ease. "We're going home!" she bubbled. "Donovan's going to relocate his security business. After all"—she looked around the table, her affectionate gaze lingering for a few seconds on each face—"we want to keep our family close, always."

"That's the best news I've heard all day," Ben said with a relieved sigh.

"And what about you, Ethan?" Donovan inquired.

"I'm selling my cabin. Callie and Ben have generously offered to let me stay with them until Jes and Allie return from Baltimore. Then, I'm going to reach out to them, apologize, and do my best to be the father and grandfather I should have been all those years."

"Allie's gonna flip out... in a good way," Lee predicted. "For the last couple of days, we've been texting non-stop, so I know she's finally feeling better." He chuckled. "It's been hard to keep the secret, but I'm true to my word."

"And you're heading home tonight?" Grace asked Lee.

He grimaced but nodded. "That was the deal. I

promised to go back in time for school. I'll be glad when I'm graduated and won't have to miss any of the cool stuff."

Callie laughed and patted his arm. "You've seen more than your share of 'cool stuff' this week, Lee. We won't be far behind you."

THE FOLLOWING MORNING, on their flight to Philly, Callie and Taylor did their best to fill the rest of them in on the details of their first visit with Carozza.

"He's exceedingly bitter about what's happened to the Succouri," Callie lamented. "I know Doctor Navarro wanted to come with us today, but frankly, I'm relieved he changed his mind. I'm not sure Carozza's capable of forgiveness, though I'm hopeful, when he hears there's a way to reverse the damage and bring back the Antico, he might change his mind."

"He's endured substantial scorn and harassment," Taylor added, "including from his own wife and son. Until now, there's been no definitive way to prove his theories, so everyone's mocked him as a crazy fanatic. His son told us Carozza's wife left him because of his obsession. I hope this visit—coming face-to-face with indisputable evidence he's been correct all this time—will bring him peace at last."

"It's too bad he won't live to see it all change," Donovan said regretfully.

"But he'll get to see the beginning and meet the first benefactors of that change," Grace encouraged.

"Yes, he will," Ben agreed. "And that brings me to a matter I've wanted to discuss with you all but haven't found the right time to do so. As soon as the doctor can shift his focus away from your care, Donovan; he, Silvia, Callie, and I will begin the difficult task of tracking down and contacting every Succouri we can find and educating them on what we've learned. Doc's already spoken with Elena and Raul and they're planning to meet with us on Wednesday. I'm confident they'll join our cause as they obviously trust Doc and already know quite a bit about my unique situation. After that, we'll focus our efforts, at least initially, on persuading Succouri who are close to the ripening phase, as the urgency to convince them is greater. Though my childhood reception and transformation provide compelling evidence, the strongest proof lies with the two of you."

Ben turned to Ethan. "You experienced the first wakening. You can also verify that my Succouri is indeed spirited and that the transfer can occur through touch."

Ben shifted to Donovan. "And you are living, breathing evidence that the gift was received in that way and is thriving. If we have any chance at convincing people of this radically foreign perspective, we will need your testimonies."

Donovan leaned forward and started to speak, but Ben put up a hand. "Before you give an answer, please understand the risks involved here. Anonymity and privacy are essential safety nets in this life. Callie and I learned that lesson when we foolishly revealed our names to those we helped in the housefire. Not only did it result in unwanted publicity, but it also enabled her stalker to find us. Despite the need for it, I'm doubtful that remaining anonymous will be possible, at least not within the Succouri network. We'll have to be known to effectively bring about the kind of dramatic change we're seeking."

Apologetically, Ben looked at his father. "As you've now associated yourself closely with us, your job, reputation, and perhaps more may be at risk if we're discovered and investigated. We've already spoken to Lee, and our family has unanimously decided to stay the course as we believe this is our destined path, what we're meant to do regardless of the risks. I wish I didn't have to ask the same of each of you, but without your statements as evidence, I doubt we'll succeed. The blood transfers and the perceived right of each human host to select the inheritor of the gift are ingrained practices and ideas that some won't easily renounce. Please, before you give an answer, consider carefully what you're jeopardizing by partnering with us." He took Callie's hand. "Consider the loved ones whose lives will be impacted and make the choice that's best for you. You won't forfeit my friendship or respect if you decline."

Callie watched each face as they considered Ben's words. Surprisingly, no one appeared shaken or caught off guard by his warnings. The silence was merely a courtesy, respecting Ben's request to soberly deliberate before answering. It seemed that each of them, even Donovan and Grace, had already counted the costs that accompanied the generous gifts they'd received. Tears sprang to her eyes as her heart warmed at the invaluable friendship and selflessness of those surrounding them.

After a confirming nod from Grace, Donovan was the first to speak. "I may not be able to hear everything my Succouri whispers to me with complete clarity yet, but if there's one thing I'm absolutely sure of, it is this: just as the human part of me is forever indebted to the human part of you, Ben, for saving my life, so too the Succouri in me is eternally loyal and will remain faithful to your Succouri for bringing it back and giving it a new destiny." He chuckled at the truth in his next statement. "I literally couldn't live with myself if I... we didn't offer our unconditional, full support."

Ben lowered his head, humbled by their generosity of spirit. "Thank you both."

"But," Donovan added quickly, holding up a finger. "One of the ways I can help is by putting my skills and training to good use. There's a lot we can do to protect ourselves. Between Taylor and me, I'm confident we can put together a plan to effectively accomplish our mission while exercising caution. And even if something does go wrong, we can plan for that eventuality as well; sort of a hope for the best, but plan for the worst strategy."

"I agree, and I'm in," Taylor responded enthusiastically.

Ben sighed. "I was hoping the two of you would offer your expertise in this area. That takes a significant weight off our shoulders."

"Son..." Taylor began with conviction. "There's nothing more important to me than you and Callie: not my job, my freedom, or even my life. If sharing in your lives means sharing in your dangers, I consider it an honor and privilege to do so. No second thoughts or need for contemplation. I love you, both of you, with all my heart, and whatever I have is yours for the taking, no strings and no explanations needed."

Touched beyond words, Callie wiped at her eyes, then reached to squeeze Taylor's hand.

"Dad, I can't tell you how much that means to us," Ben said hoarsely, tears glistening in his eyes. "I never dreamed my father would turn out to be such a good man, a man well worth emulating. I'm very proud to call you 'Dad'."

As the two men grasped each other's hands, there wasn't a dry eye to be found in the group.

At long last, Ethan cleared his throat. "Ben, I want to help you, and I will do all I can, but I've spent the last fifteen years separated from my daughter and granddaughter. I don't think it's fair to immediately ask them to take that kind of risk before I've had the chance to earn their trust. They must be my priority, at least for the time being."

"I understand, and I absolutely agree," Ben said without hesitation.

"Unquestionably, I'm also indebted to your Succouri for what it did in healing me, but I owe much to them as well. Somehow, I'll need to figure out how to satisfy both obligations."

"Perhaps you can remain anonymous," Donovan suggested. "As you're no longer actively Succouri, you won't need to maintain a tight connection to the network. The revived Succouri resides in me now, so my testimony, along with an anonymous statement from my predecessor, may prove to be adequate in convincing most people. Even if we need to call on you to persuade a few holdouts, there are ways to safeguard your identity."

"Donovan's right," Taylor said. "Besides Ben and Callie, we have the doctor, Grace, Donovan, Maggie, Lee, and me as witnesses. In ninety-nine percent of cases, that will be more than enough to prove our assertions. Each time a touch transfer takes place, we'll gain more advocates. Before long, Ben and Callie will be the only ones who need to be involved in the process. I doubt it will be necessary for you to be directly involved much at all, certainly not by name."

"I know how your daughter feels about the Succouri," Callie cautioned. "We wouldn't want to provide her with additional reasons for distrusting the gift or those who possess it. I think there's great wisdom in your caution, Ethan."

"We promised to do all we could to help you restore your relationship with your family, and we will keep our word," Ben continued. "Sadly, at some point in the future, that may involve keeping your distance from us. Nevertheless, putting them first is the correct priority. You certainly don't owe me or my Succouri a single thing, Ethan. But, even if you did, this is exactly what we both want for you."

"I appreciate that." Ethan smiled at them, touched by their genuine understanding and support.

CHAPTER 14

THE VINDICATION

When they arrived at the nursing home where Carozza now resided, Taylor and Callie took the lead, knowing that they'd be quickly recognized by the ailing man. Though the facility wasn't fancy, as they approached his bedside, Callie was relieved that it was clean and safe.

Resting comfortably, Carozza didn't stir at their presence, but when she lightly touched his hand, he opened his eyes.

"Carozza," Taylor said quietly. "It's Wes Taylor and Callie Sawyer. We've returned as we promised we would."

It took him a moment to focus on their faces. "Donna Bellissima!" he exclaimed in a hoarse whisper. He turned his hand over and grasped Callie's, his grip weak, but affectionate.

Callie smiled at him as she leaned in closer. "It's good to see you again. We've brought some people who are very excited to meet you and offer you their gratitude."

Carozza's eyes opened wide. "Have you... Have you

brought him?" Carozza asked, his volume rising with hopeful anticipation.

Chuckling softly, Taylor stepped back so Ben could take his place beside Callie.

"Mr. Carozza," Callie said, her giddy voice reflecting Carozza's excitement. "I want you to meet my husband, Ben Sawyer."

Carozza's breath caught in his throat as his eyes locked on Ben's. He tried to sit up but was too weak. Swiftly, Ben reached for his arm, and when Ben touched him, Carozza gasped and put his free hand over his heart.

"Let me help you," Ben gently offered, his healing touch and supportive hold enabling Carozza to rise to a sitting position. As he continued to stare at Ben, his dark eyes filled with tears.

"It's an honor to meet you," Ben said with a smile.

"Indeed, you *are* the chosen one," he exclaimed in a breathy whisper filled with wonder and relief. "And you're... you're much more besides, Mr. Sawyer." His eyes danced with unspeakable joy. "You and your Datouri are Creatouri."

Ben looked at Callie questioningly, but she shook her head. "I don't understand."

Slowly, Carozza exhaled, closing his eyes as if savoring something too delicious to describe. "May I ask, are you both recovered?"

"We are," Ben answered.

Opening his eyes again, he focused on Callie, a coy smile playing on his lips. "And she's returned your Antico to you?"

Once more, Ben sought clarification from her, but she had no explanation to offer.

"How... how did you know about that?" Callie stammered.

A low chuckle shook his body. "At our last parting, you offered me healing, something no Datouri can do. At least, no ordinary Datouri." His gaze returned to Ben. "Has it not yet informed you?"

Initially, Ben raised his eyebrows, once again confused. But after a moment of pondering, understanding dawned. "It told us it wanted to give us a gift. That's all we know."

This time the chuckle burst forth in a full, ecstatic laugh. "Indeed! And what a gift it is! A blessing only extended a handful of times since the very beginning. How truly extravagant is your Antico's fondness for you to offer such a rare treasure!"

Callie put her hand to her heart. "What will the gift be?" she asked with reverence.

Carozza examined Callie with a satisfied smile for a long, silent moment as if trying to find something he'd lost in her eyes. "Favored Datouri. The gift has already come. Even now, you possess it."

Putting his hand to his forehead as he looked at Callie, Ben sighed. "I don't understand. What do we possess?"

"If your Antico has not yet revealed it, it is not my place to circumvent its timing, but I'm humbled to be visited by and receive strength from ones so distinctly honored, for truly, such an uncommon privilege would not be awarded without just cause."

Baffled, neither she nor Ben knew what to say. How could they have received a gift without their awareness? And, if they already had it, why hadn't their Succouri alerted them or given an explanation? These unanswered questions, along with Carozza's ecstatic delight at whatever they'd received, made Callie dizzy with confusion as she mentally searched for possible answers.

In addition, while she and Taylor had already grown somewhat accustomed to Carozza's circular way of communicating, Ben had not, and it was clear that he was caught off guard by it.

At last, Ben cleared his throat, choosing to redirect the conversation. "We came here today to thank you, Mr. Carozza. Your knowledge about the Antico saved my life, shifted my perspective about myself and my Succouri, and unlocked the calling Callie and I were meant to follow."

"It is I who is honored by your visit, but may I inquire, what have you learned?" He leaned toward them with great interest.

Callie found it puzzling that, while Carozza inherently knew many particular details about them, some of which they didn't know themselves, he was evidently unaware of their destined purpose. Perhaps, as it had been with Ben, his blind spots were direct results of his acquired prejudices. Because he firmly dismissed the possibility of repairing the damage that had been done to the Succouri, his staunch disbelief clouded his typically clear vision.

"On their last visit, you informed my father and Callie about the devastation caused by the blood transfers and how they had robbed the Antico of their will and their destinies."

Raising a tight fist in the air, Carozza's face began to redden with anger. "Traitors! All who receive this miraculous gift, then trample it under their feet deserve to suffer the worst hell can do to them." Here was the stumbling stone of bitterness that caused him to trip and fall on his path to complete understanding.

Shaking his head, Ben kept his voice soft and controlled as he countered Carozza's unjust verdict. "Without exception, every Succouri we've met, as well as those who support them, have been unaware of the truth. I don't deny that those who initiated this practice deserve blame, but neither I, nor my Antico equate innocent ignorance with intentional malice, Mr. Carozza."

Looking like a child who'd been corrected by a parent, Carozza lowered his gaze and softened his tone. "Nevertheless, the sorrow and devastation of losing an invaluable treasure forever is unfathomable."

Ben smiled. "Not forever, my friend. Because of your help, the Antico has not been irrevocably silenced."

Raising his eyes to Ben's again, he squinted in confusion. This was the first time since she'd met him that Carozza exhibited such uncertainty. Previously, he often had the answers before they asked the questions, but right now, he had no idea what Ben would say next.

Ben glanced behind them, and Grace, Donovan, and Ethan approached, lining up at the foot of Carozza's bed.

"I'd like you to meet some dear friends of ours. A week ago, Donovan was dying from traumatic injuries he sustained during his service as a Navy SEAL. Grace is Callie's best friend, and her love for Donovan kept him going through many difficult days. Ethan is a Succouri, who received his gift through blood forty years ago and recently entered the ripening stage. Before Callie and I became aware of your theories, we devised a plan to save Donavan's life through the transfer of Ethan's gift. We worked with a doctor in the network to bring everyone safely together, but before we could carry through with the procedure, things went awry with Callie and me. That's when she and my father came to see you. When they returned from their visit, they informed us of what they'd learned, and the doctor, Callie, and I began to ask ourselves some hard questions about the ethics of following through with the blood transfusion, even though not doing so meant certain death for Donovan. Just in time, our Antico gave us the answer, solved our dilemma."

Holding his breath, Carozza put a hand to his chest. If Callie weren't well aware of the strong draw Ben was enduring as he sustained the elderly man, she might believe he was suffering a heart attack as his face was pale and drawn.

Ben nodded to Ethan, and he cleared his throat.

"Through direct contact, Ben's Succouri temporarily moved into me, awakened mine, and healed the emptiness left by the death of my wife fifteen years ago."

Gaping, Carozza leaned forward so quickly that Ben almost lost contact with his arm. "Awakened? How do you know your Succouri was awakened?" His stare was intense, but not skeptical. As he definitively believed Ben to be the chosen one, his unconditional trust in him left no room for doubt, only eager curiosity.

"I experienced the change, in a big way," Ethan explained. "It was like a part of your body you've never paid much mind to—like maybe your elbow or knee—suddenly coming alive with sensations unlike anything you've ever experienced. And I heard Ben's Succouri speaking, almost as clearly as his human voice. As it accomplished its task, mine also began to speak, express itself in kind, only less... wise, less confident." Ethan shook his head in frustration. "It's hard to explain as there's no experience similar enough to provide a reasonable comparison. After Ben's Succouri returned to him, there was a time of disorientation as I sorted through the jumbled messages coming from this new, independent voice in my head. When Ben reminded me that Donovan was in trouble, it all fell into place. I understood it couldn't stay with me, and in truth, I didn't want it to. It wanted to leave, and I was ready to be human again. This mutual realization initiated an impulse to reach out to Donovan, the force of which was many times stronger than the normal urge Succouri feel to touch the suffering. This was a non-negotiable directive, like the biological mandate to breathe."

As no one in the room had heard about his experience in this much detail, Ethan had everyone's undivided attention as he continued. "When I made contact with Donovan, I felt it go. For a moment, I panicked, hoping its absence wouldn't open another hole in me similar to the one Ben's Succouri had just healed. But as it departed, it felt much more like an unburdening, a lifting of a heaviness I'd become accustomed to throughout the years." Ethan locked eyes with Carozza. "Perhaps it's because of my wife's death that I feel this way, but I've had a week to think about it, and I'm increasingly convinced that it's more than that. I don't believe I was ever meant to be Succouri. It saved my life, gave me many happy years with Lexi and my daughter, and I'm grateful for that, but if it had been the Succouri's imperative rather than my human donor, I don't believe I would have been selected. The Succouri that was awakened inside me didn't resemble me. We didn't fit together, match one another; not like Ben's does with him. When his Succouri spoke in my head, I could have sworn it was Ben, the human being standing beside my bed. The empathy, choice of words, outlook, personality, everything was distinctly Ben. If he struggles at times to differentiate its voice from his own, I believe that's simply because there's hardly a discernable difference between them. I, perhaps better than anyone ever can or will, understand why Ben was the precise one his Antico was waiting for all those centuries."

Caught off guard and overwhelmed by these revelations, Ben shifted his weight. Callie tightened her hold on his arm as she could feel the draw's effects taking a toll.

"But, Ethan, just because your personality didn't align as closely with your Succouri's nature as mine, doesn't necessarily mean you weren't meant to be Succouri."

All eyes turned to Carozza.

"Though the match will not be perfect until the Antico reaches the end of its journey, each chosen host will have some common qualities, both in personality as well as physical features." He gestured to Ben before continuing. "I've been uniquely privileged to know three hosts of Ben's Antico. Marvelously, each one has had those same unusual blue eyes, and Owen Briggs possessed a nearly identical disposition. As the Antico craves the one-of-a-kind union it will someday enjoy with its perfect counterpart, it will select hosts who, in some way, resemble him, allowing it a taste of what's to come. The closer the resemblance the faster the integration and the tighter the bond. Of course, all of this was only true before the Succouri were diminished by the blood transfers."

Recalling how Maggie had teased Ben about his blue eyes perhaps being an inheritance from his Succouri progenitor rather than his human one, Callie smiled at how she hadn't been that far off.

"Then that confirms it for me," Ethan said, crossing his arms. "Once it was revived, we both felt the awkwardness of the incompatibility. We weren't well suited, but I believe Donovan is."

"Then, your Succouri voluntarily departed?" Carozza questioned. "You didn't coerce it in any way?"

"None whatsoever. As soon as I touched Donovan, it left. Prior to that, however, as Ben suggested, I did have to make the choice to relinquish it, which was an easy decision for me. The moment I did, it began urging me to reach out to Donovan."

"Then perhaps," Ben conjectured, offering Ethan a compassionate smile. "Because of your willingness to trust and be the first to undergo the awakening and attempt the touch transfer, you were more fated to be Succouri than you realize."

As he spoke, Callie's concern for him grew as his arms began subtly trembling. This was a crucial conversation but Carozza's health was so poor that curing him was rapidly draining Ben's strength. They may never again have the chance to benefit from this man's knowledge, but her husband's wellness was her main concern.

"Are you alright," she whispered.

He wrapped his free arm around her and pulled her tightly against him, and the trembling temporarily ceased. "A few more minutes," he whispered back. She leaned her cheek against his neck, trying to offer him all she could.

"But I don't understand," Carozza exclaimed, looking very uncomfortable with the unfamiliar admission as he rubbed his nearly bald head. "How could the Succouri be revived when it had long ago lost its path? If there had still been a way to reach its intended, it would not have fallen silent in the first place."

Everyone, including Carozza, shifted their gaze to Ben. As he probed his Succouri for an answer, he struggled to concentrate through the encroaching fog of weariness. "My present understanding is that the awakening resets the

Antico's journey: assigns it a new ultimate match and a new final mission. Ethan compared the distinction between his newly awakened Succouri and my ancient one to that of a child versus an adult. This makes sense if the awakening was, in essence, a rebirth, not just a revival."

"Then how was it that Donovan, who was chosen by your human impulses, just so happened to be the correct heir for Ethan's particular Succouri?" Carozza asked.

Ben took a shaky breath and Carozza at last noticed his strain. "In this case, Callie and I are convinced it was my Antico who orchestrated the match. It is the only Succouri in existence who can restore what's been lost: reignite the Succouri's spirit and give it a new purpose. Because of this unique ability, we've come to accept that awakening the Succouri is our lifelong assignment, but convincing others to adopt this new paradigm won't be easy. To convince me and others in the network that your theories were and are correct and that the blood transfers should end, proof was required, a tangible example of a successful rebirth and touch transfer. I don't presently have the strength or time to go into all the details but trust me when I say the coincidences are too numerous and incredible to ignore or dismiss. Ethan and Donovan were intentionally selected to be the first, the authentication of what you've spent a lifetime proclaiming. I'm close to the end of my strength, so I want to say this while you're still well and able to hear it. You've been right all along, and because you spoke the truth, everything is about to change. We won't rest until every Succouri is reborn and the blood transfers are relics of the distant past. I give you my word."

Carozza's eyes filled with tears, and Ben held on, even as his body began to tremble.

Staring at the floor as if in deep concentration, Donovan

slowly walked to the opposite side of Carozza's bed. "Ben, I... I think I can help. I feel like... like I should help."

Callie stepped away from Ben and reached her hand across the bed to Donovan. When he touched her, she laughed in delight and looked at Grace. "He's ready. It's time for the adventure of a lifetime!"

Though everyone else smiled, as he released her hand, Donovan was visibly shaken.

He wiped his hand across his brow. "You weren't kidding about the draw, Ben, though 'unpleasant' isn't the word I would use to describe it. It reminds me of the torture exercises they put us through during SEAL training to test our physical endurance."

Ben grimaced empathetically. "I wish I could tell you it gets easier or that you'll get used to it with time." He shook his head. "Sorry. I can't. In fact, the draw from Callie is relatively weak. You don't have to—"

"I think you know better than anyone that I have to do this. The voice in my head isn't open to negotiation or compromise. I can take it. I passed every one of those tests with flying colors, though I can't say I enjoyed them." He offered a reassuring smile before continuing. "I'm certainly feeling substantially more gratitude for what you did for me over the last few weeks. The SEALS would have loved to have you, Ben, as you make this look easy. I had no idea. But this is what I signed up for, so I'd rather just jump into the deep end with both feet."

Though Callie already had a good idea of how agonizing and incapacitating the draw was, witnessing Donovan's shocked reaction to it, despite his background and training, filled her with fresh pride in her husband's persistent courage and sacrifice.

"Can I help him?" Grace asked, fear in her eyes.

"Not yet." Callie put a hand on her shoulder. "It takes more time to develop your gift."

Donovan sent Grace a reassuring nod and smile before placing a hand on Carozza's arm. He sucked in a slow breath of air and braced himself with his free hand, adjusting to the unfamiliar and intense pressure of the draw. Ben stayed in place for a few seconds, watching his friend carefully. Setting his jaw, Donovan flashed the 'okay' sign with his free hand, and Ben exhaled and let go of Carozza. "Thank you, my friend."

Ethan moved to Donovan's side. "Without help from a Datouri, you won't be able to hang on for long. Please, don't overdo it on your first day. You will eventually pass out if you aren't careful and recovering alone from that takes days. After using your gift for a while, you'll learn where that line is so you can avoid crossing it, but for now, you should stop when your arms begin shaking. Can you feel the kickback?"

Unable to speak as he focused on enduring the draw, he wobbled his head at Ethan.

"It's like a drop of cool water on your parched tongue, a slight, inadequate relief, but if you focus your mind on it, it sort of, grows, or at least seems to."

Covering his eyes to concentrate, Donovan slowly nodded his understanding.

Everyone, but particularly Carozza, watched with a mix of anxiety and wonder. For the first time, the old man studied Donovan carefully. "Every word Ben has said can be trusted as the integrity of those in a terminal triad is of the highest quality. He says you were the intended recipient, the next in line, and indeed, I see in your eyes a wisdom and courage that will benefit your newly reborn Succouri. It will learn quickly, however, and soon have much to teach you as well. Learn to hear its voice and guard it carefully. Don't allow anyone to silence it again. When the time comes for it to move on, you must submit to its choice no matter how tempting it may be to grasp that power. Most assuredly, there will never again be a Succouri like Ben, who can resurrect the lost, so you must be unmovable in this pledge, and you must charge your inheritor with the same."

He paused, leaning in close to Donovan and staring into his brown eyes. Though the scrutiny verged on aggressive, Donovan didn't look away. "Because the chosen one and his Antico selected you and granted life to you and your Succouri, it is your obligation, yours and your Datouri's, to stay by their side. You must walk the difficult road with them, clear their path, keep them from harm, and remain loyal for a lifetime, even after your Succouri has departed. This is the unique privilege and sacred duty you're charged with as you were the first to benefit from their calling."

"Gladly," Donovan said without hesitation.

Though profoundly moved and comforted by both the prophetic provision and the ready acceptance of the extended proposition, Ben lightly chuckled. "A few days ago, I teasingly informed him that he could repay me by being my lifelong friend. It appears that request was more than wishful thinking on my part."

Taylor stepped closer to the foot of the bed next to Grace. "Carozza, how do you know all of this? Where does your uncanny insight come from?"

Carozza's expression shifted to sly amusement. "A healing touch is not the only gift offered by the Succouri. There are secondary gifts that can come to those who do not possess an indweller, but whose ancestral bloodline has been kissed by an Antico."

"What does that mean?"

"I will say no more on that matter as to do so would demonstrate great disrespect, but I will tell you this much: I have a gift of my own. When my human pride doesn't get in the way, I can see."

"What do you see?" Callie inquired.

"Commonly prompted by touch, I see visions about the Succouri, insights into its past, present, and future.

"Like Louis," Ben mumbled, but only Callie heard him.

"I'm the only one in many generations of my family to manifest this gift, the last documented possessor living two hundred years ago."

"And I take it your son does not have the gift," Taylor said with a smirk.

"He does not. I am the last as there is no one left to carry on the bloodline. The light of my family is fading away, but"—he grinned so broadly that the expression almost looked painful—"this gift too will be reborn. I was a fool to believe the Succouri would become extinct, vanish from this world. I underestimated its wisdom and foresight, and I overestimated man's power to extinguish it." He turned pleading eyes to Ben. "Please forgive me."

BEN'S SUCCOURI STIRRED, then clearly spoke to him. Looking across the bed at Donovan, he saw the slight tremble in his hand. "Can you hold on for one more minute, my friend? There's something I'm supposed to do, but I'll need you to keep him whole while I carry it out."

Donovan nodded, gripping Carozza with both hands.

With his right hand, Ben reached for Callie, and she interlinked her fingers around his. He placed his left hand on Carozza's forehead.

Within seconds, Ben felt the shifting, much weaker

than when he'd touched Ethan, yet intense enough to leave him dizzy. Carozza sharply inhaled, but then blew a slow breath through his lips as his expression became dreamy. He stared at the ceiling, lost in a private vision that not even Ben and Callie could see.

Though there was no ominous black hole this time, Callie once again grounded Ben's mind, keeping him conscious and connected to reality. Ben was distantly aware of a nurse opening the door to Carozza's room and Taylor reacting quickly, intercepting and cleverly maneuvering her out into the hallway with an improvised question about Carozza's care.

When the stirring at last ceased, Ben removed his hand and lifted his eyes to Donovan. "You can let go now. He's at peace, and his pain is gone."

Donovan complied, and Grace pulled a chair over to him. Blowing out a relieved breath, he sat and put his head in his hands for a moment as he tried to regain his equilibrium.

"I'm going to go get you both some water," Ethan announced, patting Donovan on the shoulder before moving toward the door.

Callie put her arm around Ben's waist. Despite her small frame, she felt remarkably strong and solid as she supported him in his weakened condition. Contemplatively, he watched Carozza's face, but his eyes didn't open.

The nurse entered, followed by Taylor, and they all stepped away from the bed so she could check his vitals.

"He's fading fast," she announced. "I don't think he'll make it through the day. Are you all family?"

"Yes, we are," Ben answered, his words bearing no falsehood. The Succouri family they all now belonged to was as real as the human ones they claimed. With his wisdom and insight, Carozza was a pillar of that family.

"It's good he'll have love around him in the end," she said with a charming southern accent. "He hasn't had visitors until today. Y'all from out of town?"

"Yes, ma'am," Ben replied.

"Well, y'all look exhausted, so don't overdo it."

"Understood." Ben offered the woman a genuine smile of appreciation for her kind concern.

When she'd gone, they circled around the bed once more, but Carozza remained still and quiet. Callie took his hand, wanting him to feel the warmth of human contact while sparing Donovan and Ben any additional draw.

Ethan returned and handed each of them a bottle of water. Unsure whether he had slipped into a coma or was simply asleep, they waited. No one considered leaving as something compelled them to maintain the silent vigil.

Half an hour passed before Carozza's eyelids finally opened, just a sliver. He weakly smiled at Callie and Ben. "It forgave me, and it took away my pain," he whispered, and they all leaned closer to hear him. "It showed me the future, how it will happen, and it provided an answer to my life-long quandary. What an extraordinary journey awaits you! I both envy and pity you, but there's never been a love or destiny like yours, and that will be your strength and joy all your days. Trust your Antico. It is infinitely wise and good. It will not lead you astray as it faithfully loves you and will always seek your well-being. Thank you for the sacrifices you have already made and the ones you will bear in the years to come. Because of you, it was worth it: every loss and each rejection. Though, throughout my life, my voice was muzzled, through you, I will sing a triumphant song that will be heard in the farthest corners of the earth."

Tears ran down Callie's cheeks and Ben set a hand on Carozza's shoulder. "You won't be forgotten. You'll be remembered as a part of our family now."

"Then I am indeed eternally blessed! *Arrivederci, amici miei.*"

With that, a full smile filled his face, and he closed his eyes and took his final breath.

CHAPTER 15

THE REUNION

On Wednesday, their meeting with Raul and Elena ended with a vow of full support and an offering of assistance in carrying out their mission to contact and instruct every Succouri in the network on what they'd discovered. Though the positive experience encouraged them, they didn't dare to hope that all their attempts to win over fellow Succouri would go so smoothly. There was already a solid foundation of trust between them, and when Elena's father spoke with strong conviction and emotion about his regrets, Elena's eyes filled with tears.

After talking with Donovan, Raul was anxious to awaken his Succouri and was disappointed to learn that he would have to wait until the ripening. Nevertheless, Raul pledged to seek out Ben's assistance as soon as the first signs of the phase manifested and to yield to his Succouri's choice for an inheritor.

Ben could see in Raul's eyes how this new knowledge changed his perspective of the gift. As Ben had, Raul perceived it as an inanimate tool, unquestionably extraordinary but not interactive or autonomous. It had been Ben's resentment that blocked his Succouri's voice, but once that was gone, he began hearing it and benefiting from the close relationship. It saddened him that others wouldn't get that chance until the ripening, and at that point, they would have a short time to enjoy it before the Succouri transferred to its next host.

Besides Donovan, it would be a long time until there were others who could relish the experience of a full partnership with their Antico. Even then, besides Callie, there likely wouldn't be anyone else who could share the pleasures of being part of a fully united terminal union. Each night, as they lay together in one another's arms, they excitedly chatted about new revelations and experiences, knowing the other would truly understand.

"Ben," Callie whispered in the dark as she lay pressed up against his warm body. "What do you think the gift is?"

Ben chuckled as he played with her curls, twisting them gently around his fingers. "I can't figure it out. If we already possess it, how can we not know about it, and why is our Antico holding back? It's shared so much with us but it's keeping this one to itself."

"Do you think it's another special ability, something else only our Succouri can do?"

Ben thought about it for a moment before answering. "I didn't get that impression when it told me about it from the reflecting pool. It was more like something for us, the human us. When Carozza spoke about it, he focused on you, Callie. I was hoping... I guess I wished it was permanent healing for your eyes, not that I mind holding your hand." He lifted her hand to his lips. "I wouldn't touch you any less if you could see perfectly without me, but I would get a lot of comfort and pleasure from knowing that, even when I'm not beside you, you could still see."

She leaned in to kiss the side of his mouth. "Since Carozza said we already have the gift, that rules out that possibility. Besides, I think this gift is for both of us."

"Oh, trust me, that gift would have brought me as much happiness as it would you."

Smiling, she lifted onto her elbow to look down into his eyes. "The other thing he said that keeps echoing inside my head is the comment about his bloodline." She pressed her lips together, recalling his exact words. "'Kissed by an Antico'. What in the world could that mean?"

"Carozza certainly had a way of talking in code. I'm impressed with how much you and Dad took away from your first visit, as I was lost for most of our conversation with him. We may never know what he meant unless our Succouri chooses to reveal it or unless we meet another seer like Carozza. It's a shame we came to know him so late in his life. I'm positive there was a lot more we could have learned from him."

"At least we were able to comfort him and ease his fears before it was too late. He looked at you like... like you were his hero. I know meeting the host of a final match was a lifelong dream."

"I don't think I'll ever understand or get used to the idea of being chosen." He shrugged and grimaced. "I'm just an ordinary man who's been given some extraordinary gifts, the most precious of which is lying in my arms right now." He smiled lovingly at her.

"There's nothing remotely ordinary about you, Ben Sawyer. Without a single magical gift, you have the most beautiful soul I've ever known." She winked flirtatiously and ran her hand slowly up his chest. "Wrapped up in an irresistibly handsome package."

Letting go of her curls, he took her in his arms. Then, in one quick motion, he rolled them over, and she giggled in surprise and delight. Taking his time, he brushed her skin with soft kisses from her shoulders up her neck, at last finding her lips. "There's nothing in this universe as irresistibly lovely as you," he whispered as his touch sent thrilling waves of heat through her body. In blissful surrender, she closed her eyes and allowed his love to enrapture her: heart, soul, and body.

If it were possible, she would choose to remain always in his arms, happily discarding any other pleasures life offered as none could come close to the ecstasy she found there. The more she was with him, the more she dreamed of him, day and night, and she knew he felt the same unquenchable passion for her. Though they'd had plenty to distract them in the last few weeks, the challenges and uncertainties drew them together more frequently and fervently as they found a lasting peace and refreshing joy available nowhere else.

Looking back, Callie couldn't fathom how she'd survived before she met him, or how they'd ever resisted the insatiable need for one another. She wondered if this was how all couples felt, or at least all Succouri couples. Carozza had said there had never been a love like theirs, so perhaps this incurable addiction to one another was unprecedented. But she would happily remain hooked on loving him forever. She had no desire to cure her habit. Ben was hers and she was his, and her greatest wish was to freely indulge in loving him for the rest of her life.

When she opened her eyes the following morning and

saw Ben sitting on the edge of the bed, dressed, and looking anxious, she abruptly sat up.

"Sweetheart. Are you alright?" he asked, reaching to stroke her cheek.

When she looked at him with confusion, he pointed to the clock on the nightstand. She was stunned to see that it was after ten.

"For the last few days, you've seemed unusually tired, which is understandable given what we've been through, but is that all there is to it?"

Putting her palm to her forehead, she shook her head. "I'm not sure. I don't think I've ever slept this much in my life. I just always feel tired, even though I'm getting plenty of rest."

"Maybe a few additional tests from the doc would be prudent, but we'll need to do that today." A sorrowful expression shadowed his face.

"Ben? What's wrong?"

"I just got a call from Lee. Louis passed away last night. The funeral will be in a few days."

"Oh no!" she exclaimed, putting a hand over her heart. "Poor Ms. Essie! We need to go home."

She threw off the covers and started to get out of bed, but Ben put his hands on her shoulders. "I've arranged a flight for us tomorrow. We have the day to pack, settle things here, and get those tests done."

Sighing as tears sprang to her eyes, Callie slumped, and Ben pulled her to him. "We'll all be there for her. Everyone's flying back with us, and Dad will join us for the funeral. Allie and Jessica will be back home soon as well, so we'll get Ethan there in plenty of time to prepare for that reunion."

"This place has come to feel like home, too," she mumbled against his chest.

Besides her childhood home, Callie had never so readily adapted to a house before. Though it was unquestioningly beautiful, there was something warm and endearing about it. The sounds of the ocean and the constant breezes that floated through the open windows soothed her soul, and every moment she'd spent there with Ben had been blissfully happy.

"I had a notion you'd like this place. I do, too, and there aren't any ghosts from my past hanging around, so we can fill it with our own beautiful memories. Consider it our second home. I think we'll have plenty of opportunities to use it. I was thinking..."

"Yes?"

"I'd like to get my pilot's license. We seem to be flying around the country with increasing frequency, and I don't see that changing anytime soon. It would be convenient to have our own plane and be able to fly us myself. Who knows, it may also come in handy someday if we have to make a quick escape."

She smiled, happy to see him excited about accomplishing a uniquely human dream. "That's a wonderful idea!"

Leaning her away from him, he looked at her with surprise. "Really? I wasn't sure you'd be comfortable with it."

Playfully, she swiftly kissed his lips. "I'd be completely comfortable flying in a plane with you at the... wheel?" She scrunched up her face. "Or whatever you call the steering thingy on a plane."

Ben laughed. "Perhaps we both need lessons. After all, I will need a copilot."

With a giggle, Callie shook her head. "I may not know much about planes, but I'm pretty sure you'll need both hands to fly one. I think a blind copilot would not be your best choice."

Grinning confidently, he took her hands in his. "We can do anything, Callie Sawyer. We'll figure it out."

"Whatever you say, beloved," she acquiesced, not doubting for a moment that they would.

Louis Jones' funeral was packed. It seemed to Ben and Callie that the entire community had come out to honor the revered hero. Touching stories were told about his days on the force and his faithful love for his wife. Those who had been saved by Louis' Succouri touch were cautious in their wording, protecting his secret even in death.

Ben spoke briefly about his mentor, his admiration and affection for the man audible in his voice and the tears glistening in his eyes.

"Louis and Ms. Essie rescued me. They didn't let me lose hope or give up on love, even when I felt utterly unworthy. Louis spoke hope directly to my soul during a time when mine was running dry. His last words to me were to take every opportunity to love my wife, do good, and live out my purpose, and I will honor his memory by doing my very best to follow that advice as I can't imagine there's any wiser counsel."

Though Ms. Essie cried during the testimonials, she was remarkably strong, extending compassion to everyone even in her unbearable grief.

Though Callie and Ben checked on her each day, bringing her flowers or something sweet, for now, they kept quiet about what they'd learned during their time in Cape Cod. They wanted her heart to begin to heal before shocking her with the new revelations about the Succouri.

Through Lee's communication with Allie, they learned that she and her mother had returned to town the day after Louis' funeral. Allie's recovery was going well, and the doctors were optimistic about her long-term prognosis. She was anxious to see them again, and even her mother seemed amenable to the idea.

After taking a few days to arrange for the sale of his cabin and the storage of his personal belongings, Ethan took Ben and Callie up on their offer and came to stay with them. Strategizing how to set up the initial reunion was complicated. They didn't want to deceive Jessica, but on the other hand, they didn't want her to outright reject a meeting with Ethan before giving him the chance to explain and apologize. In the end, the three of them decided to invite Jessica to their home for lunch while Lee went to the Hughes home to visit with Allie. Callie placed the phone call, and though Jessica sounded confused by the arrangement, she ultimately agreed to come.

When she arrived at their door, Callie and Ben warmly greeted her. Though still guarded, her demeanor was softer than their last encounter. When they had settled in the living room, Jessica spoke up quickly. "I want to thank you. I was expecting an astronomical bill for that transport flight." Momentarily looking down, she nervously pushed a strand of black hair behind her ear. "I was baffled when my bill arrived with the words 'paid in full' across the top, so I looked into it. Doctor Karl told me what you did." She put her palms together and lifted them to her chin, as she shook her head. "Truthfully, I had no idea how I was going to pay for the bills, especially that one, but my daughter is my whole world, so I figured even if I had to file for bankruptcy, if she recovered, it would be well worth it."

A single tear hung in the corner of her eye. "You can't

know how relieved I am to have that weight taken off my shoulders." She lowered her hands to her lap. "I don't know what more to say besides, thank you."

Leaning forward, Ben smiled. "It was an honor to meet you and your daughter and be a part of your journey. We couldn't be happier to hear how well she's doing."

Though she smiled back at them, she wrinkled her forehead in confusion. "She's anxious to see you again, and she can't stop talking about the Succouri. After meeting the two of you, she asked me a hundred questions. We could have met at my house so you could have seen her. I would have been happy to—"

"We're anxious to see her again, but we had something important we wanted to discuss privately with you first," Callie interjected, keeping her voice steady.

"Oh?" Jessica straightened, uncertainty triggering her defenses.

"Something truly wonderful can come of it, if you're willing to open your heart," Callie encouraged, and Jessica's shoulders relaxed, though her suspicious expression remained in place.

Rising, Ben went to the fireplace and lifted two photographs off the mantle. "When Callie and I met, her father had just suffered a severe stroke. Doctor Karl did everything he could, but in the end, we lost him." He brought the pictures back to the couch and handed the one of Ronald LeVray to Jessica.

Still puzzled, she politely took it and studied the image. "He looks a lot like you and Lee, especially the eyes and smile," she said to Callie.

As she spoke, Callie's smile faded. "My mother also had green eyes, and Lee got his red hair from her."

Ben exchanged pictures with Jessica. As she took in the

image of Molly LeVray, vague recognition flashed in her expression, though she hadn't yet put all the pieces together.

"She looks familiar. I feel like I've met her before." She looked up at Callie. "But then, you look so much like her, so that's probably it. I remember you telling me you lost her years ago. I'm sorry."

Anxiously, Callie bit her lip, and Ben took her hand. "Mrs. Hughes," Ben started, but Jessica put up her hand.

"Please call me Jessica."

"Alright, Jessica. Molly LeVray died in a car accident fifteen years ago. She was driving under the influence and hit another car, killing a woman instantly."

Jessica dropped the photograph onto her lap and put a hand over her mouth.

"Molly LeVray?" she said, wide-eyed like she'd just seen a ghost.

Callie sighed and nodded. "My maiden name is Callie LeVray."

"She... She killed my mother," she whispered, looking at the ground.

"Yes. Jessica, I'm deeply sorry." As she had with Ethan, Callie recounted the story of her mother's alcoholism and how it had impacted her father as well as her and Lee. Callie pleaded for forgiveness for her mother's irresponsible act, which had resulted in tragedy and pain. When she was finished, crying softly as Ben held her close, Jessica sat stoic and silent, staring blankly.

As their hearts ached, Jessica's eyes grew cold, and she abruptly pointed her finger accusingly at Ben. "Is this why you paid for the flight, to try to make up for—"

"Absolutely not," Ben replied gently but firmly. "We didn't discover the connection to you and Allie until several days after we left you in Baltimore. Callie's father never told her the name of the woman who was killed, as she and Lee were young children when this happened."

Jessica lowered her head into her hands. "Molly LeVray killed my mother, but she also destroyed my father. My father was Succouri, so losing her broke him, destroyed him. He ran away and left me to deal with her death. He's never even met Allie. Even after Gordon died, he didn't reach out to help me or comfort us. I don't have a mother or a father anymore thanks to Molly LeVray and the Succouri." Through her anger, Callie heard the sobs that rose from the core of her being, evidence of an abiding pain that had been locked away for far too long.

"Jes, you still have a father."

Every eye in the room looked up. Ethan Devereaux stood in the doorway, making no attempt to wipe away the tears that dripped into his beard. Slowly, he approached Jessica.

"Dad?" Jessica stood to her feet, blinking at him as if unconvinced that the man before her was really her father.

"Yes, honey. It's me. How do I begin to explain, to beg for your forgiveness for the years I've wronged you and Allie? I—"

"No!" Jessica shouted, backing away and balling her hands into fists. "You don't get to do this. You don't get to walk in here after fifteen years of outright neglect: no help, no support, no... nothing, and apologize." She grabbed her purse off the chair and rushed from the room. Ben and Callie rose, but stayed where they were, letting Ethan take the lead.

"Jes, please, just hear me out," Ethan pleaded.

Jessica spun around, her eyes ablaze with rage. "How could you! I had to go to the morgue to identify her body. I had to plan her funeral. I had to sell the house, manage everything all alone while you ran like a coward. You didn't even care about meeting your granddaughter. You betrayed me and Allie, and you betrayed Mom's memory." The rage gave way to sorrow as she continued to shout through her sobs. "Did you even know that Gordon died? Cancer ate him from the inside out, little by little. Where were you? Where was my father? Then Allie got sick. I've spent the last year working double shifts to pay for her medical bills while sitting up worrying night after night that I might lose the very last person in my life I love and who connects me to Mom." She gritted her teeth as her body trembled. "You think your Succouri curse caused you pain? I've had nothing but pain and loss for fifteen years, Dad, but I've had to keep going and take care of my husband and daughter. I couldn't selfishly walk away and throw myself a private pity-party for a decade and a half. I took care of everyone alone."

She sat down on the bench in the foyer and wept bitterly. Callie's heart broke. Though she knew the comfort she extended might be unwanted, she couldn't stand by and watch Jessica suffer without at least trying to console her.

Crossing the room, she sat beside her and put an arm around her trembling shoulders. Not knowing what she could possibly say to ease her pain, she remained silent, even when Jessica surrendered and collapsed against her shoulder. Ben approached Ethan and patted his back, encouraging him to hang on and not run away from the consequences of the hurt he'd caused his daughter.

Both she and Ben hoped that Ethan's willingness to accept the blame and remain humbly available for reconcil-iation would be the evidence Jessica would need to prove that he'd undergone a genuine change of heart. She expected him to withdraw, which was all the more reason to stand firm. This was the only way to earn her trust, but it was difficult to watch their mutual pain play out in front of their eyes.

After a few minutes, Jessica's weeping subsided. She leaned away from Callie, reached into her purse to retrieve a Kleenex, and wiped at her nose and eyes. Without looking at her father, she stood and flung her purse over her shoulder. "I have to go. I can't deal with this right now."

"If... if you change your mind and want to talk," Ethan said hoarsely. "I'll be here. I'm not going anywhere. I promise."

For a second, she made eye contact, studying him carefully. Then, without another word, she turned her back to him and left.

Stumbling into the living room, Ethan slumped into a chair and Ben and Callie sat across from him.

"Remember that tight ball of resentment and pain I predicted might come your way?" Ben asked, and Ethan nodded and sighed. "She needed to let that out, get it off her chest. It's part of the healing process. Don't get discouraged."

Ethan swiped his thumb under his eyes. "I don't think she'll ever forgive me, and I don't know if she should. She's absolutely right about everything."

Ben crossed his arms. "Callie also thought you would never forgive her that morning when you stormed out of the Navarro house after learning Molly LeVray was Callie's mother. You needed time, not just to get over the shock, but also to sort through your feelings. It's the same with Jessica."

"She'll give you a chance to explain, Ethan," Callie

comforted. "If she wasn't interested in setting things right, she would have left immediately. She stuck around long enough to let you see her hurt. If she truly didn't care, she wouldn't have bothered."

"I hope you're right," Ethan replied, looking largely unconvinced despite their assurances.

THE FOLLOWING DAY, Callie was unpacking from their trip and reorganizing their closet when she came across a large white tube in one of the boxes Ben hadn't yet unpacked. She carried it to the gray couch and pulled off the lid, feeling oddly guilty about going through his belongings, even though he was her husband and everything they owned belonged to both of them.

Inside the tube was a large, rolled-up paper. Though she couldn't see it well without Ben's touch, she recognized it as an architectural drawing. She smiled, as she'd never seen his work before.

A few minutes later, he came looking for her and found her curled up on the couch studying the plans as best she could. Chuckling, he leaned against the doorframe and crossed his arms. "Would you like some help with that, sweetheart?" he inquired with amusement.

Grinning up at him a little sheepishly, she patted the spot next to her on the couch. "Yes, please. Sorry, but I've never seen your work before. What is this?"

He crossed the room, sat next to her, and put an arm around her shoulders, shifting the curled paper so it was spread open across both their laps. "There's no need to apologize. Everything I am and everything I have is yours. During those miserable nights the week before our wedding, I didn't sleep. Every time I drifted off, I dreamed someone was hunting you, and I couldn't see them. It was so disturbing that I just stayed up, but that gave me a lot of free time, so..." He tapped the page with his finger.

As her vision focused, though she still didn't understand many of the architectural markings, she was impressed by the detail and obvious skill in the work. "Ben, I don't know anything about architecture, but this looks... It's beautiful. What kind of building is this?"

"What do you imagine I was dreaming about days before marrying you?"

Raising her eyebrows, she gazed at him as she tapped a finger on her chin. "A... A house?"

Still grinning, he winked at her.

Looking back at the drawing, she whistled. "This would be a fabulous house, but Ben, don't we already have a lot of those?"

"Not one that's uniquely ours, planned and designed by you and me."

She leaned back a few inches so she could read the expression on his face. "Do you want that?"

Excitement flashed in his eyes, but then he looked away and shrugged. "I'm content to live with you anywhere." He started rolling up the paper. "It was just something to do to kill time while—"

Countering his progress, she rolled the page back out, securing it firmly with both hands. "Let's do it!"

"What? No, Callie, really I—"

"I want to live in a house designed by my husband." Tilting her head she tapped her finger on the paper. "Nearby, but out in the country. Maybe on a lake or with a large pond." She paused to nod definitively. "That's my dream now. You can't take it back." She smiled up at him.

"But what about this house? You... We have so many memories here and Lee—"

"Lee is going to love the idea. He hates the city. And we can keep this place. We're about to have a steady flow of visitors coming to awaken their Succouri. This can be a guest house. Or perhaps your father will want to retire here or Rosa and Leo. We'll have plenty of uses for it. But I love the idea of our own memories, a home that's yours and mine right from the start. And I can't wait to see your skills in action." She giggled at her unintentionally suggestive choice of words. "Your architectural skills, that is."

As he recognized that her enthusiasm was entirely genuine, a new light began to shine in his eyes, and she delighted in witnessing an old passion, another which was distinctly human, rise again. So much of their lives from now on would be focused on their Succouri calling. Staying connected to his human dreams would bring an essential sense of balance.

"A place out of town is what I had in mind as well, both for privacy and security. And if we designed it from the ground up, we could work with Donovan on including state-of-the art security systems to keep you safe if I'm ever—"

His enthusiastic brainstorming was interrupted by the buzzing of his phone. He retrieved it from his pocket.

"The doctor," he informed her as he accepted the call. Though Ben and the doctor were anxious to embark on their mission, Ben had asked him to give Callie and him a few days to settle back home and mourn the loss of Louis before jumping in with both feet. Though this was a bit sooner than they'd expected, the doctor never called unless he had a good reason.

"Afternoon, Doc... We're doing fine. Everything alright

with you and Silvia?... Yes, she's here. I'll put you on speaker."

Ben set the phone on top of the house plans and sent Callie a look of curiosity.

"Okay, we're both listening."

The doctor cleared his throat and when he spoke, his tone was almost giddy, which was something they'd never heard from him before. "I need you both back in my lab as soon as you can manage it." The words were ominous, but the tone countered that impression.

"Um, I don't understand. Is something wrong?" Ben asked.

"I found something unexpected in Callie's blood work, quite by accident as I wasn't looking for it. I need to confirm my findings and we need to... we'll need to take some further steps once I'm certain that I'm correct."

Ben rubbed his forehead, looking distressed despite the doctor's positive demeanor. "Is this a concern, a problem?"

Silence lingered on the line before the doctor finally responded. "That's not how I would characterize it. Let me ask you, has Callie experienced anything out of the ordinary lately; any unusual symptoms?"

"As we told you the day before we left, I've been more tired than usual, but I think I'm still recovering from what we went through during and after Ben's collapse. Otherwise, I feel fine," she answered.

The doctor chuckled. "That sounds exactly right. The two of you just keep surprising me. I'm quite gratified to still have some services that are of use to you."

Though he knew the doctor couldn't see him, Ben put up his hands, totally bewildered and a bit frustrated by the lack of direct answers. "Come on, Doc. You've gotta give us something. Is this more fallout from our unexplained illness or something entirely different?"

"I want to be one hundred percent sure before I reveal what I've found. You'll understand my reasons for caution once I tell you. But let's just say that if my findings are confirmed, we'll have an explanation for why a portion of your Succouri left you and then suddenly returned." He chuckled again. "It isn't at all what any of us theorized, and it most assuredly was not an illness."

CHAPTER 16

THE HEALING

Ben booked a flight for them to return to Cape Cod the following morning. For now, they decided to keep the trip to themselves, with the exception of Lee. They hoped to be there and back in a day or two, and as the doctor hadn't given them much information, they had no concrete details to share anyway. When Callie informed Lee about it, she was casual, telling him that the doctor had a matter he felt more comfortable discussing in person rather than over the phone. At this point, Lee had accepted that his sister and brother-in-law would need to spend much of their time back east and his only complaint was being tied down to school for another month, preventing him from adventuring with them.

That evening, as they were packing, the doorbell rang, and when Ben opened the door, he was surprised to find Jessica Hughes standing there.

"Jessica, come on in," he invited with a smile. "Your father's running an errand, but he should be back any minute."

"That's alright. I'd like to talk with you and Callie first

anyway." Ben tried to interpret the expression on her face, but there wasn't much to read. The anger seemed to have calmed, but she was straight lipped and stoic.

Ben retrieved Callie from the bedroom, and she warmly embraced Jessica before they settled, once again, in the living room. As they were unsure of the motivations behind her visit, they waited patiently for Jessica to begin.

"I'd like to know how you became acquainted with my father. You said you didn't know about the connection between Callie's mother and my family until after the transport flight, but I don't understand how that could be."

Ben folded his hands in his lap and spoke softly. "Before the flight, Callie and I worked with a doctor in the Succouri network to find a donor for my dearest friend, Donovan, who was on the medical flight with us. It was the only hope we had to save his life. This doctor had met your father a while back when he came to inquire about ridding himself of the gift, as it was tormenting him due to the loss of a bond. Because of his isolation, he hadn't selected an inheritor, even though he had entered the ripening stage. With my unique background, the doc believed I might be able to make a connection with him, perhaps help him in his grief. You see, I also lived for fifteen years as Succouri without a bond. I understand what your dad went through."

"Went through?" Don't you mean is going through?" Jessica questioned.

"That's another story and something you should talk with him about. But to clarify our role in this, it wasn't until after the transport flight that we at last met him and discovered that he was your father."

"Did you tell him about Allie?"

"I did, and about your husband as well. Perhaps that

wasn't my place, but he needed hope, something to motivate him to keep going and find new purpose."

Ben set his hand on top of Callie's. "Jessica, I know it's hard to understand, but the grief a Succouri suffers at the loss of a partner isn't remotely like what a human goes through. Not to say that human grief isn't terrible, but there is a process, a healing, and, with time, the pain eases. But not for Succouri. The pain never diminishes, never relents. It's a perpetually open wound. Your father knew that you would gradually recover, and he felt that his sorrow would stall that process, keeping you from finding peace and happiness. I know it's hard to accept this, but I believe your father's absence was his way of protecting you. Watching him grieve your mother's death day after day with no progress toward healing would have been an unfair burden to place on you. He wanted you to have a good life, filled with joy. I understand that, unfortunately, circumstances didn't entirely allow for that, but it was his hope for you and his reason for keeping his distance."

Attempting to control her emotions as tears welled up in her eyes, she gripped her knees and stiffened her posture. "But it isn't fair. I was born to two human parents. For fifteen years, I've needed my human father, not one whose mind and heart were controlled by some—forgive me— alien overlord. I know it saved his life, but it took his life too, and it separated me from the human parents I deserved." She shifted her gaze to Callie. "Just as alcohol robbed you of your mother, the Succouri robbed me of my father."

For the first time, Ben began to understand why Succouri couldn't have children. Though tainted by bitterness, Jessica's expectations were reasonable. Ethan had been human first, and he and his wife had become parents.

The obligation to care for their daughter didn't terminate when he became Succouri. But once he took on that identity, the consequences of that life impacted his ability to live up to his human responsibilities. Though Ben's new knowledge and experiences countered her negative characterization of his indweller, it was nevertheless a fact that being Succouri shifted the direction of one's life.

Ben couldn't help but wonder if Ethan had been right. If he'd possessed a spirited Succouri and it had been in control of selecting an inheritor, would it have chosen a man with such binding, pre-existing human obligations? Though following their new calling required a significant course change, Ben was grateful that that shift didn't cause them to neglect any prior commitments. If he'd been a father, his duties as such would come first, but how would he have held onto that ideal when the calling of his Succouri life would certainly have interfered significantly?

Yet, overshadowing all considerations and complications was the garish truth that if Ethan had not become Succouri, he would have died forty years ago and been unable to fulfill any obligations, parental or otherwise.

"It isn't the same thing," Callie responded, her voice gentle. "Alcohol was a poison. By no means can you fairly place the Succouri in that category. Your father's life was saved by it. It's true that tragedy brought about unanticipated consequences, but there was no malice involved. Ethan's Succouri wasn't out to hurt your father or you. That's not the nature of the gift. They're healers: that's what they do. The bond is beautiful, benefiting the human as much as the Succouri. Because it's such a treasure, so incomparably special and rare, its loss is devastating. My mother is the one who brought pain and tragedy into all our lives. But even her sin didn't involve malevolence. She didn't set out to kill anyone. She made a series of foolish choices that ended in heartbreak. Without a doubt, we should all take to heart the lesson that can be learned concerning the costs of our poor decisions. But I was born blind, and that was no one's doing, so I suppose it's also an unfortunate reality that sometimes bad things happen, and we find ourselves in the middle of trials and sorrows, even when we've done nothing to warrant our place there. But that's the very reason why the Succouri were gifted to humanity. They're the flip side, the counterpoint. Just as unexpected pain befalls us all, so too unexpected miracles come across our path when we least expect them. As someone who's been touched by both unmerited hardship as well as unmerited healing, I can say that I'm infinitely blessed by and eternally grateful for the Succouri."

Ben squeezed her hand, moved by her passionate defense of and pride in his gift as well as her wisdom and clear insight.

Also touched, Jessica lowered her gaze.

"Jessica, your father loves you very much," Callie said. "Staying away was his gift to you, his way of protecting you from more pain."

Ben nodded in agreement. "My father did the same for twenty-seven years. His job was dangerous and could have put me in harm's way. He wanted a relationship with me, and I certainly would have benefited from having him in my life, but if he'd selfishly pursued that desire, I could have been killed. There are times when separation is an act of love."

"Did you forgive him?" Jessica asked, looking up at Ben as a tear traced down her cheek.

Ben smiled. "I did, though it wasn't easy at first. It took a little while for my heart to believe he truly loved me and begin to trust him. Our relationship is still a work in progress, but I'm very glad I opened my heart and gave him a second chance. He's a good man, and so is your father, Jessica."

"Did"—she paused, looking almost afraid to ask the question—"Did he save your friend?"

"Yes, he certainly did," Ben replied. "Donovan is healthy, permanently cured of his injuries and pain because of your father."

"So, he's not Succouri anymore?"

Just then, they all heard the front door open, and within seconds, Ethan stepped into the room, his face registering surprise at seeing his daughter there. Ben and Callie stood, and Ben gestured for Ethan to take their place on the couch.

"We'll let him speak for himself," Ben said, patting Ethan's shoulder as they left the two of them alone to begin the process of healing.

Thirty minutes later, Ethan knocked on the door to their bedroom. A contented smile lit up his face. "Jessica and I wondered if you two might be willing to visit Allie with us. She wants to see you. Your established rapport with her, as well as your moral support, would be of great help and much appreciated."

"You got it!" Ben said as tears of joy filled their eyes.

When Ben and Callie stepped into Allie's bedroom, she clapped her hands and giggled in delight.

She sat in her bed, surrounded by layers of frilly pillows in different shades of purple. The walls of her room were also pale lavender.

Her face was radiant, her cheeks glowing with a lovely light pink hue, and her hair attractively styled. She'd even applied some soft, natural-looking makeup. Though she was pretty before, her return to health allowed her beauty to shine nearly as brightly as her appealing personality.

No wonder her brother couldn't stop talking about Allie Hughes, Callie thought as they approached her bed.

"You finally came!" she exclaimed delightedly as she held one hand out for Ben and one for Callie.

"Of course we did," Ben responded.

"It's good to see you again," Callie added. "You look wonderful, Allie. You must be feeling much better,"

Allie wrinkled her brow and looked up at Ben, a question in her eyes. "What does your Succouri tell you about how I'm doing?"

Ben chuckled. "Almost no draw, so I'd say you're nearly back to normal."

Letting go of their hands, she folded her arms, looking annoyed. "Tell my mother that, would you please? She won't let me out of this bed, and I'm going stir crazy. If it weren't for Lee's visits, I think I'd have lost my mind by now."

"It won't be long," Ben assured her. "Lee's already planning some fun adventures for us as soon as you've fully recovered. You've got a lot to look forward to."

"Good," she said with a sigh. "Lee told me Donovan is well now, but he wouldn't give me the details and I suspect there's a terrific story there that I'm missing out on. I want to know all there is to know about the Succouri, and I want to help the two of you in your... work, or whatever your plan is to save people, like you did for Donovan and for me. I know I'm not technically family, but I think I'm connected with the Succouri somehow."

She leaned to the side to open the drawer of her nightstand. Retrieving a worn picture frame, Allie held it out to them. Ben took it, and he and Callie studied the image of a striking woman with long, straight black hair and dark eyes. She looked like Jessica, only younger and with fewer signs of stress and pain on her face.

"This was what I wanted to show you, Ben. I'm pretty sure that's my grandmother. I found it in my mother's closet years ago. She still doesn't know I have it." She pointed to the woman's face. "Look at her eyes. She looks, Succouri, like you, Mrs. Sawyer. My mom says women can't be Succouri, but…"

Callie was astonished by Allie's insight, and she began to wonder if she might possess the gift of seeing, like Carozza. "Please, call me Callie. And your mom is right. Women can't be Succouri, but we can be Datouri. That's what our role is called."

"Datouri," she repeated excitedly.

"And, trust me, Allie, that role is essential, just as important as that of a Succouri," Ben emphasized as he affectionately placed his hand on Callie's back.

Once again, Allie clapped her hands and her eyes danced. "Then if she was Datouri, my grandfather was Succouri. Right?"

Ben and Callie looked at one another, but neither answered.

Ignoring that fact, Allie continued. "I wonder what happened to them. My mother won't talk about it, but it must have been something terrible because she hid the pictures, and she gets all… weird and quiet when I ask about them. I really need to know. Do you think you could help me find out?"

Callie smiled, but Ben blew a slow breath through his lips. "I don't think that's our place, Allie, but—"

"Please. I know I'm not eighteen yet, but I have the right to know where I came from."

Once more, Ben glanced at Callie, and she nodded in response. "I'll be right back," he said, patting Allie's hand.

"Where's he going?" Allie asked in confusion as Ben left the room.

"You'll see," Callie said with a twinkle in her eye.

After a few seconds, Ben reentered the room with Jessica, and Allie sat up straighter, staring at them. "Mom?"

The picture of Allie's grandmother still lay in her lap, and she quickly flipped it over.

"It's alright." Jessica smiled. "I know you have that photograph, and I'm glad you do."

Allie crinkled her nose. "You do? How long have you known?"

"Probably since you took it out of my closet. The memories of her were too painful to face, but I'm glad you feel a connection to her. I may look like her, but you have her spirit."

Callie joined Ben behind Jessica, giving her the space to approach her daughter's bedside. She sat down and took Allie's hand. "I should have told you about them long ago. I'm sorry I didn't."

For a breath, Allie looked stunned and disoriented, but it didn't take her curiosity long to overcome the shock of her mother's sudden change of heart. "Were they Succouri? Well, I guess, Succouri and Datouri?" She corrected herself, smiling at Callie.

"They were. They loved each other very much and they helped a lot of people."

"Like they do?" Allie asked, pointing at Ben and Callie.

"Your grandparents were a lot like them."

"So, what happened to them?" Allie asked, looking a little nervous about the inquiry.

"When I was pregnant with you, your grandmother died in a car accident." Jessica sniffled and rubbed her eyes. "She was so excited about meeting you. She had everything planned out, the nursery and even names." She lightly laughed. "Your dad and I were a little worried she might not give us the chance to make any choices for ourselves. She loved you, even though she never got the chance to meet you. Always remember that, Allie."

"I will," Allie whispered, hugging the picture to her chest. "And my grandfather?"

Jessica turned to Ben, and he and Callie took a step forward. "Allie, when a Succouri loses his partner, it breaks something inside him. It isn't like regular grief; it's many times worse than that. He can't get over it or move on."

"So, he died because my grandmother died?" Allie asked, blinking hard as a few tears slid down her cheek.

"In a way," Ben said. "He didn't want you or your mother to suffer the unending pain that he did. He wanted you to heal, move on with your lives, and find joy again. Even though he couldn't do that, he knew you could, and he didn't want to interfere with your healing."

Allie shook her head, confused by his explanation.

"He ran away, honey," Jessica clarified. "He's been living alone with his grief for the last fifteen years."

Empathetic sorrow shadowed Allie's youthful face.

Abruptly, she threw off the covers and started to get out of bed.

"What are you doing?" Jessica asked in a panic.

"I have to find him, Mom, help him. He shouldn't be alone. Maybe I can bring him here, and Ben and Callie can help him somehow. I have to do something."

Everyone in the room smiled at this wonderful girl's generous, forgiving heart. It had taken her no time at all to accept the truth and want to reach out. Jessica put a hand on Allie's shoulder. "You don't have to find him, honey. Ben and Callie already did. He's here."

Allie's eyes grew wide. Ben went to the doorway, gestured into the hall, and Ethan Devereaux stepped into the room.

Nervously, he rubbed his palms together as he looked at his granddaughter for the first time. "Hi, Allie. You... You have your grandmother's eyes. I'm very happy to meet you. I'm sorry it's taken me so long."

As her mother assisted her, Allie got out of bed and walked toward him, her eyes never straying from his. When she was about two feet away, Ethan held out his hand, but Allie stepped to him, throwing her arms around his neck in an unhindered embrace.

A small gasp caught in his throat just before the tears came. Tenderly, he embraced his granddaughter and softly wept, as did everyone in the room. Ben put his arm around Callie, and she leaned her head against his shoulder, her heart so full of joy it felt like it would explode.

"I love you, Grandpa," Allie whispered. "I'm sorry about Grandma and the pain her absence has caused you, but I'm glad you're here with us now. Thank you for coming home."

Ethan leaned down and kissed the top of Allie's head as tears dripped off his chin. "I love you too, Allie, and I'm glad I'm here with you and your mom." There was profound relief in his voice, but also deep regret at the years he'd lost with this precious girl.

As she watched the exchange, Jessica covered her face with her hands, allowing refreshing tears of healing and forgiveness to flow unhindered. Her daughter's open heart had opened hers as well.

'*And a child will lead them*', Callie thought, recalling a Bible verse she'd heard long ago. She had no doubt that the restoration of this family would be led by this extraordinary fourteen-year-old girl.

Moments passed, sacred ones filled with meaning and new beginnings. At last, Allie returned to her bed, holding fast to her grandfather's hand. Jessica stood, giving Ethan her spot beside Allie. It didn't take long before the questions came, fast and unending. Ben smiled at Callie, glad that the girl would, at last, have someone nearby who could answer every one of them and connect her to her Succouri heritage.

Quietly, they slipped from the room, wanting to give this new family the chance to bond and enjoy one another, but before they left the house, Jessica caught up with them.

"Dad told me about how you helped him, even when you two were suffering yourselves. He told me, Callie, how you asked for forgiveness for your mother's actions, and he told me how your Succouri took away his emptiness. He said if it weren't for the two of you, he never would have left that cabin, and he wouldn't have come home whole, freed from his Succouri burden. He owes you an unpayable debt and so do I. My daughter"—she swallowed hard against another sob—"My daughter loves you both very much, as well as Lee. I have a ways to go in releasing the blame and anger I've heaped on the Succouri for fifteen years, but I want you to know I don't feel that way about the two of you. You're the real deal, genuine heroes. Please, accept my sincerest apologies for the way I've treated you and my deepest gratitude for putting my family back together again."

Callie stepped forward, embracing her warmly, and Jessica returned the affection. Ben did the same, as they all continuously wiped the tears from their cheeks.

"You and I have much in common, Jessica. I spent fifteen years resenting my Succouri, so I know how you feel. But I couldn't have been more wrong about its motives. When bad things happen, I think sometimes it's easier to deal with the pain if we can channel it into anger and place blame, but, in the end, it isn't good for us. It keeps us from facing the truth and healing. I'm thankful you've opened your heart. Please believe me when I say that being a part of your family's story has been a joy and privilege. Your father trusted us, and he saved my best friend's life. Now that he can heal from the wounds of the past, you'll be able to lean on him, trust in him." Ben smiled. "You have your human father back, and neither of you will need to be alone anymore."

A peaceful smile lingered on Jessica's lips. "Please, stay in touch, and let us know what we can do to help you as I understand you have a challenging journey ahead. We want to do what we can, especially after all you've done for us."

"You owe us nothing," Ben stated emphatically, "But you can count on our friendship, always."

With one last round of embraces, Ben and Callie left the Hughes home, confident that each heart dwelling inside would find the healing and wholeness it had sought for far too long.

CHAPTER 17

THE LEGACY

On the flight to Cape Cod, Ben and Callie reflected on the joyous events of the previous evening.

"Our Antico continues to amaze me," Ben mused.

"In what way?"

"When we spoke to Jessica, just before leaving the house, it told me that the healing it had provided Ethan was as much for her as it was for him. Through my eyes, it saw her pain, her anger toward the Succouri, and it wanted to offer her something to repair the damage that had been done. Instead of being offended by her unfair accusations, it was moved by her suffering." He sighed. "For so many years, I was terribly wrong about it, harshly judging its intentions. But, as with Jessica, it had nothing but compassion and empathy for my plight, holding no grudge against me for my shortsightedness."

Smiling, Callie patted his knee.

"But you've believed in its virtuousness all along, haven't you?" Ben placed his hand on top of hers and softly chuckled.

"Because I know you, I know our Succouri. From the moment we learned about it from Ms. Essie, I understood that the two of you share the same heart, the same gentle kindness for the broken, whether in body or spirit. Perhaps it's just easier to see from the outside in, rather than from the inside out."

"Thank you for being patient with me, giving me the time and space to discover and accept who I am. When I met you, I thought it would be you who would need time to adjust to my unique identity and life. It turns out, I had it backward. My insecurities sprang from my own misgivings about it. Since I've let all that go, I've found a freedom and peace I didn't believe possible."

"I know, my love. I see it in your eyes, and nothing gives me greater joy."

He smiled, then began unconsciously stroking her hand with his thumb as he contemplated. "However, I'll freely admit there's still a lot I don't understand."

"Like why we're on our way to Cape Cod right now?" she conjectured with a light laugh.

"Callie, what in the world could the doctor have found that was urgent enough for him to want to tell us about it in person, yet harmless enough for him to chuckle about it and seem almost... excited?"

She shrugged. "I have no idea, but I think we know the doctor well enough now to be confident that it's nothing to be alarmed about. Over the last few weeks, he's run dozens of tests on us both. I don't think he can make heads or tails of most of his findings, but perhaps there's finally something he does understand and he's anxious to share what he's learned."

"Maybe," he murmured, though he sounded doubtful about her proposed explanation.

. . .

When they arrived at the Navarro home, the doctor's and Silvia's broad grins further eased their concerns. The doctor took another blood sample from Callie as well as a urine sample. As he studied the results, they waited on the sage couch. Anxiously, Callie shifted and Ben drummed his fingers on his knee.

When Ben got up and began pacing, Callie laughed. "We're behaving just like Lee, you know?"

Sighing, he sat back down beside her. "When it comes to your health and well-being, I don't do patient very well."

She reached for his hand. "I'm alright, beloved. Of that, I'm absolutely certain. I actually feel stronger, better than usual, and I think the tiredness is all but gone. Whatever the doctor's found, it's nothing serious. I promise you."

Ben's posture only slightly relaxed at her words of assurance.

When the doctor walked into the room carrying a folder, his ecstatic expression made their hearts pound, but not from fear.

He sat across from them, shaking his head repeatedly and chuckling.

"Alright, Doc," Ben pleaded. "Please put us out of our misery. What's going on?"

Leaning forward, he placed the folder on the coffee table, opened it, and tapped it three times. "Triple confirmation, so there's absolutely no doubt."

"No doubt about what?" Callie asked, her voice shaking with anticipation.

Shifting his gaze between them, he held out both hands, as if giving them a gift. "Ben, Callie, I'm bewildered, but very happy to inform you that you're going to be parents. Callie is pregnant."

No one moved or breathed. Ben's mind went blank. What did he say? He couldn't have heard that right.

"Wh... What did you say?" Ben stuttered.

Doctor Navarro laughed at their dumbfounded expressions. "Callie's pregnant. You're going to have your very own miracle baby."

"I... I don't understand." Callie stammered, putting her hand to her heart. "How is that possible?"

"That's a confounding mystery, but I do have a fairly solid theory if you'd like to hear it."

"Um... I..." Ben fumbled for words. He turned to look at Callie, even as he addressed the doctor. "You're sure? No chance this is some kind of false reading?"

Again, the doctor tapped the folder in front of him. "No chance, Ben. This is a certainty. Callie is pregnant."

Ben watched Callie's face as the news fully registered in her heart. With a new kind of beauty, she began to glow, and her bright smile made his heart soar. She cradled her stomach with both hands and looked down adoringly, as if she were already holding their child.

Their child! At that moment, Ben's disoriented mind at last interpreted the doctor's announcement, and, as it had the day he'd married Callie, the rhythm of his heart shifted, leaving him breathless. Almost audibly, he heard his Succouri speak. "*The gift!*" it exclaimed in a voice that resounded with his uncontainable joy.

"Callie!" he managed hoarsely as tears filled his eyes. He took her in his arms, and she clung to him, laughing and crying as they celebrated news they'd never expected to hear.

After rejoicing together for a long time, Callie at last

spoke. "Ben! A baby! Our baby; yours and mine. Conceived in love. Part of you and part of me united in one beautiful new person. He'll be our very own to love, keep, and cherish forever!" She took his face in her hands, nearly bouncing out of her seat as she continued. "And he'll have your eyes, I know he will." She laughed and kissed his face repeatedly.

Laughing with her, Ben stroked her arms and returned her kisses. "And your curls and beautiful heart."

Leaning their foreheads against one another's, their thoughts united, and fresh tears flowed as Callie felt the depths of Ben's happiness.

"Yes!" she exclaimed in response to his thoughts. "You *will* have the chance to be a father, after all. And you'll be a great one, Ben."

Then, she heard the whispered voice of their Succouri, speaking directly to her this time. With wonder, she gasped and leaned back to look into Ben's eyes. "The gift! Our Succouri did this? It... I don't understand," she said, though her smile never faded.

Simultaneously, they looked to where the doctor had been sitting, but he wasn't there.

Ben laughed. "How long have we been celebrating?"

Giggling, Callie shrugged. "Longer than it seemed, I guess."

Before calling the doctor back into the room, Ben gently placed his hand on Callie's stomach, and she put hers on top of his. "I love you, Callie Sawyer. I can't express how happy I am right now. Besides you, this is the best gift I've ever received. With all my heart, I already love our little miracle. I don't understand how this happened or why we've been granted such favor, but I swear to you that I will protect and care for you both with all my strength, always."

Circling her arms around his neck, she kissed him, and

he responded in kind, lingering in another hallowed moment they'd forever treasure in their memories.

When they at last called the doctor back into the room, he reclined in his chair, smiling at them for a long moment.

"We know for certain our Succouri did this," Ben explained. "It already told me that we fell ill because it wanted to give us a gift. That made no sense, and I still don't understand the how and why, but there's no question that this was premeditated: a pure, extravagant offering of love."

"It is extraordinary and entirely unexpected! I think even Carozza would agree with that."

"He told us the gift we'd been given had only been extended a handful of times since the beginning," Ben recalled.

"Creatouri!" Callie suddenly exclaimed.

Ben and the doctor looked at her questioningly.

"Carozza said we were Creatouri. I looked it up and it means creators. How did we not guess this? We never even considered it, even though all the signs were there."

"When we found out we wouldn't be able to have children, I think we grieved and moved on, accepting the fact and resolving to build a wonderful life regardless." Ben chuckled. "It seems our acceptance was so thorough that it precluded us from considering the possibility."

"I don't blame you," the doctor said. "As I told you on the phone, despite all my tests, I was in no way looking for this outcome. It was happenstance that I caught it."

Ben gestured toward the doctor. "So, let's hear it. What's your theory about how this miracle came about?"

Still grinning, the doctor focused his gaze on Ben. "In simplest terms, Callie conceived because, for a short period of time—perhaps less than twenty-four hours—you were human enough to accomplish the task. It likely happened during that brief window of time when you lost your healing touch. The active Succouri presence in your body was at a critical low, causing you both a lot of discomfort and trauma, but" —he grinned slyly— "also opening the door to an otherwise impossible opportunity. I don't mean to pry, but to legitimize my hypothesis, I need to know if, during that time—just a few hours— you two..." He cleared his throat and shifted uncomfortably. "I recognize that you are still newlyweds, but you were very ill that day. Nevertheless, I have to ask If you two engaged in... had the occasion to..." he held out his hand and sent them a wink.

Callie smiled knowing the answer immediately, but it took Ben a few seconds to remember that morning, just hours after Ben awoke from his long night of unconsciousness. Grieving the loss of their bond, struggling with their physical pains, and recovering from the time they'd spent separated by six feet of distance, they'd found some much-needed comfort in one another's arms. It was the one and only time they'd made love without the union of their minds. Ironically, afterward, he remembered thinking how uniquely human the encounter had been.

Feeling awkward, Ben nodded, answering the doctor's question. "But that was only about three weeks ago."

"Plenty of time for the pregnancy to show up on these tests." Leaning back, looking satisfied that his theories were proving plausible, he tapped his fingertips together in front of him as he explained. "As soon as I discovered the pregnancy, it was also my supposition that your Antico planned this entire affair. It wanted to give the two of you a child, a gift, as you say. To do so, it needed to make Ben more human and less Succouri; as human as possible without killing him. It certainly stepped right up to that line, but somehow managed not to cross it. To accomplish this, it was necessary for it to—at least in part—evacuate from your blood and systems, but it had nowhere to go that would be compatible, except Callie. Callie's blood has already been altered to work with the Succouri part of your physiology. Not as dramatically altered as yours, Ben, but sufficient for this short-term transfer. It was an impressively ingenious plan!"

He paused to shake his head as he marveled at the intelligence of their Antico. "What I don't know for certain is whether the occupation of Callie was solely related to its need to vacate Ben's system, or whether it also had a task to perform in her body to enable her to successfully conceive. As we can't scientifically understand why Succouri couples can't have children—whether it's a problem with the Succouri, Datouri, or both—we might never learn the answer to that quandary. Nevertheless, your spirited Succouri carefully and consciously strategized to bring this wondrous miracle to you. It may have taken weeks to orchestrate the ideal conditions to make it possible, and it certainly put the two of you through significant torment, but I'm betting you're feeling it was well worth it right about now."

"Well worth every minute of it," Ben answered quickly, and Callie nodded her agreement.

"It saves its best gifts for the Succouri and Datouri of the terminal match." Callie mumbled the words spoken by Carozza, and Ben and the doctor smiled at her.

"Indeed, it did," the doctor concurred. "This also explains why the condition suddenly reversed itself. Once the task was accomplished, there was no further need for your Succouri to reside in Callie, so it returned both of you to normal. Well, almost normal," he said whimsically. "I am keenly curious about your Succouri's particular ability to travel, to move out of you and into another, as it also did when it transferred to Mr. Devereaux. Apart from the permanent transfer that takes place at the ripening, I've never witnessed or heard of a Succouri possessing this capability. Clearly, it is severely distressing to you, both physically and mentally, but you survived it. I wouldn't have guessed that possible."

"Only because of Callie," Ben emphasized. "She filled in the gap left by its absence. Without her, there's no way I'd live through it."

"Aw! I see!" he exclaimed, putting up a finger. "So her partnership was required for this new skill to emerge and become viable. Fascinating! I wonder if this ability is exclusive to yours or if it is something all spirited Succouri can achieve?"

Ben smiled, glad to see that the doctor's enthusiastic curiosity had fully returned. "I'm not entirely sure. But my instincts tell me it is a rare skill, perhaps something only available to a terminal triad because the bonding is so tight. Even for the three of us, I don't believe that, until very recently, the tie was strong enough to enable us to successfully accomplish it. And without that ability, it wouldn't be possible for our Succouri to awaken the others. The timing of all of this was no accident."

"Remarkable!" Ben could see in the doctor's eyes that he had more questions, but he sighed and refocused. "Returning to the situation at hand, it seems your Antico also took this opportunity to deal with matters that needed to be resolved between you and it," the doctor said to Ben. "I suppose there's no better time to find peace with oneself and one's purpose than before becoming a parent. That way you can offer your child all you have to give, without obstacles or barriers."

Humbled by his Antico's manifest kindnesses, Ben bowed his head. "Doc, will our baby be normal... fully human?"

"That's another yet unanswerable mystery," the doctor admitted, evidently already having thought in depth about Ben's question. "Your Succouri allowed you to become human enough to make conception possible, but, Ben, even at that point, your physiology wasn't..." The doctor desperately sought a kind way to finish his thought.

"Understood." Ben raised a hand, indicating that there was no need to explain further.

"As for you, Callie, as we just discussed, your blood's been modified significantly as well. The test results on blood I took from you after you returned Ben's Succouri are nearly as incomprehensible as Ben's. I can no longer compare you to other Datouri, no matter how long they've carried that title. You're in a category of your own now. Your body's not dramatically transformed like Ben's, but your blood more closely resembles his than anyone else's."

"And that doesn't worry you, Doc?" Ben asked.

"Not in the least," he exclaimed confidently. "As you have, I've come to trust your Antico. If what you say is true and its fate is linked to both of yours, it's not about to do anything to harm either of you. Even if its survival wasn't dependent on yours, it's more than obvious at this point that it has your best interests at heart, to say the least."

Putting his arm around Callie's shoulders, Ben leaned back with her, relaxing in the unquestionable truth. "Agreed."

"But given the reality of your physiologies, it's difficult to believe that your child won't be... special in some way, but I just can't say with certainty. In a few weeks, we can begin performing ultrasounds and more, if you desire. I'm not sure how much we can learn from testing and there may be associated risks, but even determining the sex might provide some clues."

"It doesn't matter to me," Callie interjected, shaking her head. "I mean, it might be nice to know if it's a boy or a girl, but otherwise, I don't need to know more until he's born, and I'm not going to take any chances of doing him harm. This child is a miracle, meant to be and do something extraordinary, whether it's fully human or"—she shifted her gaze to Ben— "kissed by our Antico. It won't change my love for him in the slightest. Just like everything else in our lives, we'll have to simply live day by day, take what comes, and stand back and wonder at the miracle of it all."

As Ben listened, ever in awe of his wife's accepting heart, the glow on her face brightened.

"I'm in complete agreement with Callie," Ben declared without reservation. "Our son or daughter will be perfect. No need to put him or her through any unnecessary trauma."

"Alright then," the doctor said, his full support and pleasure at their decision clear in his smile. "We'll just do the normal healthy mom and baby checks and let the rest work itself out. Though"—he squinted as he grinned—"I will need to make some changes to my lab and augment my medical supplies. I never imagined I'd have the privilege of practicing obstetrics again."

"Send us the bill for all of it, Doc. And don't hold back. Let's do whatever's necessary to ensure that Callie and the baby make it safely through this pregnancy, delivery, and beyond."

"We'll work out a fair deal, Ben. I assure you, I'll

prepare for every eventuality, and do everything in my power to bring this child into the world healthy and thriving and keep Callie comfortable and well, too. It's an honor to be a part of this, a once-in-a-lifetime opportunity. I'm assured that no Succouri alive today has been granted this gift. Being present to witness this miracle; that's worth more to Silvia and me than I'll ever be able to express."

Before they left, they worked out a schedule of regular visits, and Ben and Callie made the decision to spend the last month of her pregnancy at their Cape Cod home so they'd be nearby when it was time for the delivery.

As they headed for the door, Silvia met up with them and embraced them. "It's so wonderful!" she gushed. "What a beautiful miracle for two well-deserving people!"

Doctor Navarro gripped their shoulders affectionately. "My guess is this will be an easy pregnancy, Callie. With Ben around, there's no chance of morning sickness or even pain during delivery. You're a very lucky woman in that regard. I look forward to enjoying the journey with you. Congratulations to you both!"

"Thank you for everything, Doctor," Callie replied.

"We'll be in touch. I don't know how this affects the other goals we're working toward," Ben admitted. "Let me sleep on it, and I'll reach back out to you soon."

"Take your time. Relish the joy of this news. There's plenty of time to worry about the rest."

THEY DECIDED to stay overnight at their place in Cape Cod so they could rest up and celebrate privately. As they drove, Callie continually caught herself resting her hand on her stomach, still finding it difficult to believe she carried their miracle child in her body. Several times, Ben reached with his free hand, placing it on hers as he smiled blissfully.

When they arrived at the house, Lee called, and Callie did her best to assure him that all was fine while avoiding revealing anything or making him suspicious. For that one night, she wanted the news to be theirs alone.

When she completed the call, she went looking for Ben, at last finding him leaning on the railing of the private deck in their bedroom. Lost in thought, she startled him when she came up behind him and put her arms around his waist.

Quickly, he turned and pulled her close, kissing the top of her head. Though she could feel his abiding joy, there was something else, too; something that was worrying him.

"What is it?" she asked, looking up into his eyes.

"Nothing important, sweetheart. I couldn't be any happier than I am right now, I promise. I'm just..."

"Please, tell me."

"I'm just trying to sort it all out, line up my priorities properly, and listen to our Antico for guidance."

Stepping back, she took his hands in hers. "This doesn't change our mission, Ben."

"Perhaps it should. When we were speaking with Jessica yesterday, there was a moment when I understood why Succouri can't have children. It wasn't wrong of her to expect her father to put her first, care for her needs above any other considerations. But his Succouri life prevented him from doing so. I don't want it to be that way for our child."

Protectively, he placed his hand on her stomach. "We're parents now, and you have my word that, after my responsibility to you as your husband, being our child's father will be my highest priority." He lowered his gaze. "I'm just trying to figure out how my Succouri calling fits in with that.”

Lovingly, she pushed several strands of hair away from his forehead, still as captivated by his extraordinarily handsome face as the day she’d first seen it clearly. “Our Succouri calling,” she corrected. “Do you believe that our Antico gave us this calling?”

“Of course.”

“And do you believe the timing was exactly right?”

“I do,” he answered, looking at her with curiosity.

“Do you also believe our Antico planned this pregnancy, this child for at least weeks, maybe since the day we met?”

“I don’t think there’s any question about that.”

“So then, the timing of the calling and the timing of our child aren’t coincidental. They’re destined. Why would our Antico give us two blessings at exactly the same time if one obstructed the other?”

Ben just blinked at her, having no good answer to her question.

“I don’t understand exactly how yet, though I could venture some exciting guesses, but I’m absolutely sure this baby will, in no way, keep us from living out our purpose. In fact, I think he will help us fulfill it.” She put a hand on her hip. “Now, undoubtedly, we are going to need help, a lot of it.” She resumed her smile. “It’s a good thing we have more family than we know what to do with. Ms. Essie, Maggie, your father, and Rosa and Leo, not to mention Lee are going to get more than they bargained for when they offered to help us. But how wonderful will that be! Our child will have so many people who love him, he’ll never be wanting for affection. We might even have to worry about him being spoiled,” she conjectured with a laugh.

"But what if things get dangerous, Callie? What if what we do puts our child at risk?"

She traced her finger down the line of his tight jaw. "Have faith, my love. Unlike Ethan and Lexi, we didn't have this child before we were Succouri. We didn't even plan to have it now. Our Antico selected us to be parents, at this exact moment in time, knowing full well what we'll face in the future. Remember, it showed Carozza a vision of our lives. It didn't promise us a smooth road, but Carozza said our love and destiny would give us strength. This child is unquestioningly a big part of that destiny, and he was surely conceived in love. He's our legacy, Ben, the part of our love story that will carry on long after our journey is over. Carozza told us to trust our Antico. It wouldn't give us a gift as wonderful as this unless it had a plan for him, to make him part of that story."

Surrendering to her wisdom, Ben relaxed and looked at her with so much admiration that she had to temporarily divert her eyes as she felt unworthy of his lavish praise.

"When I think about my life over the last months since I met you, my mind can't conceive how much you've changed my world, Callie Sawyer. I was a lost soul, devoid of hope, love, and purpose. I had no clue who I was, and the burdens of past pain bent my back, like a ton of bricks I carried wherever I went, inhibiting me from lifting my head and glimpsing the horizon. Then, this beautiful woman stepped into my darkness, lit up my entire world with her unfailing love, and willingly walked beside me through countless days of fire and pain. Without hesitation, you continued to want me when you believed doing so would leave you without children of your own, and even when it meant dying by my side. Because of you, I let go of my past, found my father, embraced my Succouri gift, discovered my destiny, and now"—he shook his head as a tear escaped the corner of his eye—"now you're giving me a legacy, a future beyond this life. How can I ever hope to repay you? I can only offer this." He took her face in his hands as his brilliant blue eyes stared deep into her soul. "I will love you with all my heart, soul, and strength forever and ever."

She smiled at him, and stepped closer, wrapping her arms around his neck. "That's all I'll ever want or need, Ben Sawyer."

After a tender kiss that dispelled any remaining doubt, Ben put his mouth to her ear. "You keep calling our baby 'he'. Do you know something I don't?"

Leaning back, she giggled, her expression mischievous. "Perhaps. Wait and see, beloved."

NOTE TO READER

Thank you for reading *All I Have to Keep* by Meridith Gibbens.

Please kindly consider leaving a review of this novel at your place of purchase or other book review websites like Goodreads or Bookbub.

This concludes the *All I Have* Series, but Ben and Callie will return as the Succouri Saga continues with exciting, new adventures in future series. Sign up for my newsletter to stay informed about new releases.

Sign-up link: https://dashboard.mailerlite.com/forms/ 665700/103487653988533291/share

BOOK LIST

The Succouri Saga Books

List of books in the *All I Have* Series:
    Book 1: *All I Have to Give*
    Book 2: *All I Have to Lose*
    Book 3: *All I Have to Love*
    Book 4: *All I Have to Keep*

About the Author

As an Adjunct Professor of Communication for more than two decades, writing has always been a part of Meridith's life and career. Her novels combine her love for romance and imaginative storytelling with her communication and writing background. Legally blind since birth, Meridith's unique point of view and experiences bring intriguing and fresh perspectives to her storylines and characters. Beyond simple romance novels, Meridith writes unforgettable, epic love stories that sweep readers off their feet.

Meridith resides in Kansas with her husband, Jason, and her two sons.